Now these

Odde

PRAISE FOR *Oddly Enough:*

AN ALA BEST BOOK FOR YOUNG ADULTS
AN ALA QUICK PICK FOR RELUCTANT YOUNG ADULT READERS

"Fans of the author's perky popular novels will be
surprised and rewarded by this collection of nine
provocative, and very different, short stories."
—*The New York Times Book Review*

"This is Coville's first collection of short stories and
they give young readers an amazing variety in their
tone and style."—*BookPage*

"Satisfying and unsettling stories."—*Booklist*

PRAISE FOR *Odder Than Ever:*

★ "Richly satisfying, and there are a few
surprises...An immensely enjoyable and
thought-provoking collection."
—*School Library Journal* (starred review)

"An intriguing collection...Shows Coville's range and
versatility in a way his novels never can."
—*Booklist*

"A consummate storyteller, Coville writes with
a light touch...Both fantastical and thought-
provoking."—*VOYA* (5Q—highest rating)

ODDS ARE GOOD

OTHER BOOKS BY BRUCE COVILLE

Armageddon Summer (with Jane Yolen)

The Prince of Butterflies

The Monsters of Morley Manor

The Unicorn Treasury

Thor's Wedding Day

THE MAGIC SHOP BOOKS

The Monster's Ring

Jeremy Thatcher, Dragon Hatcher

Jennifer Murdley's Toad

The Skull of Truth

Juliet Dove, Queen of Love

ODDS ARE GOOD

AN *Oddly Enough* AND
Odder Than Ever OMNIBUS

Stories by
Bruce Coville

Magic Carpet Books
Harcourt, Inc.

Orlando   Austin   New York   San Diego   Toronto   London

Requests for permission to make copies of any part of the work
should be mailed to the following address: Permissions Department,
Harcourt, Inc., 6277 Sea Harbor Drive, Orlando, Florida 32887-6777.

www.HarcourtBooks.com

First Magic Carpet Books edition 2006

Magic Carpet Books is a trademark of Harcourt, Inc., registered in
the United States of America and/or other jurisdictions.

Library of Congress Cataloging-in-Publication Data
Coville, Bruce.
Odds are good: an Oddly enough and Odder than ever
omnibus/Bruce Coville.
p. cm.
Summary: A collection of eighteen previously published short stories
featuring such creatures as a ghost, a giant, a unicorn, and a werewolf.
1. Horror tales, American. 2. Children's stories, American.
[1. Horror stories. 2. Short stories.] I. Coville, Bruce. Oddly enough.
II. Coville, Bruce. Odder than ever. III. Title: Oddly enough.
IV. Title: Odder than ever. V. Title.
PZ7.C8344Odh 2006
[Fic]—dc22 2005050343
ISBN-13: 978-0-15-205716-9 ISBN-10: 0-15-205716-1

Permission acknowledgments begin on page 329 and
constitute a continuation of the copyright page.

Text set in Bembo
Designed by Cathy Riggs

A C E G H F D B

Printed in the United States of America

For Helen Buckley Simkewicz,
who told me I could write when it was the thing
I needed most in the world to hear. Many thanks.

AND

For Dick Decker,
with profound thanks for urging me to stretch
my wings and set sail on uncharted seas.

CONTENTS

HOW ODD TO KNOW MR. C.

Oddly enough, Bruce Coville and I have been friends for almost thirty years. Thirty odd years. For the first year and a half of our friendship, I spelled his last name wrong and he kindly pointed it out to me again and again until I finally got it right. Not *Colville*, but *Coville*. He was so forgiving, I am glad to finally set that record straight.

We have comforted each other through sickness and bad reviews. We have written a book together, edited stories written by the other, dedicated books to each other. Oh yes, and we have tried to open sacred boxes, flown high with the butterflies, cooked magical biscuits, and been chased by monsters out of deep dark woods.

No...

Wait...

Those are stories. Bruce's fantasy stories. Only when I read them, they have such a ring of truth that I *want* them to be real. I want to find a world in which each house has a water room, where a giant's tongue is "coarse and soggy, like a bed of rain-soaked ferns," where I can have an annoying brownie to keep my house clean, and where I can turn into a wolf and "hear the voles rustling in the soil beneath me."

"I desired dragons," J. R. R. Tolkien once wrote. "I desired dragons with a profound desire. Of course, I in my timid body did not wish to have them in the neighborhood, intruding into my relatively safe world...I never imagined that the dragon was of the same order as the horse."

Bruce Coville knows this deep in his bones. It is what makes his stories so magical. Not the dragons and unicorns and monsters and aliens. That's only on the outside of any story. But the desire for the unknown, that ache for the great Truth beyond us, the understanding that we are all—as the old song goes—stardust. Such a desire drives his tales. He shows us how inside we are part of a universe that is deeply weirder, deeply odder, and much more beautiful than history and science can tell us.

And he does this while often making us laugh. I dare you to read "Duffy's Jacket" once or even a dozen times without laughing uproariously at the end. I dare you to read "Am I Blue?" without howling at the villain's perfect comeuppance. I dare you to keep a straight face when the Kwarkissian class lets out a group fart.

My own personal favorites? "The Box" for its deep beauty, "Duffy's Jacket" for its sheer cheek, and "Am I Blue?" for its brilliant daring, though I love them all. But, as we like to say in science fiction circles, "YMMV: Your Mileage May Vary," meaning you will probably have your own favorites. And that's just fine, too. There's plenty of Coville magic around. (As long as you spell his name right!)

—JANE YOLEN, PHOENIX FARM, 2005

ODDS ARE GOOD

THE BOX

Once there was a boy who had a box.

The boy's name was Michael, and the box was very special because it had been given to him by an angel.

Michael knew it had been an angel because of the huge white wings he wore. So he took very good care of the box, because the angel had asked him to.

And he never, ever opened it.

When Michael's mother asked him where he had gotten the box, he said, "An angel gave it to me."

"That's nice, dear," she answered, and went back to stirring her cake mix.

Michael carried the box with him wherever he went. He took it to school. He took it out to play. He set it by his place at mealtimes.

After all, he never knew when the angel would come back and ask for it.

The box was very beautiful. It was made of dark wood and carved with strange designs. The carvings were smooth and polished, and they seemed to glow whenever they caught the light. A pair of tiny golden hinges, and a miniature golden latch that Michael never touched, held the cover tight to the body of the box.

Michael loved the way it felt against his fingers.

Sometimes Michael's friends would tease him about the box.

"Hey, Michael," they would say. "How come you never come out to play without that box?"

"Because I am taking care of it for an angel," he would answer. And because this was true, the boys would leave him alone.

At night, before he went to bed, Michael would rub the box with a soft cloth to make it smooth and glossy.

Sometimes when he did this he could hear something moving inside the box.

He wondered how it was that something could stay alive in the box without any food or water.

But he did not open the box. The angel had asked him not to.

One night when he was lying in his bed, Michael heard a voice.

"Give me the box," it said.

Michael sat up.

"Who are you?" he asked.

"I am the angel," said the voice. "I have come for my box."

"You are not my angel," shouted Michael. He was beginning to grow frightened.

"Your angel has sent me. Give me the box."

"No. I can only give it to my angel."

"Give me the box!"

"No!" cried Michael.

There was a roar, and a rumble of thunder. A cold wind came shrieking through his bedroom.

"I must have that box!" sobbed the voice, as though its heart was breaking.

"No! No!" cried Michael, and he clutched the box tightly to his chest.

But the voice was gone.

Soon Michael's mother came in to comfort him, telling him he must have had a bad dream. After a time he stopped crying and went back to sleep.

But he knew the voice had been no dream.

After that night Michael was twice as careful with the box as he had been before. He grew to love it deeply. It reminded him of his angel.

As Michael grew older the box became more of a problem for him.

His teachers began to object to him keeping it constantly at his side or on his desk. One particularly thick and unbending teacher even sent him to the principal. But when Michael told the principal he was taking care of the box for an angel, the principal told Mrs. Jenkins to leave him alone.

When Michael entered junior high he found that the other boys no longer believed him when he told them why he carried the box. He understood that.

They had never seen the angel, as he had. Most of the children were so used to the box by now that they ignored it anyway.

But some of the boys began to tease Michael about it.

One day two boys grabbed the box and began a game of keep-away with it, throwing it back and forth above Michael's head, until one of them dropped it.

It landed with an ugly smack against the concrete.

Michael raced to the box and picked it up. One of the fine corners was smashed flat, and a piece of one of the carvings had broken off.

"I hate you," he started to scream. But the words choked in his throat, and the hate died within him.

He picked up the box and carried it home. Then he cried for a little while.

The boys were very sorry for what they had done. But they never spoke to Michael after that, and secretly they hated him, because they had done something so mean to him, and he had not gotten mad.

For seven nights after the box was dropped Michael did not hear any noise inside it when he was cleaning it.

He was terrified.

What if everything was ruined? What could he tell the angel? He couldn't eat or sleep. He refused to go to school. He simply sat beside the box, loving it and caring for it.

On the eighth day he could hear the movements begin once more, louder and stronger than ever.

He sighed, and slept for eighteen hours.

When he entered high school Michael did not go out for sports, because he was not willing to leave the box alone. He certainly could not take it out onto a football field with him.

He began taking art classes instead. He wanted to learn to paint the face of his angel. He tried over and over again, but he could never get the pictures to come out the way he wanted them to.

Everyone else thought they were beautiful.

But they never satisfied Michael.

Whenever Michael went out with a girl she would ask him what he had in the box. When he told her he didn't know, she would not believe him. So then he would tell her the story of how the angel had given him the box. Then the girl would think he was fooling her. Sometimes a girl would try to open the box when he wasn't looking.

But Michael always knew, and whenever a girl did this, he would never ask her out again.

Finally Michael found a girl who believed him. When he told her that an angel had given him the box, and that he had to take care of it for him, she nodded her head as if this was the most sensible thing she had ever heard.

Michael showed her the pictures he had painted of his angel.

They fell in love, and after a time they were married.

Things were not so hard for Michael now, because he had someone who loved him to share his problems with.

But it was still not easy to care for the box. When he tried to get a job people would ask him why he carried it, and usually they would laugh at him. More than once he was fired from his work because his boss would get sick of seeing the box and not being able to find out what was in it.

Finally Michael found work as a night custodian. He carried the box in a little knapsack on his back, and did his job so well that no one ever questioned him.

One night Michael was driving to work. It was raining, and very slippery. A car turned in front of him. There was an accident, and both Michael and the box flew out of the car.

When Michael woke up he was in the hospital. The first thing he asked for was his box. But it was not there.

Michael jumped out of bed, and it took three nurses and two doctors to wrestle him back into it. They gave him a shot to make him sleep.

That night, when the hospital was quiet, Michael snuck out of bed and got his clothes.

It was a long way to where he had had the accident, and he had to walk the whole distance. He searched for hours under the light of a bright, full moon, until finally he found the box. It was caked with mud, and another of the beautiful corners had been flattened in. But none of the carvings were broken, and when he held it to his ear, he could hear something moving inside.

When the nurse came to check him in the morning, she found Michael sleeping peacefully, with a dirty box beside him on the bed. She reached out to take it, but his hand wrapped around the box and held it in a grip of steel. He did not even wake up.

Michael would have had a hard time paying the hospital bills. But one day a man came to their house and saw some of his paintings. He asked if he could buy one. Other people heard about them, and before long Michael was selling many paintings. He quit his night job, and began to make his living as an artist.

But he was never able to paint a picture of the angel that looked the way it should.

One night when Michael was almost thirty he heard the voice again.

"Give me the box!" it cried, in tones so strong and stern that Michael was afraid he would obey them.

But he closed his eyes, and in his mind he saw his angel again, with his face so strong and his eyes so full of love, and he paid no attention to the voice at all.

The next morning Michael went to his easel and began to paint. It was the most beautiful picture he had ever made.

But still it did not satisfy him.

The voice came after Michael seven times that year, but he was never tempted to answer it again.

Michael and his wife had two children, and they loved them very much. The children were always curious about the box their father carried, and one day, when Michael was napping, the oldest child tried to open it.

Michael woke and saw what was happening. For the first time in his memory he lost his temper.

He raised his hand to strike his son.

But in the face of his child he suddenly saw the face of the angel he had met only once, so long ago, and the anger died within him.

After that day the children left the box alone.

Time went on. The children grew up and went to their own homes. Michael and his wife grew old. The box suffered another accident or two. It was battered now, and even the careful polishing Michael gave it every night did not hide the fact that the carvings were growing thin from the pressure of his hands against them so many hours a day.

Once, when they were very old, Michael's wife said to him, "Do you really think the angel will come back for his box?"

"Hush, my darling," said Michael, putting his finger against her lips.

And she never knew if Michael believed the angel would come back or not.

After a time she grew sick, and died, and Michael was left alone.

Everybody in his town knew who he was, and when he could not hear they called him Crazy Michael, and whirled their fingers around their ears, and whispered that he had carried that box from the time he was eight years old.

Of course nobody really believed such a silly story.

But they all knew Michael was crazy.

Even so, in their hearts they wished they had a secret as enduring as the one that Crazy Michael carried.

One night, when Michael was almost ninety years old, the angel returned to him and asked for the box.

"Is it really you?" cried Michael. He struggled to his elbows to squint at the face above him. Then he could see that it was indeed the angel, who had not changed a bit in eighty years, while he had grown so old.

"At last," he said softly. "Where have you been all this time, Angel?"

"I have been working," said the angel. "And waiting." He knelt by Michael's bed. "Have you been faithful?"

"I have," whispered Michael.

"Give me the box, please."

Under the pillow, beside his head, the battered box lay waiting. Michael pulled it out and extended it to the angel.

"It is not as beautiful as when you first gave it to me," he said, lowering his head.

"That does not matter," said the angel.

He took the box from Michael's hands. Holding it carefully, he stared at it, as if he could see what was inside. Then he smiled.

"It is almost ready."

Michael smiled, too. "What is it?" he asked. His face seemed to glow with happiness. "Tell me what it is at last."

"I cannot," whispered the angel sadly.

Michael's smile crumpled. "Then tell me this," he said after a moment. "Is it important?" His voice was desperate.

"It will change the world," replied the angel.

Michael leaned back against his pillow. "Then surely I will know what it is when this has come to pass," he said, smiling once again.

"No. You will not know," answered the angel.

"But if it is so important that it will change the world, then..."

"*You* have changed the world, Michael. How many people know that?"

The angel shimmered and began to disappear.

Michael stretched out his hand. "Wait!" he cried.

The angel reached down. He took Michael's withered hand and held it tightly in his own.

"You have done well," he whispered.

He kissed Michael softly on the forehead.

And then he was gone.

DUFFY'S JACKET

If my cousin Duffy had the brains of a turnip it never would have happened. But as far as I'm concerned, Duffy makes a turnip look bright. My mother disagrees. According to her, Duffy is actually very bright. She claims the reason he's so scatter-brained is that he's too busy being brilliant inside his own head to remember everyday things. Maybe. But hanging around with Duffy means you spend a lot of time saying, "Your glasses, Duffy," or "Your coat, Duffy," or—well, you get the idea: a lot of three-word sentences that start with "Your," end with "Duffy," and have words like *book, radio, wallet,* or whatever it is he's just put down and left behind, stuck in the middle.

Me, I think turnips are brighter.

But since Duffy's my cousin, and since my mother and her sister are both single parents, we tend to do a lot of things together—like camping, which is how we got into the mess I want to tell you about.

Personally, I thought camping was a big mistake. But since Mom and Aunt Elise are raising the three of us—me, Duffy, and my little sister, Marie—on their own, they're convinced they have to do man-stuff with us every once in a while. I think they read some book that said me and Duffy would come out weird if they don't. You can take him camping all you want. It ain't gonna make Duffy normal.

Anyway, the fact that our mothers were getting wound up to do something fatherly, combined with the fact that Aunt Elise's boss had a friend who had a friend who said we could use his cabin, added up to the five of us bouncing along this horrible dirt road late one Friday in October.

It was late because we had lost an hour going back to get Duffy's suitcase. I suppose it wasn't actually Duffy's fault. No one remembered to say, "Your suitcase, Duffy," so he couldn't really have been expected to remember it.

"Oh, Elise," cried my mother, as we got deeper into the woods. "Aren't the leaves beautiful?"

That's why it doesn't make sense for them to try to do man-stuff with us. If it had been our fathers, they would have been drinking beer and burping and maybe telling dirty stories instead of talking about the leaves. So why try to fake it?

Anyway, we get to this cabin, which is about eighteen million miles from nowhere, and to my surprise, it's not a cabin at all. It's a house. A big house.

"Oh, my," said my mother as we pulled into the driveway.

"Isn't it great?" chirped Aunt Elise. "It's almost

a hundred years old, back from the time when they used to build big hunting lodges up here. It's the only one in the area still standing. Horace said he hasn't been able to get up here in some time. That's why he was glad to let us use it. He said it would be good to have someone go in and air the place out."

Leave it to Aunt Elise. This place didn't need airing out—it needed fumigating. I never saw so many spiderwebs in my life. From the sounds we heard coming from the walls, the mice seemed to have made it a population center. We found a total of two working lightbulbs: one in the kitchen, and one in the dining room, which was paneled with dark wood and had a big stone fireplace at one end.

"Oh, my," said my mother again.

Duffy, who's allergic to about fifteen different things, started to sneeze.

"Isn't it charming?" asked Aunt Elise hopefully.

No one answered her.

Four hours later we had managed to get three bedrooms clean enough to sleep in without getting the heebie-jeebies—one for Mom and Aunt Elise, one for Marie, and one for me and Duffy. After a supper of beans and franks we hit the hay, which I think is what our mattresses were stuffed with. As I was drifting off, which took about thirty seconds, it occurred to me that four hours of housework wasn't all that much of a man-thing, something it might be useful to remember the next time Mom got one of these plans into her head.

Things looked better in the morning when we went outside and found a stream where we could go wading. ("Your sneakers, Duffy.")

Later we went back and started poking around the house, which really was enormous.

That was when things started getting a little spooky. In the room next to ours I found a message scrawled on the wall. BEWARE THE SENTINEL, it said in big black letters.

When I showed Mom and Aunt Elise they said it was just a joke and got mad at me for frightening Marie.

Marie wasn't the only one who was frightened.

We decided to go out for another walk. ("Your lunch, Duffy.") We went deep into the woods, following a faint trail that kept threatening to disappear but never actually faded away altogether. It was a hot day, even in the deep woods, and after a while we decided to take off our coats.

When we got back and Duffy didn't have his jacket, did they get mad at him? My mother actually had the nerve to say, "Why didn't you remind him? You know he forgets things like that."

What do I look like, a walking memo pad?

Anyway, I had other things on my mind—like the fact that I was convinced someone had been following us while we were in the woods.

I tried to tell my mother about it, but first she said I was being ridiculous, and then she accused me of trying to sabotage the trip.

So I shut up. But I was pretty nervous, especially when Mom and Aunt Elise announced that they were going into town—which was twenty miles away—to pick up some supplies (like lightbulbs).

"You kids will be fine on your own," said Mom cheerfully. "You can make popcorn and play Monopoly. And there's enough soda here for you to make yourselves sick on."

And with that they were gone.

It got dark.

We played Monopoly.

They didn't come back. That didn't surprise me. Since Duffy and I were both fifteen they felt it was okay to leave us on our own, and Mom had warned us they might decide to have dinner at the little inn we had seen on the way up.

But I would have been happier if they had been there.

Especially when something started scratching on the door.

"What was that?" said Marie.

"What was what?" asked Duffy.

"That!" she said, and this time I heard it, too. My stomach rolled over, and the skin at the back of my neck started to prickle.

"Maybe it's the Sentinel!" I hissed.

"Andrew!" yelled Marie. "Mom told you not to say that."

"She said not to try to scare you," I said. "I'm not. *I'm* scared! I told you I heard something following us in the woods today."

Scratch, scratch.

"But you said it stopped," said Duffy. "So how would it know where we are now?"

"I don't know. I don't know what it is. Maybe it tracked us, like a bloodhound."

Scratch, scratch.

"Don't bloodhounds have to have something to give them a scent?" asked Marie. "Like a piece of clothing, or—"

We both looked at Duffy.

"Your jacket, Duffy!"

Duffy turned white.

"That's silly," he said after a moment.

"There's something at the door," I said frantically. "Maybe it's been lurking around all day, waiting for our mothers to leave. Maybe it's been waiting for years for someone to come back here."

Scratch, scratch.

"I don't believe it," said Duffy. "It's just the wind moving a branch. I'll prove it."

He got up and headed for the door. But he didn't open it. Instead he peeked through the window next to it. When he turned back, his eyes looked as big as the hard-boiled eggs we had eaten for supper.

"There's something out there!" he hissed. *"Something big!"*

"I told you," I cried. "Oh, I knew there was something there."

"Andrew, are you doing this just to scare me?" said Marie. "Because if you are—"

Scratch, scratch.

"Come on," I said, grabbing her by the hand. "Let's get out of here."

I started to lead her up the stairs.

"Not there!" said Duffy. "If we go up there, we'll be trapped."

"You're right," I said. "Let's go out the back way!"

The thought of going outside scared the daylights out of me. But at least out there we would have somewhere to run. Inside—well, who knew what might happen if the thing found us inside.

We went into the kitchen.

I heard the front door open.

"Let's get out of here!" I hissed.

We scooted out the back door. "What now?" I wondered, looking around frantically.

"The barn," whispered Duffy. "We can hide in the barn."

"Good idea," I said. Holding Marie by the hand, I led the way to the barn. But the door was held shut by a huge padlock.

The wind was blowing harder, but not hard

enough to hide the sound of the back door of the house opening, and then slamming shut.

"Quick!" I whispered. "It knows we're out here. Let's sneak around front. It will never expect us to go back into the house."

Duffy and Marie followed me as I led them behind a hedge. I caught a glimpse of something heading toward the barn and swallowed nervously. It was big. Very big.

"I'm scared," whispered Marie.

"Shhhh!" I hissed. "We can't let it know where we are."

We slipped through the front door. We locked it, just like people always do in the movies, though what good that would do I couldn't figure, since if something really wanted to get at us, it would just break the window and come in.

"Upstairs," I whispered.

We tiptoed up the stairs. Once we were in our bedroom, I thought we were safe. Crawling over the floor, I raised my head just enough to peek out the window. My heart almost stopped. Standing in the moonlight was an enormous, manlike creature. It had a scrap of cloth in its hands. It was looking around—looking for us. I saw it lift its head and sniff the wind. To my horror, it started back toward the house.

"It's coming back!" I yelped, more frightened than ever.

"How does it know where we are?" asked Marie.

I knew how. It had Duffy's jacket. It was tracking us down, like some giant bloodhound.

We huddled together in the middle of the room, trying to think of what to do.

A minute later we heard it.

Scratch, scratch.

None of us moved.

Scratch, scratch.

We stopped breathing, then jumped up in alarm at a terrible crashing sound.

The door was down.

We hunched back against the wall as heavy footsteps came clomping up the stairs.

I wondered what our mothers would think when they got back. Would they find our bodies? Or would there be nothing left of us at all?

Thump. Thump. Thump.

It was getting closer.

Thump. Thump. Thump.

It was outside the door.

Knock, knock.

"Don't answer!" hissed Duffy.

Like I said, he doesn't have the brains of a turnip.

It didn't matter. The door wasn't locked. It came swinging open. In the shaft of light I saw a huge figure. The Sentinel of the Woods! It had to be. I thought I was going to die.

The figure stepped into the room. Its head nearly touched the ceiling.

Marie squeezed against my side, tighter than a tick in a dog's ear.

The huge creature sniffed the air. It turned in our direction. Its eyes seemed to glow. Moonlight glittered on its fangs.

Slowly the Sentinel raised its arm. I could see Duffy's jacket dangling from its fingertips.

And then it spoke.

"You forgot your jacket, stupid."

It threw the jacket at Duffy, turned around, and stomped down the stairs.

Which is why, I suppose, no one has had to remind Duffy to remember his jacket, or his glasses, or his math book, for at least a year now.

After all, when you leave stuff lying around, you never can be sure just who might bring it back.

HOMEWARD BOUND

Jamie stood on the steps of his uncle's house and looked up. The place was tall and bleak. With its windows closed and shuttered, as they were now, it was easy to imagine the building was actually trying to keep him out.

"This isn't home," he thought rebelliously. "It's not home, and it never will be."

A pigeon fluttered onto the lawn nearby. Jamie started, then frowned. His father had raised homing pigeons, and the two of them had spent many happy hours together, tending his flock. But the sight of the bird now, with the loss of his father still so fresh in his mind, only stirred up memories he wasn't yet ready to deal with.

He looked at the house again and was struck by an odd feeling: while this wasn't home, coming here had somehow taken him one step closer to finding it. That feeling had to do with the horn, of course; of that much he was certain.

Jamie was seven the first time he had seen the horn hanging on the wall of his uncle's study.

"Narwhal," said his uncle, following the boy's

gaze. "It's a whale with a horn growing out of the front of its head." He put one hand to his forehead and thrust out a finger to illustrate, as if Jamie were some sort of an idiot. "Sort of a seagoing unicorn," he continued. "Except, of course, that it's real instead of imaginary. I'd rather you didn't touch it. I paid dearly to get it."

Jamie had stepped back behind his father without speaking. He hadn't dared to say what was on his mind. Grown-ups, especially his uncle, didn't like to be told they were wrong.

But his uncle *was* wrong. The horn had not come from a narwhal, not come from the sea at all.

It was the horn of a genuine unicorn.

Jamie couldn't have explained how he knew this was so. But he did, as surely—and mysteriously—as his father's pigeons knew their way home. Thinking of that moment of certainty now, he was reminded of those stormy nights when he and his father had watched lightning crackle through the summer sky. For an instant, everything would be outlined in light. Then, just as quickly, the world would be plunged back into darkness, with nothing remaining but a dazzling memory.

That was how it had been with the horn, five years ago.

And now Jamie was twelve, and his father was dead, and he had been sent to live with this rich, remote man who had always frightened him so much.

Oddly, that fear didn't come from his uncle. Despite his stern manner, the man was always quiet and polite with Jamie. Rather he had learned the fear from his father. The two men had not been together often, for his uncle frequently disappeared on mysterious "business trips" lasting weeks or even months on end. But as Jamie had watched his father grow nervous and unhappy whenever his brother was due to return, he came to sense that the one man had some strange hold over the other.

It frightened him.

Yet as scared as he was, as sad and lonely over the death of his father, one small corner of his soul was burning now with a fierce joy because he was finally going to be close to the horn.

Of course, in a way, he had never been apart from it. Ever since that first sight, five years ago, the horn had shimmered in his memory. It was the first thing he thought of when he woke up, and the last at night when he went to sleep. It was a gleaming beacon in his dreams, reassuring him no matter how cruel and ugly a day might have been, there was a reason to go on, a reason to be. His one glimpse of the horn had filled him with a sense of beauty and rightness so powerful it had carried him through these five years.

Even now, while his uncle was droning on about the household rules, he saw it again in that space in the back of his head where it seemed to reside. Like a shaft of never-ending light, it tapered through the darkness of his mind, wrist thick at its base, ice-pick sharp at its tip, a spiraled wonder of icy, pearly whiteness. And while Jamie's uncle was telling him the study was off-limits, Jamie was trying to figure out how quickly he could slip in there to see the horn again.

For once again his uncle was wrong. No place that held the horn could be off-limits for him. It was too deeply a part of him.

That was why he had come here so willingly, despite his fear of his uncle. Like the pigeons, he was making his way home.

Jamie listened to the big clock downstairs as it marked off the quarter hours. When the house had been quiet for seventy-five minutes he took the flashlight from under his pillow, climbed out of bed, and slipped on his robe. Walking softly, he made his way down the hall, enjoying the feel of the thick carpet like moss beneath his feet.

He paused at the door of the study. Despite his feelings, he hesitated. What would his uncle say, or do, if he woke and caught him here?

The truth was, it didn't matter. He had no choice. He had to see the horn again.

Turning the knob of the door, he held his breath against the inevitable click. But when it came, it was mercifully soft. He stepped inside and flicked on his flashlight.

His heart lurched as the beam struck the opposite wall and showed an empty place where the horn had once hung. A little cry slipped through his lips before he remembered how important it was to remain silent.

He swung the light around the room, and breathed a sigh of relief. The horn—the alicorn, as his reading had told him it was called—lay across his uncle's desk.

He stepped forward, almost unable to believe that the moment he had dreamed of all these years was finally at hand.

He took another step, and another.

He was beside the desk now, close enough to reach out and touch the horn.

And still he hesitated.

Part of that hesitation came from wonder, for the horn was even more beautiful than he had remembered. Another part of it came from a desire to make this moment last as long as he possibly could. It was something he had been living toward for five years now, and he wanted to savor it. But the biggest part of his hesitation came from fear. He had a sense that once he had touched the horn, his life might never be the same again.

That didn't mean he wouldn't do it.

But he needed to prepare himself. So for a while he simply stood in the darkness, gazing at the horn.

Light seemed to play beneath its surface, as if there was something alive inside it—though how that could be after all this time he didn't know.

Finally he reached out to stroke the horn. Just stroke it. He wasn't ready, yet, to truly embrace whatever mystery was waiting for him. Just a hint, just a teasing glimpse, was all he wanted.

His fingertip grazed the horn and he cried out in terror as the room lights blazed on, and his uncle's powerful voice thundered over him, demanding to know what was going on.

Jamie collapsed beside the desk. His uncle scooped him up and carried him back to his room.

A fever set in, and it was three days before Jamie got out of bed again.

He had vague memories of people coming to see him during that time—of a doctor who took his pulse and temperature; of an older woman who hovered beside him, spooning a thin broth between his lips and wiping his forehead with a cool cloth; and most of all of his uncle, who loomed over his bed like a thundercloud, glowering down at him.

His only other memories were of the strange dream that gripped him over and over again, causing him to thrash and cry out in terror. In the dream he was running through a deep forest. Something was behind him, pursuing him. He leaped over mossy logs, splashed through cold streams, crashed through brambles and thickets. But no matter how he tried, he couldn't escape the fierce thing that was after him—a thing that wore his uncle's face.

More than once Jamie sat up in bed, gasping and covered with sweat. Then the old woman, or the doctor, would speak soothing words and try to calm his fears.

Once he woke quietly. He could hear doves cooing outside his window. Looking up, he saw his uncle standing beside the bed, staring down at him angrily.

Why? wondered Jamie. *Why doesn't he want me to touch the horn?*

But he was tired, and the question faded as he slipped back into his dreams.

He was sent away to a school, where he was vaguely miserable but functioned well enough to keep the faculty at a comfortable distance. The other students, not so easily escaped, took some delight in trying to torment the dreamy boy who was so oblivious to their little world of studies and games, their private wars and rages. After a while they gave it up; Jamie didn't react enough to make their tortures worth the effort on any but the most boring of days.

He had other things to think about, memories and mysteries that absorbed him and carried him through the year, aware of the world around him only enough to move from one place to another, to answer questions, to keep people away.

The memories had two sources. The first was the vision that had momentarily dazzled him when he touched the horn, a tantalizing instant of joy so deep and powerful it had shaken him to the roots of his being. Hints of green, of cool, of wind in face and hair whispered at the edges of that vision.

He longed to experience it again.

The other memories echoed from his fever dreams, and were not so pleasant. They spoke only of fear, and some terrible loss he did not understand.

Christmas, when it finally came, was difficult. As the other boys were leaving for home his uncle sent word that urgent business would keep him out of town throughout the holiday. He paid the headmaster handsomely to keep an eye on Jamie and feed him Christmas dinner.

The boy spent a bleak holiday longing for his father. Until now his obsession with the horn had shielded him from the still-raw pain of that loss. But the sounds and smells of the holiday, the tinkling bells, the warm spices, the temporary but real good-will surrounding him, all stirred the sorrow inside him, and he wept himself to sleep at night.

He dreamed. In his dreams his father would reach out to take his hand. "We're all lost," he would whisper, as he had the day he died. "Lost, and aching to find our name, so that we can finally go home again."

When Jamie woke, his pillow would be soaked with sweat, and tears.

The sorrow faded with the return of the other students, and the resumption of a daily routine. Even so, it was a relief when three months later his uncle sent word that Jamie would be allowed to come back for the spring holiday.

The man made a point of letting Jamie know he had hidden the horn by taking him into the study soon after the boy's arrival at the house. He watched closely as Jamie's eyes flickered over the walls, searching for the horn, and seemed satisfied at the expression of defeat that twisted his face before he closed in on himself, shutting out the world again.

But Jamie had become cunning. The defeat he showed his uncle was real. What the man didn't see, because the boy buried it as soon as he was aware of it, was that the defeat was temporary. For hiding the horn didn't make any difference. Now that Jamie had touched it, he was bound to it. Wherever it was hidden, he would find it. Its call was too powerful to mistake.

Even so, Jamie thought he might lose his mind before he got his chance. Day after day his uncle stayed in the house, guarding his treasure. Finally, on the morning of the fifth day, an urgent message pulled him away. Even then the anger that burned in his face as he stormed through the great oak doors, an anger Jamie knew was rooted in being called from his vigil, might have frightened someone less determined.

The boy didn't care. He would make his way to the horn while he had the chance.

He knew where it was, of course—had known from the evening of the first day.

It was in his uncle's bedroom.

The room was locked. Moving cautiously, Jamie slipped downstairs to the servants' quarters and stole the master key, then scurried back to the door. To his surprise he felt no fear.

He decided it was because he had no choice; he was only doing what he had to do.

He twisted the key in the lock and swung the door open.

His uncle's room was large and richly decorated, filled with heavy, carefully carved furniture. Above the dresser hung a huge mirror.

Jamie hesitated for just a moment, then lay on his stomach and peered beneath the bed.

The horn was there, wrapped in a length of blue velvet.

He reached in and drew the package out. Then he stood and placed it gently on the bed. With reverent fingers he unrolled the velvet. Cradled by the rich blue fabric, the horn looked like a comet blazing across a midnight sky.

This time there could be no interruption. Hesitating for no more than a heartbeat, he reached out and clutched the horn with both hands.

He cried out, in agony, and in awe. For a moment he thought he was going to die. The feelings the horn unleashed within him seemed too much for his body to hold. He didn't die, though his heart was racing faster than it had any right to.

"More," he thought, as images of the place he had seen in his dreams rushed through his mind. "I have to know more."

He drew the horn to his chest and laid his cheek against it.

He thought his heart would beat its way out of his body.

And still it wasn't enough.

He knew what he had to do next. But he was afraid.

Fear made no difference. He remembered again what his father had said about people aching to find their true name. He was close to his now. *No one can come this close and not reach out for the answer,* he thought. *The emptiness would kill them on the spot.*

And so he did what he had to do, fearful as it was. Placing the base of the horn against the foot of the massive bed, he set the tip of it against his heart.

Then he leaned forward.

The point of the horn pierced his flesh like a sword made of fire and ice. He cried out, first in pain, then in joy and wonder. Finally the answer was clear to him, and he understood his obsession, and his loneliness.

"No wonder I didn't fit," he thought, as his fingers fused, then split into cloven hooves.

The transformation was painful. But the joy so far surpassed it that he barely noticed the fire he felt as his neck began to stretch, and the horn erupted from his brow. "No wonder, no wonder—no, it's all wonder, wonder, wonder and joy!"

He reared back in triumph, his silken mane streaming behind him, as he trumpeted the joyful discovery that he was, and always had been, and always would be, a unicorn.

And knowing his name, he finally knew how to go home. Hunching the powerful muscles of his hind legs, he launched himself toward the dresser. His horn struck the mirror, and it shattered into a million pieces that crashed and tinkled into two different worlds.

He hardly noticed. He was through, and home at last.

No, said a voice at the back of his head. *You're not home yet.*

He stopped. It was true. He wasn't home yet, though he was much closer. But there was still more to do, and further to go.

How could that be? He knew he was, had always been, a unicorn. Then he trembled, as he realized his father's last words were still true. There was something inside that needed to be discovered, to be named.

He whickered nervously as he realized all he had really done was come back to where most people begin—his own place, his own shape.

He looked around. He was standing at the edge of a clearing in an old oak wood. Sunlight filtered through the leaves, dappling patches of warmth onto his flanks. He paused for a moment, taking pleasure in feeling his own true shape at last.

Suddenly he shivered, then stood stock-still as the smell of the girl reached his nostrils.

The scent was sweet, and rich, and he could resist it no more than he had resisted the horn. He began trotting in her direction, sunlight bouncing off the horn that jutted out from his forehead.

He found her sitting beneath an apple tree, singing to herself while she brushed her honey-colored hair. Doves rustled and cooed at the edges of the clearing. They reminded him of the pigeons his father had raised.

As he stood and watched her, every fiber of his being cried out that there was danger here. But it was not in the nature of a unicorn to resist such a girl.

Lowering his head, he walked forward.

"So," she said. "You've come at last."

He knelt beside her, and she began to stroke his mane. Her fingers felt cool against his neck, and she sang to him in a voice that seemed to wash away old sorrows. He relaxed into a sweet silence, content for the first time that he could remember.

He wanted the moment to go on forever.

But it ended almost instantly as the girl slipped a golden bridle over his head, and his uncle suddenly stepped into the clearing.

The man was wearing a wizard's garb, which didn't surprise Jamie. Ten armed soldiers stood behind him.

Jamie sprang to his feet. But he had been bound by the magic of the bridle; he could neither run, nor attack.

Flanks heaving, he stared at his wizard uncle.

"Did you really think you could get away from me?" asked the man.

I have! thought Jamie fiercely, knowing the thought would be understood.

"Don't be absurd!" snarled his uncle. "I'll take your horn, as I did your father's. And then I'll take your shape, and finally your memory. You'll come back with me and be no different than he was—a dreamy, foolish mortal, lost and out of place."

Why? thought Jamie. *Why would anyone want to hold a unicorn?*

His uncle didn't answer.

Jamie locked eyes with him, begging him to explain.

No answer came. But he realized he had found

a way to survive. Just as the golden bridle held him helpless, so his gaze could hold his uncle. As long as he could stare into the man's eyes, he could keep him from moving.

He knew, too, that as soon as he flinched, the battle would be over.

Jamie had no idea how long the struggle actually lasted. They seemed to be in a place apart, far away from the clearing, away from the girl and the soldiers.

He began to grow fearful. Sooner or later he would falter and his uncle would regain control. It wasn't enough to hold him. He had to conquer him.

But how? *How?*

He couldn't win unless he knew why he was fighting. He had to discover why his uncle wanted to capture and hold him.

But the only way to do that was to look deeper inside the man. The idea frightened him; he didn't know what he would find there. Even worse, it would work two ways. He couldn't look deeper into his uncle, without letting his uncle look more deeply into him.

He hesitated. But there was no other way. Accepting the risk, he opened himself to his uncle.

At the same time he plunged into the man's soul.

His uncle cried out, then dropped to his knees and buried his face in his hands, trembling with the humiliation of being seen.

Jamie trembled too, for the emptiness he found

inside this man could swallow suns and devour planets. This was the hunger that had driven him to capture unicorns, in the hope that their glory could fill his darkness.

Then, at last, Jamie knew what he must do. Stepping forward, he pressed the tip of his horn against his uncle's heart.

He had been aware of his horn's healing power, of course. But this was the first time he had tried to use it. He wasn't expecting the shock of pain that jolted through him, or the wave of despair that followed as he took in the emptiness, and the fear and the hunger that had driven his uncle for so long.

He wanted to pull away, to run in terror.

But if he did, it would only start all over again. Only a healing would put an end to the pursuit. And this was the only way to heal this man, this wizard, who, he now understood, had never really been his uncle, but only his captor. He had to be seen, in all his sorrow and his ugliness; seen, and accepted, and loved. Only then could he be free of the emptiness that made him want to possess a unicorn.

Jamie trembled as the waves of emptiness and sorrow continued to wash through him. But at last he was nearly done. Still swaying from the effort, he whispered to the man: "Go back. Go back and find your name. And then—go *home*."

That was when the sword fell, slicing through his neck.

It didn't matter, really, though he felt sorry for his "uncle," who began to weep, and sorrier still for the soldier who had done the deed. He knew it would be a decade or so before the man could sleep without mind-twisting nightmares of the day he had killed a unicorn.

But for Jamie himself, the change made no difference. Because he still was what he had always been, what he always would be, what a unicorn had simply been an appropriate shape to hold. He was a being of power and light.

He shook with delight as he realized that he had named himself at last.

He turned to the wizard, and was amazed. No longer hampered by mere eyes, he could see that the same thing was true for his enemy—as it was for the girl, as it was for the soldiers.

They were *all* beings of power and light.

The terrible thing was, they didn't know it.

Suddenly he understood. This was the secret, the unnamed thing his father had been trying to remember: that we are all beings of power and light. And all the pain, all the sorrow—it all came from not knowing this simple truth.

Why? wondered Jamie. *Why don't any of us know how beautiful we really are?*

And then even that question became unimportant, because his father had come to take him home, and suddenly he wasn't just a unicorn, but was all unicorns, was part of every wise and daring being that had worn that shape and that name, every unicorn that had ever lived, or ever would live. And he felt himself stretch to fill the sky, as the stars came tumbling into his body, stars at his knees and at his hooves, at his shoulder and his tail, and most of all a shimmer of stars that lined the length of his horn, a horn that stretched across the sky, pointing out, for anyone who cared to look, the way to go home.

WITH HIS HEAD TUCKED UNDERNEATH HIS ARM

Fifteen kings ruled the continent of Losfar, and each one hated the others. Old, fat, and foolish, they thought nothing of sending the children of their subjects off on war after war after war, so that the best and the bravest were gone to dust before they ever really lived.

The young men left behind fell into two groups: those who escaped the wars for reasons of the body—the weak, the crippled, the maimed—and those who avoided the wars for reasons of the mind; those too frightened, too smart, or simply too loving to be caught in the trap the kings laid for them.

This last category was smallest of all, and a dangerous one to be in. Questioning the wars outright was against the law, and standing up to declare they were wrong was a quick route to the dungeons that lay beneath the palace. So it was only through deceit that those who opposed the wars could escape going off to kill people they had never met, and had nothing against.

One such was a cobbler's son named Brion, who had avoided the wars by walking on a crutch and pretending that he was crippled. Yet he chafed under the role he played, for he was not the sort to live a lie.

"Why do I have to pretend?" he would ask his friend Mikel, an older man who was one of the few who knew his secret. "Why must I lie, when I am right, and they are wrong?"

But Mikel had no answer. And since much as Brion hated the lie, he hated even more the idea of killing some stranger for the sake of a war he did not believe in, he continued to pretend.

One afternoon when Brion was limping through the marketplace on his crutch, he saw an officer of the king's army beating a woman because she had fallen in his path. The sight angered him so much that without thinking he stepped in to help the woman. "Leave her alone!" he cried, grabbing the officer's arm.

The man pushed Brion away and raised his hand to strike the woman again.

"Help!" she wailed. "He's killing me!"

Brion hesitated for but a moment. Though he knew it would reveal his lie, he sprang to his feet and felled the man with a single blow.

In an instant he was surrounded by soldiers.

Within an hour he found himself chained to a dungeon wall, with no one for company save the occasional passing rat, and no music save the trickle of the water that dripped endlessly down the cold stones.

As the days went by Brion began to wonder if he had been forgotten and would simply be left in his cell to rot. But late one afternoon he heard the clink of keys in the lock. Two uniformed men came into his cell, unlocked his chains, and dragged him to his feet. Gripping his arms in their mailed gloves, they hustled him to the throne room, to face the king.

"Is it true that you refuse to fight for me?" asked the king angrily.

At the moment, Brion's main fight was with the lump of fear lodged in his throat. But he stood as straight as he was able and said, "It is true. I cannot kill a man I have never met for the sake of a war I do not believe in."

The king's jowly face grew scarlet with rage. "Let the court see the treason of this speech. Let it be recorded, so that all will understand why this rebellious youth is being put to death."

Three days later Brion was marched to the public square. His weeping mother stood at the front of the crowd, shaking with sorrow as the guards escorted her son up the steps to die. Pushed to his knees, Brion laid his head on the block. He heard his father's voice cry out. But the words were lost to him, because the executioner's ax had fallen.

The crowd roared as Brion's severed head tumbled into the waiting basket.

Body and head were buried in a shallow grave far outside the city, in a corner of the boneyard reserved for traitors.

Brion was about as mad as a dead man can be, which may explain why three nights later he climbed out of the ground. Reaching back, he plucked his head from the grave, gave it a shake to rid it of loose dirt, then tucked it under his arm and started for the city.

It was the quietest part of the night when he reached the palace. Most of the guards were nodding at their posts, but even the few who were still alert did not see him enter.

The dead have their ways.

Slowly Brion climbed the stairs to the king's bedchamber. When he entered the room he stood in silence. But his presence alone was enough to trouble the king, and after a moment the fat old man sat up suddenly, crying, "Who dares to disturb my sleep?"

"I dare," said Brion, "because I know you for what you really are: a murderer and a thief, not fit to be king. You have been stealing your subjects' lives, and I have come to set things right."

Then he crossed the room and stood in a shaft of moonlight that flowed through the window next to the king's bed. When the king saw the body of the young man he had ordered killed just three days earlier standing next to him, saw the severed head with its still-raw wound, he began to scream.

"Silence!" ordered Brion, raising his head to hold it before the king's face. "Silence, if you wish to see the morning!"

Trembling beneath his blankets, the king pleaded with Brion to spare his life. "I will do anything you ask," he whimpered. "Anything at all."

The head smiled. Then Brion told the king what he wanted him to do.

The next day the king's advisors were astonished to hear the king announce that the war was over, and that he was calling the armies back from the field.

"Why, your majesty?" they asked. They were deeply disturbed, for they loved their game of war and were sad to see it end.

But the king would say nothing of his reasons.

Now life in the kingdom began to change slowly for the better. The youths who returned from the war began to take a useful part in the life of their homeland. With strong young hands to till the fields, the farms grew more productive. Some of those who returned from the wars were artists and poets; some were builders and thinkers. New ideas came forward, new designs, new ways of doing things. As time went on the kingdom grew stronger, happier, and more prosperous than any of those surrounding it.

And in all this time Brion never left the king to himself. Though the guard was doubled, and doubled again, somehow they always slept when Brion walked the halls—as he did every night when he came to visit the king's bedchamber. And there, with his head tucked underneath his arm, he would instruct the king on what to do next.

When morning came, Brion would be gone. But the smell of death lingered in the room. The servants began to whisper that the king was ailing, and would not live much longer. But live he did, and for the next three years he continued to do as Brion told him.

In that time the kingdom grew so prosperous that the other kings on Losfar grew jealous. They began to plot together and soon decided to attack the rebellious kingdom that had left the wars.

"After all," said King Fulgram, "the only reason they have so much is that they have not been spending it to defend themselves, as have we. Therefore, a share of it should be ours."

"A *large* share," said King Nichard with a smile.

When Brion heard that the armies of Losfar were marching on his homeland, he did not know what to do. He certainly did not want a war. But neither did he want to let the outsiders tear down all that had been built. And he knew he could not let them murder his people.

"Send a message of peace to the enemy camp," he told the king a few nights before the enemy was expected to arrive.

The king sneered, but, as always, did as he was told.

The messenger was murdered, his body sent back as a warning of what was to come.

Panic swept the kingdom.

That night, when Brion stood by the king's bedside, the old man began to gloat over the coming war. "See what you have brought us to," he taunted. "We are no better off, and in fact far worse, than when you started. Before, we fought on *their* soil, and it was *their* homes that were destroyed. In two days' time the enemy will be upon us, and this time it is *our* city that will burn."

Brion said nothing, for he did not know what to do.

Later, when he was walking back to his grave, Brion met another traveler on the road. Brion recognized him as the murdered messenger by the stray bits of moonlight that flowed through the holes in his chest (for the king had described the man's wounds with savage delight).

The messenger turned from his path to walk with Brion. For a time the two men traveled in silence.

Brion felt a great sorrow, for he blamed himself for the messenger's death. Finally he began to speak, and told the man everything that had happened since his own beheading.

"Don't feel bad," replied the messenger. "After all, your heart was in the right place—which is more than I can say for your head," he added, gesturing to the grisly object Brion carried beneath his arm. It was sadly battered now, for dead flesh does not heal, and in three years it had suffered many small wounds and bruises.

Brion's head began to laugh, and before long the two dead men were staggering along the road, leaning on each other as they told bad jokes about death and dying.

After a time they paused. Standing together, they stared into the deep and starry sky.

"I am so tired," said Brion at last. "How I wish that I could be done with this. How I wish that I could rest."

"You cannot," said the messenger. "You must finish what you have started."

Brion sighed, for he knew that his new friend was right. "And what of you?" he asked. "Why do you walk this night?"

"I was too angry to rest," said the messenger. "I wish that those fools could know how sweet life is. But perhaps only the dead can know that."

"More's the pity," said Brion. And with that he left the messenger and returned to his grave.

But the messenger's words stayed with him, and the next night when he rose, he knew what to do. Finding the grave of the messenger, he called him forth, saying, "I have one last message for you to deliver."

Then he told him his plan. Smiling, the messenger agreed to help. And so the two men went from grave to grave, calling the dead with these words:

"Awake, arise! Your children are in danger, your parents may perish, your childhood homes will burn. All that you loved in life is at peril. Awake, arise, and walk with us."

Not every soul gave back an answer. Some were too long dead, or too tired, or too far away in the next world. Some had never cared about these things in life. But for many, Brion's call was all that was needed to stir them from their place of rest. The earth began to open, and up from their graves rose the young and the old, the long dead and the newly buried. And each that rose took up the message and went to gather others, so that two became four, and four became eight, and eight became a multitude, shaking the earth from their dead and rotted limbs for the sake of all that they had loved in life.

When the army of the dead had gathered at the gate of the graveyard, Brion stood before them and took his head from beneath his arm. Holding it high, he told them all that had happened.

He told them what he wanted of them.

Then he turned and headed for the camp of the enemy.

Behind him marched the army of the dead. Some moaned as they traveled, remembering the sweetness and the sorrow of the living world. Some were no more than skeletons, their bones stripped clean by their years in the earth. Others, more recently dead, left bits and pieces of themselves along the way.

Soon they reached the camp of the enemy, which was all too close to the city. Following Brion's lead, they entered the camp. It was easy enough to pass the sentries. The dead *do* have their ways. Then, by ones and twos, they entered the tents of the living, where they began to sing to them of death's embrace.

"Look on me, look on me," they whispered in the ears of the sleeping men. "As I am, soon you shall be."

When the soldiers roused from their dreams of killing and dying to find themselves looking into the faces of those already dead, fear crept into their hearts.

But the dead meant them no harm. They had come only to speak to them, slowly and softly, of what it is to be dead; how it feels to be buried in the earth; what it is like to have worms burrow through your body.

"This will come to you soon enough," they whispered, extending their cold hands to stroke the faces of the living.

Some of the dead women held out their arms. When the men cried out and cowered from their touch, they whispered, "If you fear my embrace, then fear the grave as well. Go home, go home, and there do good. Choose life, choose life, and leave this place in peace."

One by one, the terrified men slipped from their tents and fled across the hills to their homes, until the invading army had vanished like a ghost in the night.

Then the army of the dead returned to the cemetery. They laughed as they went, and were well pleased, and chuckled at their victory. For though they had spoken nothing but the truth, they had not told all that there was to tell. The departing men would learn that in good time; there was no need for them to know *all* the secrets of the world beyond too soon.

As dawn drew near, Brion stood at the edge of his grave and stared into it with longing. At last the time had come to discover what came next, the secrets and surprises he had denied himself for three long years.

Tenderly he placed his head in the grave. Then crawling in beside it, he laid himself down and died.

CLEAN AS A WHISTLE

Jamie Carhart was, quite possibly, the messiest kid in Minnesota. The messiest kid in her town, no doubt. The county? She pretty well had that sewed up, too. And her mother was convinced that, were there a statewide competition, Jamie would easily be in the top ten, and might, indeed, take first place.

Not that Mrs. Carhart was amused by this fact.

"This room is a sty!" she would say at least once a day, standing in the doorway of Jamie's room and sighing. Then she would poke her foot at the mess that threatened to creep out into the rest of the house, sigh again as if the whole thing was far too much for her to cope with, and wander off.

So it was a shock for Jamie to come home from school on the afternoon of April 17 and find her room totally, perfectly, absolutely neat, clean, and tidy.

"Aaaaaah!" she cried, standing in her doorway. "Aaaaaah! What happened? Who did this?"

Jamie didn't really expect an answer. Her parents both worked and wouldn't be home for another two hours.

For a horrible moment she wondered if her grandmother had come to visit. Gramma Hattie was perfectly capable of sneaking into a kid's room and cleaning it while that kid wasn't looking. Heaven alone knew where *she* might have put things. Even Jamie's mother found Gramma Hattie hard to cope with.

But Gramma Hattie lived in Utah (which in Jamie's opinion was a good place for her), and now that Jamie thought of it, she was off on a trip to Europe. Besides, if she had done this, she would have pounced by now, crowing at her victory over disorder.

So it wasn't her.

Jamie hesitated, wondering if she dared go in.

"Anyone here?" she asked timidly.

No answer.

"Anyone?"

Silence, though she did notice that the cat was on her bed. This did not please her. Actually, she always longed to have the cat in her room. But Mr. Bumpo normally refused to come through her door. Jamie's mother claimed this was because the cat was too neat and couldn't stand the mess. Jamie denied this, usually quite angrily. So she wasn't amused to find Mr. Bumpo here now that the room was so clean; his gently purring presence seemed to confirm her mother's horrible theory.

Jamie looked around nervously as she entered the room. After a moment she dropped her books on her bed. She waited, half expecting someone to come dashing in and pick them up.

"What is going on here?" she asked the cat, scratching its orange-and-black head.

Mr. Bumpo closed his eyes and purred louder.

When Mrs. Carhart arrived home and came up to say hello to Jamie, she grabbed the edges of the doorway and staggered as if she had been hit between the eyes with a two-by-four.

"What," she asked in astonishment, "got into you?"

"What are you talking about?" asked Jamie sourly. She was sitting at her desk, working on a small clay project. She had generated a minor mess with the work, and managed to create a tad of clutter here and there. But overall the room was still so clean as to be unrecognizable.

"I mean this room," said her mother. She squeezed her eyes shut then opened them again, as if to make sure that she wasn't hallucinating. "It's so... so... *tidy!*"

Jamie looked at her suspiciously. "Didn't you hire someone to come in here and clean it?" she asked. She was still fairly angry about the invasion of her privacy (and not about to admit that she was delighted to find her clay-working tools, which had been missing for some six months now).

Her mother snorted. "The day we can afford a housekeeper, he or she takes on some of *my* work first."

"Then who did this to me?" asked Jamie.

Her mother looked at her oddly. "You are the strangest child," she said at last. "But thanks anyway."

Before Jamie could reply, Mrs. Carhart turned and left. Jamie growled and stabbed a long metal tool through the little clay man she had been making. She knew what her mother was thinking. She was thinking that she, Jamie, had cleaned up the room but was too embarrassed to admit it. She was also thinking that if she pushed the issue Jamie would never do it again. Which meant that when Jamie claimed she had nothing to do with this...this *catastrophe,* her mother would simply think that she was playing an odd game, and the more she tried to convince her otherwise, the more Mrs. Carhart would be convinced that she was right in her assumption. Jamie groaned. It was hopeless.

Of course, the other possibility was that her mother was lying and really had hired someone to clean the room. Jamie considered the idea. "Unlikely," she said out loud.

But what other explanation was there? Some demented prowler who broke into people's houses to clean rooms when no one was at home? Jamie glanced around nervously, then shook her head.

———

Dinner that night was interesting. Mrs. Carhart had clearly warned Mr. Carhart that he was not to make a big deal over the clean room for fear that Jamie would never do it again.

By the time the meal was over, Jamie wanted to scream.

By the time the night was over, she *did* scream. "I just want you to know that I am *not* responsible for this!" she bellowed, standing at the top of the stairs. "I had nothing to do with it!"

She heard her father chuckle.

Furious, she returned to her room, slamming the door behind her. When she undressed for bed she tore off her clothes and scattered them about the floor. Once she was in her nightgown she went to the door, opened it a crack, and yelled "Good night!"

Then she slammed it shut and climbed between the sheets.

When Jamie got home the next afternoon, yesterday's clothes (which she had studiously avoided touching that morning) had disappeared from her floor. Her clay-working tools were lined up in an orderly fashion on her desk. The bits of clay that she had left around had been gathered together and rolled into a ball.

The cat was curled up in the middle of her bed, sleeping peacefully.

"Did you do this?" she asked, looking at him suspiciously. She was perfectly aware of what a stupid question it was. On the other hand, when things got this weird, stupid questions began to make sense.

Mr. Bumpo blinked at her, but said nothing. She reached out to stroke him and realized that his fur, which normally had a number of tangles and knots, was perfectly groomed.

"This is creepy," she said. "And I don't like it." She tossed her backpack on the bed and began to search the room for some clue or sign as to who might have done this. Under her bed she found only that the rapidly breeding colony of dust bunnies had become extinct. She checked her closet next, where she saw something she had not laid eyes on in over three years: the floor. When she looked in her dresser she found that every item of clothing had been neatly folded. This was even worse than it had been the day before!

What she did not find was any sign of who had done this terrible thing to her.

She sat on the edge of her bed for a long time, stroking Mr. Bumpo and listening to him purr. Finally she decided to go back to her clay working. Remembering a sketch for a new project she had made during math class, she overturned her pack and emptied it on the bed. Out tumbled a mixture of books, crumpled papers, pens and pencils in various stages of usefulness, candy wrappers, rubber bands, sparkly rocks she had picked up on the way to and from school, three crayons stuck together with a piece of used chewing gum, and a moldy sandwich.

Jamie dug her way through the mound of stuff until she found the sketch. She carried it to her desk and smoothed it out, then picked up the ball of clay and began to work. After about half an hour she decided to go get a snack.

When she got up from her desk and turned around she let out a yelp of astonishment.

Her bed was perfectly clean! The mess she had dumped onto it had been organized and tidied into meek submission. The crumpled papers had vanished, the pencils were lined up in a tidy row, the crayons unstuck, the gum that held them together mysteriously gone. Even the backpack's straps had been neatly folded beneath it.

"What is going on here?" she cried.

The only answer was a yawn from Mr. Bumpo.

Goose bumps prickling over her arms, Jamie wondered if she should run for her life. But nothing about what was happening was threatening. It was just... *weird*.

She stared at her bed for a while, then made a decision. Stomping over to it, she snatched up the neat piles and tossed them into the air. Mr. Bumpo yowled in alarm, bolted from the bed, and ran out of the room. Jamie stirred the mess around a bit more, rumpled the bedcovers for good measure, then went back to her desk and picked up her tools. She pretended to work. What she was really doing was trying to look over her shoulder while bending her neck as little as possible.

For several minutes nothing happened except that her neck got sore. In a way, she was glad nothing happened; part of her had been afraid of what she might see. Eventually the pain in her neck got to be too much, and she was forced to straighten her head. When she turned back she saw a brown blur out of the corner of her eye.

"Gotcha!" she cried, leaping to her feet.

But whatever it was had disappeared.

Jamie stood still for a moment, wondering what had happened. *Under the bed!* she thought suddenly.

Dropping to her knees, she crept to the bed and lifted the edge of the spread. All she saw was clean floor, and a ripple of movement at the other side of the spread. Whatever had been there had escaped.

"That little stinker is fast," Jamie muttered, getting to her feet. She stared at the bed, which was still a mess, and made a decision. Leaving the room, she headed for the kitchen.

When Jamie returned to her room the bed had been remade and the things from her pack were in perfect order. This did not surprise her.

She went to the far side of the bed, the side from which whatever-it-was had disappeared. She opened the bottle of molasses she had taken from the kitchen, then poured a thick line of the sticky goo the length of the bed, about a foot from the edge. Replacing the lid, she once again messed up everything on top of the bed. Then she returned to her desk.

It wasn't long before she heard a tiny voice cry, "What have you done, what have you done?"

Turning, she saw a manlike creature about a foot-and-a-half tall. He was jumping up and down beside her bed. Covered with brown fur, he looked like a tiny, potbellied version of Bigfoot. The main differences were a long tail and a generally more human face.

"Wretched girl!" cried the creature, shaking a hazelnut-sized fist at her. "What's the matter wi' you?"

"What's the matter with *you?*" she replied. "Sneaking into a person's room and cleaning it up when you're not invited is perverted."

"I was too invited," snapped the creature. Sitting down, he flicked his tail out of the way and began licking molasses from the bottom of his right foot.

"What a liar you are!" said Jamie.

"What a Messy Carruthers you are!" replied the creature. "And you don't know everything, miss. I was sent here by one of your blood. That counts as invitation if she is close enough—which she is."

Jamie scowled, then her eyes opened wide. "My grandmother!" she exclaimed. "*She* sent you, didn't she?"

"That she did, and I can see why, too. Really, this place is quite pathetic. I don't understand why you wouldn't welcome having someone clean it up. I should think you'd be grateful."

"This is my room, and I liked it the way it was," said Jamie.

This was not entirely true. Jamie did sometimes wish that the place was clean. But she felt that she couldn't admit that without losing the argument altogether. Besides, she mostly did like it her way; and she most certainly did *not* like having someone clean it without her permission. She felt as if she had been robbed or something. "What are you, anyway?" she asked, by way of changing the topic.

The creature rolled his eyes, as if he couldn't believe her stupidity. "I'm a brownie," he said. "As any fool can plainly see."

"Brownies don't exist."

"Rude!" cried the creature. "Rude, rude, rude! Your grandmother warned me about that. 'She's a rude girl,' she said. And she was right."

"I think it was rude of my grandmother to talk about me like that in front of a complete stranger," replied Jamie.

"I'm not a complete stranger. I've been the Mac-Dougal family brownie for nearly three hundred years."

"That shows what you know!" said Jamie. "I'm not a MacDougal, I'm a Carhart."

"Aye, and what was your mother's name before she was married?"

"Chase," said Jamie smugly.

"And her mother's name?"

Jamie's sense of certainty began to fade. "I don't have the slightest idea," she said irritably.

"Rude, and irreverent as well! No sense of family, have you girl? Well I'll tell you what you should have known all along. Your grandmother's maiden name was MacDougal—Harriet Hortense Mac-Dougal, to be precise."

"What has that got to do with me?" asked Jamie.

"Everything," said the brownie. Having finished licking the molasses from his feet, he scooted over to her desk. Moving so fast she barely had time to flinch, he climbed the desk leg and positioned himself in front of her, which made them face-to-face (though his face was barely the size of her fist). "The last of your family in the old country died last year, leaving me without a family to tend to. Your grandmother, bless her heart, came to close up the house. There she found me, moaning and mournful. 'Why brownie,' she says (she being smart enough to know what I am, unlike some I could mention), 'Why brownie, whatever is the matter with you?'

"'My family is all gone,' I told her. 'And now I've naught to care for, so I shall soon fade away.'

"Well, right off your grandmother says, 'Oh, the family is not all gone. I've a daughter in the States, and *she* has a daughter who could more than use your services.'"

"Thanks, Gramma," muttered Jamie.

"I wasn't much interested in coming to this barbarian wilderness," said the brownie, ignoring the interruption. "But things being what they were, I didn't have much choice. So here I am, much to your good fortune."

Jamie wondered for a moment why Gramma Hattie had sent the brownie to her instead of to her mother. It didn't take her long to figure out the answer. Jamie's mother would have been as happy to have someone clean her house as Jamie was annoyed by having her room invaded. Gramma Hattie would never have wanted to do anything that pleasant.

"What will it take to get you to leave me alone?" she asked.

The brownie began to laugh. "What a silly girl you are!" he cried. "You won't ever be alone again!"

Great, thought Jamie, rolling her eyes. *My grandmother has sent me an eighteen-inch-high stalker.* Aloud, she asked, "Are you saying I don't have any choice in this?"

"It's a family matter," replied the brownie. "No one gets to choose when it comes to things like that."

"But I don't want you here!"

The brownie's lower lip began to quiver and his homely little face puckered into what Jamie's mother called "a booper."

"You really don't want me?" he asked, sniffing just a bit.

Jamie felt her annoyance begin to melt, until she realized what the brownie was trying to do to her. (It wasn't hard to figure it out, since she tried the same thing on her parents often enough.) "Oh, stop it," she snapped.

Instantly the brownie's expression changed. Crossing his arms, he sat down on her desk and said, "I'm staying, and that's final."

"You're going, and I mean it," replied Jamie. But she realized even as she said it that she had no way to make the threat stick. The smug look on the brownie's face told her that he was well aware of this.

Now what was she going to do? Totally frustrated, she said, "I'm going to tell my mother about you." She hated talking like that; it made her feel like a little kid. But she couldn't think of anything else.

It didn't make any difference. "She won't believe you," said the brownie, looking even smugger.

"Wouldn't you like to go to work for her?" pleaded Jamie. "She'd be more than happy to have you."

The brownie looked wistful. "I would be delighted," he replied. "But the oldest female in the family has assigned me to you. I have no choice in the matter."

For a day or two Jamie thought she might be able to live with the situation—though with the brownie taking up residence in her closet she made it a point to do her dressing and undressing in the bathroom.

The worst thing was the way her mother smiled whenever she passed the room. Jamie ground her teeth, but said nothing.

By the third day she was getting used to having the room neat and clean. And though she hated to admit it, it was easier to get things done when she didn't have to spend half an hour looking for whatever she needed to start. But just when she was beginning to think that things might work out, the brownie did something unforgivable.

He began to nag.

"Can't you do anything for yourself?" he asked petulantly when she tossed her books on the bed one afternoon after she arrived home from school. "Am I expected to take care of *everything* around here?"

Jamie looked at him in astonishment. "I didn't ask you to come here!" she exploded. "And I certainly didn't ask you to be messing around with my stuff all the time!"

"I am not messing," said the brownie primly. "I am *un*messing."

"I don't care!" she screamed. "I want you to go away. I don't like having you here all the time. I don't like knowing you're in my closet. I don't like having my room look the way you and my grandmother think it should look instead of the way I think it should look."

"Messy Carruthers," muttered the brownie.

"Nosey Parker!" snapped Jamie, accidentally using one of her grandmother's favorite phrases.

She stomped to her desk. The brownie disappeared into the closet. A heavy silence descended on the room, broken only when Jamie crumpled a sketch she didn't like and tossed it on the floor.

"You pick that up right now!" called the brownie.

Not only did she not pick up the paper, she crumpled another and threw it on the floor just to spite the creature.

That was the beginning of what Jamie later thought of as "The Great Slob War."

Immediately the brownie came dashing from the closet, snatched up the offending papers, and tossed them into the wastebasket. Muttering angrily, he stomped back to the closet (not very effective for someone only a foot and a half tall) and slammed the door behind him.

Jamie immediately wadded up another paper and threw it on the floor. The brownie dashed out to pick it up. Seized by inspiration, Jamie overturned her wastebasket and shook it out. As the brownie began scurrying around to pick up the papers, she plunked the wastebasket down and sat on it. "Now where will you put the papers?" she asked triumphantly.

Her sense of victory dissolved when the brownie gathered the trash in a pile and began to race around it. With a sudden snap, the pile vanished into nothingness. Wiping his hands, the brownie gave her the smuggest look yet. Then he returned to the closet, slamming the door behind him.

"How did you do that?" cried Jamie. He didn't answer. She threw the wastebasket at the door and began to plan her next attack.

She smeared clay on the wall.

She emptied the contents of her dresser onto her floor, tossing out socks, underwear, blouses, and jeans with wild abandon. She tracked all over them with muddy boots and crushed cracker crumbs on top. The brownie simply waited until she left for school. By the time she got home everything had been cleaned, folded, and replaced, neater than before.

Furious, she opened her pencil sharpener and sprinkled its contents all over her bed, topped them off with pancake syrup, a tangled mass of string, and the collection of paper-punch holes she had been saving all year.

The brownie, equally furious, managed to lick and pluck every one of the shavings from the thick weave of the spread with his tiny fingers. The entire time that he was doing this he muttered and cursed, telling Jamie in no uncertain terms what he thought of her, what a disgrace she was to her family, and to what a bad end she was likely to come.

Jamie tipped back her chair on two legs, lounging unrepentantly. "You missed one," she said when the brownie had finished and was heading back to the closet. He raced back to the bed, but after an intense examination discovered that she had been lying.

"What a wicked girl!" he cried. "Trying to fool a poor brownie that way."

"You're not a poor brownie!" she screamed. "You're a menace!" Suddenly days of frustration began to bubble within her. "I can't stand it!" she cried. "I can't take any more of this. I want you to leave me alone!"

"I can't leave you alone!" shouted the brownie, jumping up and down and waving his tiny fists in the air. "We are bound to each other by ancient ties, by words and deeds, by promises written in blood spilled on your family's land."

"Get out!" cried Jamie. In a frenzy she snatched up an old pillow that had come from her grandmother's house and began smacking it against her bed. The pillow burst open, exploding into a cloud of feathers. "Get out, get out, get out!"

Shrieking with rage, the brownie began trying to pick up the feathers. But the faster he moved the more he sent them drifting away from him. When Jamie saw what was happening she began waving her arms to keep the feathers afloat. The brownie leaped and turned, trying to pluck them from the air. He moved faster and faster, wild, frenzied. Finally he began racing in a circle. He went faster still, until he was little more than a blur to Jamie's eyes. Then, with a sudden *snap!* he vanished, just as the papers had the day before.

Jamie blinked, then began to laugh. She had done it. She had gotten rid of him!

And that should have been that.

But a strange thing happened. As the days went on she began to miss the little creature. Infuriating as he had been, he had also been rather cute. Moreover, the condition of her room began to irritate her.

A week after the brownie vanished she was rooting around in the disarray on her floor, trying to find her clay-working tools, which had been missing for three days. Forty-five minutes of searching had so far failed to turn them up.

"Sometimes I actually wish that brownie had stayed around," she muttered.

From the closet a tiny voice said, "A-hoo."

Jamie stood up. "Is that you, brownie?"

"A-hoo," repeated the voice; it sounded pathetically weak.

Feeling slightly nervous—ever since this started she had not been entirely comfortable with her closet—Jamie went to the door and asked, "Are you in there?"

"A-hoo," said the voice a third time. It seemed to come from the upper shelf.

"Brownie, is that you?"

No answer at all this time.

She ran to her desk. Kicking aside the intervening clutter, she dragged the chair back to the closet. By standing on it, she could reach the upper shelf.

"Brownie?" she called. "Are you there?"

"A-hoo."

The voice was coming from a shoe box. She pulled it from the shelf and looked in. The brownie lay inside. He looked wan and thin, and after a moment she realized to her horror that she could see right through him.

"I thought you had left," she said, her voice thick with guilt.

"I had no place to go." His voice seemed to come from a far-off place. "I am bound to you, and to this house. All I could do was wait to fade away."

An icy fear clenched her heart. "Are you going to die?"

"A-hoo," said the brownie. Then he closed his eyes and turned his head away.

She scrambled from the chair and placed the shoe box on her bed. *I've killed him!* she thought in horror. Reaching into the box, she lifted his tiny form. It was no heavier than the feathers he had been chasing when he had disappeared. She could see her fingers right through his body.

"Don't die," she pleaded. "Don't. Stay with me, brownie. We can work something out."

The brownie's eyelids fluttered.

"I mean it!" said Jamie. "I was actually starting to miss you."

"A-hoo," said the brownie. Opening his eyes, he gazed at her uncomprehendingly. "Oh, it's you," he said at last. Then he lifted his head and looked at her room. He moaned tragically at the disarray and closed his eyes again.

"I'll clean it up," she said hastily. "Just don't die. Promise?"

The brownie coughed and seemed to flicker, as if he was going to vanish altogether. "A-hoo," he said again.

"Watch!" said Jamie. Placing his tiny form gently on the bed, she began a whirlwind cleaning campaign, moving almost as fast as the brownie himself when he was in a cleaning frenzy. Along the way she found her clay-working tools, the pendant her nice grandmother had sent her, two dollars and forty-seven cents in change, and the missing homework that had cost her an F the day before. She kept glancing at the brownie while she worked and was encouraged to see that he seemed to be getting a little more solid. When she was entirely done she turned around and said, "There! See?"

To her enormous annoyance, the brownie had turned the shoe box over and was sitting on the end of it, looking as solid as a brick and smiling broadly. "Well done!" he said.

"I thought you were dying!" she said angrily.

"I wasn't dying, I was fading. And if you wanted me to live, why are you so angry that I'm alive?"

"Because you were faking!" she snarled.

"I never!" cried the brownie, sounding genuinely offended. "Another few minutes and I would have been gone for good, faded away like a summer breeze, like the last coals in the fire, like dew in the morning sun, like—"

"All right, all right," said Jamie. "I get the picture." She paused. Though she still wasn't sure she believed him, she asked, "What happens when you fade?"

The brownie shivered, and the look of terror on his face was so convincing that she began to suspect that he was telling the truth. "I'm just *gone*," he said.

Jamie shivered too. "Do you really have nowhere else to go?" she asked.

The brownie shook his head. "'Tis you to whom I'm bound, and you with whom I must stay until the day I fade away—or the day you become the oldest female in the family and assign me to someone else of your line."

Jamie sighed. She looked at the pendant, the tools, the change lying on her desk. "If I let you stay will you behave?"

The brownie wrapped his tail around his knees. "I am what I am," he said.

"So am I," she replied.

The brownie looked startled, as if this had not

occurred to him before. "Can you help a little?" he asked plaintively.

"If I do, will you stop nagging me?"

The brownie considered this for a moment. "Will you let me keep the closet as neat as I want?"

"Can I have my desk as messy as I want?" replied Jamie.

The brownie glanced at the desk, shivered, then nodded.

"It's a deal," said Jamie.

And so it was. They did not, it should be noted, exactly live happily ever after. The truth is, they annoyed each other a great deal over the years. However, they also learned to laugh together, and had enormous good times when they weren't fighting.

That's the way it goes with family things.

THE LANGUAGE OF BLOOD

Greetings, young one. I understand it is your turn, and they have sent you to me to learn how it is. They want me to tell you how I, Banang, came to be the one who speaks the language of blood. They want me to tell you what it cost me, and why I did it.

All right, that's fair. If you are to take my place, these are things you need to know. Take a cushion—one only!—and sit here.

I will tell you the story.

I was born outside the Glorious City. However, my parents moved within its walls before I was a year old. My mother was the ambitious one, always looking for something better. My father was a scribe. From what the elders later told me, the village missed him greatly when he came here. There, he had been the only scribe; here, he was but one among many. But as I said, my mother was ambitious.

I grew up running through the streets of the Glorious City. The neighbors all knew me, and liked me. "There goes Banang," they would say, laughing as I went racing by. "Always running! I'll wager he is the fastest boy in the city." Perhaps I was. But as I found—as you will find, my young friend—you cannot run forever. Sooner or later the world catches up with you.

For me it happened shortly after I turned seven. It was at First Night Ceremony. Oh, how excited I was to be going. The food, the singing, the fireworks—especially the food. It never occurred to me that my world would shift beneath me, that my life...But then, you know all that, or else you would not be here. In fact, you know much more, my young friend, than I did when I was in your place. It has taken me most of my life to convince the Pyong Myar that there was no point in keeping you as ignorant as they kept me.

Still, it is sweet to remember, even now—sweet and terrible to think of how we put on our robes of yellow and crimson and made our way through the streets with all the others. My family went with our neighbors. Their daughter Shula was my best friend, and she held my hand as we wound through the streets.

We laughed together at the bloody clowns along the way.

We were that innocent.

I still remember standing with the crowd at the foot of the temple, looking up at each level. The first seemed so much higher to me then—twice man height, it was nearly four times my size. How I loved to see the guards standing on it all in a row, their weapons at the ready. Then, ten feet behind it and twelve feet higher, the second level with the costumed maidens in their robes and scarlet feathers. Then the third level with the priests, the fourth with the watchers, the fifth where the Pyong Myar stood waiting.

The Pyong Myar. I see the cloud that passes over your face. He is frightening, is he not? Do the children still tell each other stories of what he will do to them in the night if they are bad? I feared him with that delicious fear of childhood that made me want to hide when his name was mentioned at the same time that I wanted, *hungered,* to hear more about him.

This was the first time I had ever seen him. I shivered happily at the sight, since I was clinging to my mother's skirts and therefore believed myself to be safe.

The Pyong Myar stood at the top of the temple, surrounded by a ring of fire and holding two huge knives above his head as if he planned to carve a hole in the sky. The trumpets blared, the people shouted, and to my utter horror, the Pyong Myar began to walk down the great line of steps that runs up the center of the temple.

What was he doing?

A silence fell over the crowd. The watchers, the priests, the maidens, the guards became motionless.

The Pyong Myar continued his slow progress down the steps, ritually crossing and uncrossing his knives as he walked.

Shula whimpered next to me, and received a sharp rap on the head from her father's knuckles for the transgression.

The Pyong Myar was the tallest man I had ever seen, an effect that was heightened by his fantastic headgear. His crimson robe flowed behind him. Though he was well over a hundred and seventy-five years old, the muscles that shifted beneath the leather straps of his chest harness were those of a young man.

"What is he doing?" I whispered to my mother. "Why is he coming down here?"

This earned me the same treatment that Shula's whimpers had earned her.

The guards dropped to one knee when the Pyong Myar reached their level. My own knees began to buckle, and I must actually have started to drop, for my mother grabbed my shoulder.

The crowd was stiff and silent, and young as I was I could feel the tension among them. As the Pyong Myar began the descent from the first level of the temple to the ground a murmur of astonishment rose, then quickly died. The only sound in the entire city was the metallic hiss of the Pyong Myar's knives as the blades slid back and forth, back and forth, across each other's surface.

We were standing some fifteen feet from the

front of the crowd. The Pyong Myar placed his knives together, upright, then spread them apart. At this gesture the crowd separated as smoothly as if some invisible blade had thrust among us, slicing us into two groups. We jostled back in eerie silence, leaving a path about five feet wide through which the Pyong Myar could pass. I stared across that space at Shula, who stood shivering next to her father.

The Pyong Myar began to walk down the aisle he had created, glancing from side to side. To my horror I realized that his eyes were blue, and glowing. I clung still closer to my mother as he approached, my fear so great I could hardly breathe. Once he had passed us by I nearly collapsed with relief.

But he had not gone more than eight paces past us when he turned and walked back to where we stood.

He stopped directly in front of me. I tried to back away, but there was no hole in the solid wall of flesh behind me, no nook or cranny into which I could escape.

He stared down at me. Awe-stricken, I gazed up at him.

He extended the knives, placing one on either side of my neck. "You!" he said. Then he drew the knives forward, slicing two lines— See? I have the scars still—along my jaw.

My mother shouted in triumph.

My father began to weep.

The Pyong Myar reached down and took my hand. His grip was utterly unlike anything I had ever felt before, and I did not even know the word for it until my third year in the temple when I was given some ice from the top of the mountain. His grip was *cold.*

My mother pushed me forward. The crowd was silent, save for Shula, who whispered, "Good-bye, Banang!" as the Pyong Myar led me away from my parents and my childhood, up the stairs of the temple.

I was hard put to keep up with the Pyong Myar, for the steps were too large for my childish legs. It was a terrifying climb. With no warning I had been pulled from the crowd by this fearsome stranger and taken from my family, who I was quite sure I would never see again. Something dark and mysterious had reached out and chosen me to be part of it; something that was only whispered about in the city. Yet such was the awe in which we held the temple ceremonies, and the power that emanated from the Pyong Myar, that I did not cry out, did not resist, only did as I was expected. I tried to do this with some dignity, but it was not easy when I could barely negotiate the steps, and I was crying out inside with loss and terror, as well as the pain of the cuts on my jaw.

The guards, already on their knees, bowed their heads to the ground as we crossed the broad terrace on which they stood. Despite my terror, part of me wondered if this display of respect was for the Pyong Myar, or for me. For little as I knew what was in store, I knew that children chosen in this fashion were considered rare and precious.

As we mounted the next level of steps, I turned to glance behind me. I could still see my parents in the crowd below. A fierce tug from the Pyong Myar brought me face forward again.

The maidens bowed in the same way the guards had, though I noticed at least one of them secretly glancing up to get a better look at me. The priests, too, touched their heads to the ground as we passed. Only the watchers in their blue robes did not move but stared intently, as if burning my image into their brains.

At the top level of the temple, the level where the Pyong Myar had stood alone, he turned me to face the mob below. Carefully, almost tenderly, he set the huge knives on a stone table. Then he put his hands around my waist, which was wet with my own blood, and lifted me above his head.

The crowd roared its approval.

The Pyong Myar turned and carried me through a dark door.

As you know, it is ten strides from that door to the Pyong Myar's private apartments. Were you as astonished as I at the luxury of them? I had not known what to expect, but the lavish tapestries, pillows, rugs, fountains, polished woods, and silky curtains were a surprise.

My new master placed me upon a table, and though he did not tell me to stay, I knew better than to attempt to move.

It was a relief when he removed that terrifying headdress and I saw that beneath it he was only a man after all. A remarkable man, but a man nonetheless.

"Do you know why I have brought you here?" he asked.

I shook my head. I had some vague idea, but no certainty, and no voice with which to say so.

He smiled, which did nothing to make his face any less frightening. "Carna and Sangua spoke to me. 'We have sent the next Speaker,' they whispered in my mind. 'Go and find him, and train him, so that he may serve the people.'" He paused, and for an instant—I will never forget it, for I never saw it again—a look of weariness passed over his features, and they seemed to sag with age. "It has been too long since a Speaker appeared," he said. "I have been worried for the people. It is good that you are here."

I nodded, feeling a little bit better. I wanted to be good.

He looked at me, and I saw the second thing that I have never seen in him again. It was pity, and it terrified me.

"Do you know what the Speaker does?" he asked.

It took me a moment to answer, for my tongue seemed to be sealed to the roof of my mouth. "He has visions," I said at last. "Visions that guide the people."

"And do you know how he does it?" asked the Pyong Myar.

I shook my head, relieved to be able to answer without words.

He closed his eyes and sighed. But he said nothing more on the matter. A moment later two women came to the door, and I sensed that it was with some relief that he gave me into their care. They washed my wounds and smeared them with an ointment that burned like fire. Then they tucked me into a strange bed, and sang me to sleep with songs I had never heard before.

This was my entrance into the Red Temple.

My life in the temple soon fell into a pattern. The women who had taken me from the Pyong Myar's rooms, Lala and Ariki, became my guardians, and—more important—my teachers. They began by teaching me the history of our city, the stories of our wars and our victories, and the tales of our enemies, the terrible enemies that are always waiting, lurking, ready to overwhelm us. They told me stories of those who speak the language of blood, and how their words have ever and again saved us from surprise, helped us avert disaster, led us to salvation.

They told me that I was to be the next Speaker. But they did not tell me what that meant, nor how I was to make this transition. That knowledge was kept from me for the time being.

My only dissatisfaction was that I was kept within the temple walls, a prisoner in a golden cage. I did have other children to play with, children of the guards and the temple women. One, especially, became a friend. His name was Mam, and he was Ariki's nephew, an arrogant scamp who somehow managed to sneak out of the temple and roam the city on a regular basis. Mam loved to tell me what was going on outside our walls, and after a time I begged him to look in on my family, and on my friend Shula.

He, in turn, tried to convince me to sneak out with him. The night I agreed to try we were caught, of course. He was severely beaten. I was not, and while my escape from punishment was a great relief, it also left me feeling extremely guilty.

Mam was far too much the scapegrace to hold this against me, but he no longer suggested that I accompany him on his adventures. It was clear to me that whoever ruled our lives did not care if Mam entered the city, and cared a great deal whether I even attempted such a thing.

The night before my eleventh birthday Lala took me aside and said, "Tomorrow you will be initiated into the next level of the temple. A man will come to take you away. Go bravely, and do not shame your second mothers, Lala and Ariki." She closed her eyes and drew me to her. "It is possible we will not see you again, my little one, my Banang," she whispered. The tremor in her voice frightened me, and I threw my arms around her and wept.

The next day the two women dressed me in my finest clothes. The rest of my things were packed in a wooden chest. Late in the afternoon the chest and my trembling self were set outside the doors of our apartments. Lala and Ariki each embraced me and told me to be good, wise, and brave. Then they closed the door. I could hear two things. The snick of the metal as they slipped the bolt and locked me out, and their cry of lamentation as they mourned my loss.

I stood and waited, trying to be brave.

It was not easy.

After a long time, or at least what seemed like a long time, the Pyong Myar came to me. I had not seen him since the night he delivered me to Lala and Ariki. He was naked, save for a black cloth tied around his waist and a red cape that flowed from his shoulders.

"Are you ready, Banang?" he asked. His terrible voice was gentle, almost worried.

When I nodded he reached down and took my hand. "Someone will come later to get your things," he said. Side by side we walked along the corridor. Because I had a feeling it might be a long time before

I came here again, I stared hard at the images carved on the walls, the pictures of gods and heroes, trying to burn them into my mind.

We stopped before a carving of a tree. The Pyong Myar reached out with his free hand and pressed one of the fruits. To my surprise, a large section of the wall slid open, revealing another corridor beyond. I had walked past this hidden door hundreds of times without ever knowing it was there.

"You will learn many secrets before this day is over," said the Pyong Myar. "This is but the least of them."

The corridor was lit by oil lamps. Between them hung tapestries woven with pictures from the stories I had been taught by Lala and Ariki.

The Pyong Myar led me to a room that was as large and comfortable as his own. Yet it felt close and still. It took me a moment to realize that this was because it had no windows.

In the center of the room stood a table made of stone. The Pyong Myar told me to lie down upon it.

A moment later a slender, dark-eyed man entered the room. He was nearly as tall as the Pyong Myar. He looked young, except for his eyes, which seemed very, very old.

"This is Banang," said the Pyong Myar, gesturing to me. "Your successor."

The man smiled and nodded to me. "I have been waiting for you for a very long time," he said. He sounded weary, a little sad. I felt guilty, though I had no idea what I could have done to hurry things along.

As if he had read my mind, the man said, "Do not worry, Banang. It is not your fault. The world turns as it will. Sometimes relief comes sooner, sometimes later. I still have years to wait. But knowing you are here and ready to begin makes my heart lighter."

I nodded, said nothing.

The man turned to the Pyong Myar. "Leave us," he said. "I will do what must be done."

To my astonishment, the Pyong Myar turned and left. I would not have believed that anyone could give him an order.

"My name is Naranda," said the man. "I am the one who speaks the language of blood. This is not an easy thing, but it must be done. I do it for the people. It is you who will do it when I am gone."

I stared at him, eyes wide, but said nothing. I am not sure I could have spoken had I wanted to.

"To do this, you must be prepared," continued Naranda. "That is why you are here today. What I do to you today, you will do to others later. Almost always you will take from them. Only once in all the years that follow will you give as I am about to give to you."

His eyes were powerful, his voice soothing. He was moving closer to me. As he spoke, his eyes began to change. Soon they were glowing, deep red, like coals in a firepit. Then he smiled, and I saw for the first time the sharp fangs that curved down from beneath his upper lip.

I wanted to scream, but found that I could not, could not move, could not resist.

Naranda bent over me. My heart was pounding so fast that I feared it would explode. Drawing back his lips, he plunged his fangs into my neck.

A spasm wracked my body. Fire seemed to pour into my veins.

Then the world disappeared and I found myself floating in a strange nothingness. Odd shapes, made of mist and edged with fire, whirled past me. Voices whispered in my ears.

I thought I was dying, but knew that I could not be that lucky. The agony was exquisite.

Then all went black.

When I woke, Naranda was sitting nearby. He looked tired, gray, worn-out. He raised his head, and the eyes that had glowed red when he first approached me now seemed empty, as if the fire had consumed what was there, and only cold ashes were left.

"You live," he whispered.

I nodded.

"I was afraid you might not." His voice sounded like dried corn husks rustling in the wind.

I wanted to rage at him for what he had done to me. But his weakness was like a poultice, drawing out the sting of my anger. Whatever his purpose, his action had clearly cost him as much, possibly more, than it had cost me.

"Are you all right?" I asked.

"I'll live. I have to, until you are mature yourself. Who else will speak the language of blood until then, if I do not? Can you stand?"

I tried, and found that I could—found, in fact, that I felt surprisingly strong.

"Help me up," said Naranda.

"What is the language of blood?" I asked, as I drew him to his feet.

"It is the language to which you were born, Banang," he answered. "It is words of warning, whispers of prophecy; tomorrow itself singing a song that only the drinkers of blood may hear and repeat, only the Pyong Myar interpret."

I did not understand, nor did he expect me to. At his command I led him to a pallet. It was covered by a finely woven robe. When he lay upon it I noticed, with a shudder of revulsion, the line of dried blood that ran from the side of his mouth. My blood. Looking more closely I saw that traces of it circled his lips as well. As if aware of what I was looking at, he flicked his tongue at the corners of his mouth, trying to clean away the brown flakes.

"Tell me what you have done to me," I said, my voice quavering.

"I have made you a man of the people," he replied. "When I am gone, it is you who will read the secrets written in the language of blood."

I stared at him, saying nothing.

"When the time comes for your change, your body will grow in the ways that all young men's bodies do—with this addition. Like me, you will have the bloodteeth." And here he drew back his lips to show the fangs with which he had pierced my neck.

Ah—I notice you looking at me nervously. Do you want to see mine? Don't be shy; I don't mind. Here. Impressive, are they not? And never more so than when blood is in the offing.

Naranda became my teacher, and for the next three years I was trained in the ways of the Speaker. This was difficult, for at first I could not stand to be near him, as his very presence brought to mind our first meeting and what he had done to me. But after a time I grew used to him and even, I suppose, to love him. He taught me a great deal: how the Sources are chosen, and why they die after their third contribution; why those who speak the language of blood can never see the sun again; what it is to live longer than anyone save the Pyong Myar.

This and more he taught me, as I will teach you. He prepared me well to take his place, and when in the spring of my sixteenth year he finally died, I felt that I was ready. My own change had come upon me

nearly two years earlier, and as my voice had deep-
ened, my shoulders broadened, so, too, had my bloodteeth developed, just as Naranda promised.

He had prepared me for everything, except for
what I found when I climbed the stairs to meet my
first Source.

The stairs, as you will eventually see, are on the outside of the temple. They lead to a small structure on
the very top of the building. The walls of this structure are chest high—tall enough to hide what happens within them. It has no roof save the sky, and the
moon's light fills the chamber. Inside is a stone table,
much like the one in this room.

An eager dread, a mix of excitement and terror,
filled my heart as I climbed to the top of the temple.
I had been moving toward this moment all my life.
The breeze was cool. I could see the city below me
and knew that the people depended on me, on the
knowledge I would bring them. I wanted to be a
good Speaker, yet feared the act that would make me
one.

Fear turned to dread when I walked through the
door and saw my Source waiting for me on the stone
table.

It was Shula, of course. Not mere coincidence,
but the will of the Pyong Myar. This act would be
the test and the binding of my will to speak the language of blood.

She was not bound. There were no guards. She could have walked away.

But she lay waiting for me.

"It has been a long time, Banang," she whispered, as I stared at her in shock and horror. "I have missed you."

"And I have missed you," I said at last.

I felt as if two snakes were fighting in my stomach, twisting and writhing. I was torn between the fire that was stirring in my blood and my horror at using my long-lost childhood friend as my Source.

"Why do you look at me that way?" she asked. "Are you angry?"

"Why are you here?" I replied.

"They chose me. I came. Just the same as you."

"Run away," I said, my voice flat, my heart filled with shame at the betrayal of the people carried in that simple sentence.

"Will you run away with me?"

I shook my head. She shrugged, as if to ask how I could possibly expect her to do what I would not.

I sat beside her on the stone table and we talked of old times, of our families, of what had happened in the years since I entered the temple. Too soon I saw in her eyes that the moon was overhead, and I could wait no longer. I stood, turned away, turned back. My mouth ached as the bloodteeth grew for the first time, stretching down past my upper lip. She closed her eyes, extinguishing the moon, as I bent over her and pierced the smooth flesh of her neck.

Her blood pumped into my mouth, hot and fragrant, and the gods reached down to touch me. Despite my revulsion, I drank deep, sucking the blood through the wounds I had made.

Then the Fit of Prophecy came upon me. As Shula's blood released what is in me, that part that makes me a Speaker began to read the secrets of the blood, the past of our people which flows in all our veins and points to our future. Fire crawled along my limbs. The heroes whispered their messages. Images swam before me, not like a dream but like a new reality, sharper and more clear than anything seen before. I was transformed, and my heart saw into the past and the future with eyes that would shame a hawk's.

I fell to the floor, writhing and jerking, as the words flowed out of me. The tiniest part of me was aware of the Pyong Myar standing nearby, taking down everything that I said.

When finally the fit ran its course, I slept as if I were dead. When I woke, I was in my own room. The Pyong Myar was again nearby, staring at me. He smiled when I opened my eyes, and said, "You did well."

The sickness in me made it impossible to answer.

"It is always this way after the first time," he said. "You will feel better tomorrow."

What he did not know was that I suffered not

merely the sickness of the First Speaking. I suffered a sickness of the heart, a terrible guilt and fear over what I had done to Shula.

He showed me what I had spoken, the words of blood that told the future of our people. It would be a good year, but a cloud was growing on the horizon, a darkness yet unclear. Thus was the importance of the speaking reinforced. Knowing that this danger was coming, we could begin to prepare. In six months I would again speak the language of blood. Perhaps then we would know what the danger was.

Shula and I were married, of course. My first bride. How many since, I have lost count. A year for each, wed at the first speaking, taken to new heights at the second, separated by death at the third.

Six months later a new bride.

I will be glad to lay the mantle down.

Naranda, I suspect, did not find this all so difficult. In the training he gave me, there was no hint of the pain that I felt in regard to Shula. For him, it was the way it was. Maybe he had forgotten. Maybe he had never cared.

I cared. I brooded day and night about Shula's fate.

The second speaking came and went. She was pale and weak for many days afterward. But the speaking had been important. A war was brewing, enemies gathering in the distance, forces joining against us. This we needed to know; this we would not have known, save for the language of blood.

I went to visit Lala and Ariki. I could not tell them what I was thinking, that I could not do this again, not when I knew that it would mean the death of my Source, my friend, my love. They knew what I was thinking anyway, of course. They always did. Without a word they let me know that my thoughts, my doubts, were shameful.

Finally I spoke to Shula. "We should run away," I said.

"Silly Banang," she answered. "What is, is. There is no running away."

But I persisted. Every night I whispered to her that we must leave the city, flee to the jungle.

"Silly Banang," she would respond. "You have tasted the blood. You must drink now, whether we are here or in the jungle."

"I can find other blood," I replied. "It does not have to be yours. I do not want you to die. We must leave, we must leave."

Then she would put her hands on either side of my face, resting her little fingers in the scars the Pyong Myar had made the night he took me from my family. Looking deep into my eyes she would ask, "Then who will speak for the people?"

For that, I had no answer.

"Silly Banang," she would whisper. Then she would cuddle against me, and lying in my arms fall asleep.

I could not.

I noticed the Pyong Myar watching me and wondered if he knew what I was thinking. He took me aside to talk to me.

"The next time you speak the language of blood will be terribly important," he said, his face stern, his blue eyes glowing with that horrible fire. "If all goes well, you will speak of the enemy and his plans— where the army gathers, when it will attack. This is what you were born for, Banang. You will tell the city what it must know in order to survive."

I did not tell him of the hollow horror growing in my heart. I could not make the words come past my thick, rebellious tongue.

The night before my third speaking, a year since I had first tasted Shula's blood, a sunrise and a sunset before I would be called upon to drink until she died, I said to her, "We are leaving the city."

The horror in her eyes matched what was growing in my heart. But its roots were different. She could not imagine this terrible act of betrayal. "What will the people do without us?" she asked.

"I don't care," I replied. My voice was savage. "I don't care about the people. I care about you."

She looked down. She did not answer. I knew she was ashamed for me, but that she would come with me if I insisted.

I insisted. Late that night we left the temple, slipping out through the secret ways that Mam had taught me long ago, the first and only time that I had ventured into the city after the night of my calling. I feared that we would be spotted. My plan was to run. Once I had been called the fastest boy in the city. I did not know how fast I was compared to the guards, but counted on love and fear to put wings on my heels. I knew that Shula could not keep up. But if I escaped myself, at least she would live. I did not want to lose her. But better to lose her yet know she still lived than to lose her to the demands of the language of blood.

Or so I thought at the time.

No one stopped us.

We traveled far from the city, deep into the jungle.

Two nights later we found the enemy.

It might seem like the oddest of chances. It was not chance. There are no coincidences. The heroes led me there, to see what I needed to see.

We came upon the army when we climbed a hill and saw, in the valley below us, row on row on row of tents, stretching as far as the nearly full moon could show us.

These men were coming to take the city. If they were successful, they would rape the women, kill the children, loot the Red Temple.

There were no words to be said. Language was not needed. Shula took my hand and turned me around. Silently, carefully, we made our way back to the city.

The Pyong Myar stood at the temple door, the not-quite-secret door through which we had fled, through which we returned. He did not speak, only nodded, his eyes dim and sorrowful.

The next night I climbed the temple stairs to the low-walled room where Shula lay waiting on the stone table. I swallowed the rest of her life, and as she lay dying I writhed on the floor and spoke again the language of blood. All the secrets of the past, all the wisdom of the people, all the strength of the heroes flowed from my tongue. In the language of blood I told not only the location of the enemy, which I well knew, but their numbers and their plans and their secret weaknesses.

The city was saved, of course.

I have had many Sources since then.

I am more weary than I can tell you.

I am glad you are here.

So. Now you know what it is all about, know far more than I did the day I came to Naranda.

Are you ready? Place yourself here, please.

Turn your head just so.

This will only take a moment.

OLD GLORY

Donald B. Henderson
Civic Responsibility Class
Ms. Barnan
Sept. 15, 2041

ESSAY: The Day I Did My Duty

My great-grandfather was the craziest man I ever met. Sometimes it was embarrassing even to have him be part of the family.

For example: You should have seen how he acted when Congress passed the S.O.S. law last June.

He actually *turned off* the holo set!

"Well, that's the end of life as we know it," he said as the image started to fade. Then he stared at the floor and started to mutter.

"Oh, Arthur, don't be ridiculous," said my mother.

She switched the set back on and waited for the newsgeek to reappear in the center of the room.

"Ridiculous?" yelped Gran-Da. "You want to see ridiculous? I'll show you ridiculous!" He stood and pointed to the big flag that hangs over our holo set. "*That's* ridiculous! Thirteen stripes, sixty-two stars, and not a bit of meaning. After what they did today it's all gone."

"That's not so, Grampa," said my father quietly. His voice was low and soft, the way it gets when he's really angry. "Now sit down and be quiet."

That was a relief. After Gran-Da came to live with us I was always afraid he was going to get us into trouble. So I felt better whenever Dad made him be quiet. Sometimes I wished Dad would just throw him out. I didn't really want him sleeping on the streets, like all the old men I walk past on the way to school. But I didn't want to make our Uncle angry either.

Later that night, when I was going to bed, Gran-Da called me into his room.

"How you doing?" he asked.

I shrugged. "I'm okay."

Gran-Da smiled. "Are you afraid of me?"

I wanted to say no. Only that would have been a lie. So I just nodded my head.

"Afraid I'll talk dangerous?"

I nodded again. I didn't know what I would do if my friends were ever around when he started talking like he does sometimes. I knew what I *should* do, of course. But I didn't know if I could do it. I mean, he *was* my great-grandfather, even if he was crazy and wicked.

He looked sad. "Are all the kids at your school like you?" he asked.

"What do you mean?"

"Scared little sheep, afraid to talk."

"I'm not afraid to talk," I said loudly. "I just don't talk nonsense, like..."

I broke off.

"Like me?" he asked, scratching at the little fringe of white hair that circled the back of his head. (I don't know why he never got his head fixed. All the other great-grandfathers I know have full heads of hair, whatever color they want. Not mine.)

I looked away from him. Suddenly I realized what was wrong with his room. "Where's your flag?" I asked.

"I took it down."

I must have looked pretty funny. At least, the look on my face made him snort.

"How could you?" I asked in a whisper.

"It was easy," he said. "I just pulled out the tabs at the corners, and then—"

"Gran-Da!"

"Donald!" he replied. "When the government passed S.O.S., they took away the last thing that flag stood for. I don't want to look at it anymore."

He paused and stared at the floor for a while. I looked at the door, wondering if he would say anything if I just left.

Suddenly he looked up again. "Listen, Donald. I'm ninety years old. That's not that old, these days—I could probably last another thirty."

That was no news. It was one of the reasons my mother was so upset when he moved in. I felt sorry for her. Thirty years of Gran-Da was my idea of a real nightmare.

"The thing is," he continued, "I'm just a normal guy, not a hero. But sometimes there's something you have to do, no matter what it costs you."

I looked at him in horror. "You're not going to do anything crazy, are you?" I felt sick in my stomach. Didn't he understand he could get us *all* in trouble? If he wasn't careful, the Uncles might come and take us away. I glanced at the ceiling, half expecting it to open up so that a giant hand could reach down and snatch my great-grandfather then and there.

"Why are you telling me this?" I asked at last.

"Maybe I'm hoping that if I scare you enough, it will make you start to think." He shrugged. "Or maybe I just want to see what you'll do."

"Can I go now?"

"Yeah," he said bitterly. "Go on. Get out of here."

I slipped out of his room and ran down the hall to my own room. I flopped onto my bed and lay there, staring up at my beautiful flag and trembling.

I thought about Gran-Da all that night. I thought about him in school the next morning, while we were saying the pledge, and the Lord's Prayer, and reciting the names of the presidents. I remembered what Gran-Da had said the first time he heard me recite the list—that there had been more presidents than we were naming, that some of them were being left out.

I wanted to talk to my teacher, but I was afraid.

The next morning was Saturday. When Gran-Da came to breakfast he had a red band tied around his head. He was wearing a vest with fringe on it, a blue shirt, and faded blue pants; he was carrying a lumpy plastic bag. He had a button on his vest that looked like an upside-down Y with an extra stick coming out of it.

"What's that?" I asked, pointing to the button.

"A peace symbol," he said. He dropped the bag to the floor and settled into his chair.

"Really, Arthur," said my mother. "Don't you think this is carrying things a little too far?"

"S.O.S. was carrying things too far," said Gran-Da.

My father sighed. "Look, Grampa, it's not really a problem. If you don't break the rules, S.O.S. won't have any effect on you."

I was amazed to hear him say that. Then I decided he must be trying to get Gran-Da to calm down. It didn't work. Gran-Da shook his head stubbornly, and suddenly I knew what he had in the bag.

My throat got thick with fear. I couldn't finish my breakfast.

After breakfast I followed Gran-Da out of the house. He was heading for the town square. I was pretty sure I knew what he was planning. My stomach was churning. What if the Uncles thought he had polluted our whole family?

I could only think of one way to save us. I slipped into a televid booth to call my Uncle. When I told him what was happening he looked stern and shocked.

"You won't hold this against the rest of us, will you?" I asked nervously.

He shook his head. "Of course not," he said. "You've done the right thing. We'll have to come and talk to all of you when this is over, of course. But I wouldn't worry about it much."

The screen went blank. I hurried back out to the street.

I felt embarrassed, and frightened. But I was also a little excited. Would the S.O.S. men really show up? My friends would think I was a real hero. I hurried toward the town square.

Gran-Da was already there. He had climbed onto the bandstand, of all places, and he was shouting about S.O.S.

People looked at him nervously. To my surprise, a few actually stopped to listen. I stood beneath a large tree, about a hundred feet away. I didn't want to get too close.

Suddenly Gran-Da reached into the bag and pulled out the flag he had taken off his wall the night before. Holding the upper edge, he rolled it over the side of the bandstand. A slight breeze made the stripes slide and shift.

I covered my face with my hands and wished the terrible scene would end.

Where were the S.O.S. men?

"Friends!" cried Gran-Da. "When I was a boy this piece of cloth used to stand for something. Yes, it did. In fact, it stood for a whole lot of things. Ideas. Like that a man should be free to say what he thinks, and worship where he wants, and get together with other folks if it pleases him."

More people were stopping to listen now. Someone started to boo.

"But that's all over!" shouted Gran-Da. "Bit by bit, piece by piece, we've given away all the things this used to stand for. S.O.S. was the end of it. Now this poor old flag doesn't stand for anything at all.

"That being so, I think it's time I put it out of its misery."

I looked around. Where were the S.O.S. men? Why didn't they get here?

Now that people realized what Gran-Da was going to do, they started to back away. Some of them left. I could tell that others wanted to, wanted to get as far away from the terrible thing he was about to do as they possibly could. But they couldn't bring themselves to go. They wanted to see if he would really do it.

Gran-Da raised the flag and lit a match.

"Good-bye, Old Glory," he said sadly. "It was a good idea while it lasted."

He touched the corner of the flag with the match. Nothing happened, of course, since like all flags it was made of flameproof material. You can't burn a flag even if you try.

Gran-Da knew that. He wasn't stupid—just crazy. A crazy, dangerous person—the kind who could ruin the wonderful country we've built.

Suddenly I saw the S.O.S. men. They looked beautiful in their blue pants, white shirts, and red vests.

Gran-Da saw them, too. I know he did.

So it's not like it's my fault, really. He had a chance. Everyone knows that even though the new law allows for instant executions, the Shoot-On-Sight men are supposed to give a guy a chance.

But Gran-Da didn't care. When his first match went out he lit another one. He held it to the corner of the fireproof flag and just stood there, smiling at the three men.

So everyone could see that he was crazy.

The men lifted their laser rifles. The leader counted to three, and they fired in unison.

The light sliced right through the old man. He toppled over the edge of the bandstand. The flag curled around him as he fell. He was still holding it when he hit the ground.

My throat got thick. I could feel tears at the corners of my eyes. Crazy, I know. But he was my great-grandfather, after all. So I don't think it was too bad to feel a *little* sad about what had happened.

That doesn't mean I don't know I did the right thing by calling the S.O.S. guys. I mean, think about it. What would happen if other people started to believe like Gran-Da—crazy things, like that everybody should be allowed to say whatever they wanted to?

What kind of a world would that be?

THE PASSING OF THE PACK

The cave was dark. Even so, I could see well enough to know when the wolf lurched to his feet and began walking toward me. I pushed myself backward, until the cave wall stopped me. The wolf continued to advance. His eyes, locked on mine, were like the kind of coals you find late at night: nearly spent, yet still holding the power to burn—or to kindle a new flame.

I thought of red-haired Wandis, safe in some distant village, and wondered if I could somehow change my mind. But of course it was far too late for that.

The wolf lowered his head, then curled his black lips in a snarl, revealing yellow fangs that glistened with saliva. I held my breath to keep from crying out in fear.

Dying-ember eyes still locked with mine, the beast moved closer. My self-control was weakening. But before I could disgrace myself with a scream, his teeth sank into my flesh, and I fainted.

How long I lay on the floor of the cave I have no idea. It could have been an hour; it might have been days.

When I finally woke I felt drained of strength. Even opening my eyes seemed more than I could manage. Wondering if I had been a fool or—perhaps more accurately—just how much of a fool I had been, I began to review the strange events that had led me to this moment, starting with my first encounter with the great wolf.

It had happened eleven years earlier, when our little village was being battered by the worst winter in memory. I was only five at the time, but I knew it was the worst because my grandmother told me so. She seemed to take most of her pleasure from telling me how much better or worse or bigger or smaller everything had been when she was young, so if she said the howling winds and driving snow that lasted for weeks on end were the most ferocious she had ever experienced, I felt it must be true.

It must have been bad for the wolves, too, for they had never troubled us before then. But one night, when thick snow was dropping like wet feathers onto our already snow-choked village, they came, slipping through the dark as silently as whispers between friends. Their killing was quiet, too, until the warm blood emboldened them, and the village animals took fright. Then the silence was broken by a growing commotion.

I was among the first to hear it, possibly because

my sleep had already been disturbed by strange dreams that night. I didn't understand what was going on, of course. I only knew something had roused our small flock of chickens.

Even at five I was trying to fill in for the lack of a man in our house. So when I climbed down the ladder from the little loft where I had my bed, I moved as soundlessly as possible, hoping not to rouse my mother from her sleep. I slipped into my coat and pulled on the fur-lined boots my grandmother had made for me. Then I pulled open the bottom half of our door. But the way out was blocked by drifted snow. I closed the bottom of the door and opened the top. Then I fetched my stool and clambered through the opening.

I almost disappeared in the snow. Sputtering and cold, I dug my way out of the drift. Fortunately, the snow was not that deep everywhere. The same winds that had blown it against our door had cleared other places almost down to the hard-packed paths we had made over the last two months. Wading over to one of the paths, I headed for the henhouse.

After a few moments I sensed a dark form on my left. A moment later I realized there were two more on my right. A sudden fear clutched my heart. I would have turned back, but the house seemed suddenly very far away. Moreover, I had a favorite hen, a biddy with golden feathers, that I loved too dearly to lose. In my childish mind, I somehow thought I could protect her.

Or perhaps I thought that she would protect me.

Anyway, as I struggled my way to the small hen-house the surrounding commotion grew louder. I knew it would not be long before other folk came out to tend their livestock, too.

Once inside I gathered my hen in my arms. As I was trying to soothe her a dark form surged through the doorway. The light was too dim for me to see it clearly, but I had no doubt that it was a wolf. The hen squawked and struggled in my arms. It was hard to say which was beating more frantically, the hen's wings or my heart.

The wolf growled—a low, throaty sound that moved me to a new level of fear. It stalked forward. Clutching the hen as if she could protect me from the beast, I watched the wolf draw nearer, until I could smell its hot breath.

Suddenly another, larger wolf leaped into the hen-house. It hurtled forward and slammed against the first wolf. After a moment of growling and scuffling one wolf slunk away. The second wolf stepped forward. I knew it was the second because its outline, which was all I could see, was so much larger than that of the first wolf. It took my hen from my arms and closed its jaws. The bird was dead.

The wolf nudged me with its head, then turned

and trotted from the coop. Overwhelmed by its presence, I started to follow it, completely forgetting the first wolf. But it had not forgotten me; it moved in front of the door, refusing to let me pass.

The wolf kept me prisoner for only a few moments. But it was time enough for the village to finish rousing. Soon the streets were filled with shouts and screams. Then, above it all, I heard a howl that seemed to pierce my skull and shiver down my spine. I believe it was a signal of some sort, for the wolf that had been guarding me turned and ran from the coop, leaving me alone with a flock of hysterical chickens.

My mother found me soon after that. Torn between rejoicing that I was safe and wanting to beat me for my foolishness, she bundled me in her arms and carried me back inside. Then she began to cry. I felt very bad. I thought: *If I had a father, he could have taken care of this trouble.*

It was three summers before I saw another wolf. I had lost my way in the forest and was just beginning to panic when one of the creatures stepped from behind a tree. I jumped in alarm, but it simply sat and gazed at me. When it was clear that my panic had passed, the wolf came and took my sleeve between its teeth. Its grip firm but gentle, it began tugging at my arm. As it seemed to have no inclination to harm me, I followed it—though the truth is I probably didn't have much choice anyway. Before long it had led me to a familiar clearing, where I saw a village girl named Wandis gathering flowers.

I paused before stepping into the clearing. When I looked down the wolf had vanished. Pretending that I had intended to come this way all along, I stepped into the clearing. Wandis and I walked home together.

Though she was a year or so younger than I, Wandis and I became friends. Her companionship was a comfort to me, for it was not easy to be fatherless in our village, where I was often taunted as "No man's son." I blamed my mother for this, though later I began to see that it was as hard for her to raise me without benefit of a man as it was for me to grow up that way. Yet whenever I asked her about my father, she became vague and avoided answering my questions directly. This was hard, for I longed to know who had sired me.

A few times during these years I would wake in the night at some noise below me, and peering through the cracks in my floor I would see a tall, dark-haired man sitting at our table. Once he was holding my mother's hand. Another time he was kissing her.

I wanted to kill him. I wanted him to come live with us. I was angry at him for only coming at night, when I was in bed and could not get to know him.

I wanted him to love me.

———

My mother died when I was ten, and I did not see the man again. I went to stay with my grandparents.

About the time of my fifteenth birthday I began to see the wolves more often. Sometimes when I woke in the night I would draw open my window and spot one of them sitting beside the house, staring up at me. Or if I was walking home from a late visit with one of my few friends, I might hear a sound and turn to see a wolf behind me. Once spotted, it would sit and stare until I turned and went on. They never chased me, never made a move against me. But neither would they let me approach them. Whenever I tried they would bare their fangs and raise their hackles.

I did not mention them to anyone, for our village was a superstitious place. But in the end my silence was of little value; the villagers turned against me anyway.

Of all the people in the village Wandis was my closest friend. I thought her very beautiful, with her red hair and strangely blue eyes. Yet she was as much an outcast as I, somehow unable to fit properly into the life of the community. Naturally, this gave us something in common.

Sometimes when I went to the forest to gather wood, or simply to be alone, I would find Wandis on her hands and knees, examining some plant. She knew wonderful things about them. Once she showed me a small, low-growing vine called Sal-o-My-Heart; it was adorned with clusters of miniature red berries, and she claimed it could be used to make a man or woman fall in love. I asked her to give me some, teasing that I might use it on her. But she only blushed and turned my attention elsewhere.

I remember that day well, because a few weeks later one of the village women accused Wandis of witchcraft. She said Wandis had used her powers to steal her husband's love. I thought it more likely the woman's own nagging had turned her husband away, and his eyes had strayed to Wandis because she was young and very lovely. Even so, I asked Wandis if what the woman said was true. She patted my cheek, and told me not to be silly.

It was not so easy to turn aside the village elders. She could not pat *their* cheeks and tell them to go away when they came to take her. When I spoke out on her behalf, I was accused, too. ("Only a witch would defend a witch," they said.)

We were given a trial, which was a mockery, and sentenced to be burned at the stake. And this they would have done, had not the wolves come to our rescue.

It was late October. I was bound with stout ropes and thrown into a woodshed built against the side of one of the elders' homes. The space was cold and cramped, and though a little light filtered in during the daytime, after sunset it became completely black. Yet my thoughts were less of my current discomfort than of the morning, and the flame. I wondered how long it would hurt. I wondered, too, how my fellow villagers could be so cruel.

Shortly after midnight I heard something scratching outside the wall of my prison. I felt a shiver run down my spine, for I had no idea what it was, and there were many tales in our village of the strange things that wander after dark.

The noise went on for some time. It seemed to be getting closer. Then it stopped. Suddenly a great, furry shape was pressing against me. Had I not become so used to the wolves I might have died of fright right then.

The wolf began to gnaw at the ropes that held my hands and feet. It was not long before they parted under his sharp teeth. Taking the leg of my trouser in those same teeth, he guided me to the wall, where I discovered the hole he had dug to get in. It took some work to enlarge the hole enough for me to wriggle through it. By the time we were done, I was hot and sweaty and filthy. But I was also free!

The wolf whined and tugged at my trouser leg again. Obviously he wanted to get away from the village as quickly as possible. But I would not go until we had freed Wandis, too.

As it turned out, the wolves were ahead of me. A familiar voice whispered to me from nearby. Only the soft growl of warning from the wolf at my side kept me from crying out her name. I moved forward to embrace her, but two huge wolves stepped between us, barring my way.

"Don't be foolish!" I hissed angrily.

They bared their fangs. The sound that rumbled in their throats was too soft to wake those sleeping in the house. Nevertheless, the menace it contained was genuine.

The wolf that freed me had been joined by another of the beasts. They tugged at my clothing again, even as the ones beside Wandis started to pull her away from me. She looked back once as they led her into the darkness. That was my last sight of her, for the wolves beside me began herding me, just as insistently, in the opposite direction.

It was a clear night. The sky was drunk with stars and a half-moon hung low on the horizon, silvering the trees, the village, the wolves. It was darker when we entered the forest, and I had to concentrate to keep from stumbling over the great tree roots that erupted from the ground at odd intervals. I bumbled and crashed along, but the wolves seemed to make no sound at all.

Finally we came to a small cave. The wolves led me inside, then settled themselves in front of the entrance. Obviously, I was supposed to stay here. It seemed I had only traded one prison for another.

But why?

———

I was kept in the cave for two weeks, guarded by the pair of wolves that had brought me there.

As soon as I saw them in the daylight I was able to tell them apart. One had a wild eye, blue and strange, that seemed to look into another world. The other was marked by a ragged ear, which I assumed had been earned in some youthful battle.

Several other wolves came to the area during this time. Usually they brought small game for me to eat, though sometimes I got the feeling they were coming simply to look me over. I felt that I was on display.

Wild Eye and Ragged Ear escorted me to a nearby stream whenever I wanted to drink. Once, convinced that they would not hurt me, I tried to run away. But they set up a howling, and before long the woods around me were thick with wolves. I was herded back to my cave like a lamb being herded by a shepherd.

The mystery finally ended on All Hallows' Eve, when Wild Eye woke me from a sound sleep by nudging at my face.

"What do you want?" I asked crankily.

He took my arm and pulled on it.

"For heaven's sakes," I said. "It's the middle of the night!"

This didn't seem to make any difference. Realizing I wouldn't get any sleep anyway, I decided it was easiest just to follow him. Ragged Ear joined us at the entrance to the cave. Walking on either side of me, the two wolves led me deeper into the forest.

It was an eerie journey. The bright moon cast a glow over the trees that made the woodland seem entirely different than during the day. A cool breeze rustled through the leaves, heavy with the rich scent of the forest. To our left I could hear a tiny brook tinkling its way over polished stones. The silent wolves pressed against my legs.

After a time we came to another cave. A dark-haired man sat in front of it—the same man I had seen kissing my mother so many years ago. He was lean, and though there were deep lines in his face, I could see that he had once been very handsome. On closer inspection I noticed that the hair that had seemed so black was shot through with silver. His eyes were deep set, and dark as the night.

Wild Eye and Ragged Ear moved to his side.

The man stood and embraced me. "Welcome," he said. "I am glad to see you, my son."

How could I respond to this? I was glad, for my heart had reached out to this man even in those brief glimpses of him that I had had so long ago. But I also felt great anger that he had not been with me while I was growing up. I wanted to hit him. I wanted him to hold me. I wanted to say all that, but didn't know how.

"Where were you?" I whispered at last.

"Here," he said. "Where I belong."

"You belonged with us," I answered.

He shook his head sadly. "No man can do all the things he ought," he said. He returned to his seat. The wolves stayed at his side. "It is always choices," he said, resting a hand on Wild Eye's head. "I doubt any man is ever sure he has made the right one. But once you have made it, you have to live by it."

He said these last words fiercely, as if he thought them very important.

"This was your choice?" I asked. "To live in the forest instead of with your family?"

"To be where I was most needed," he answered.

"I don't understand," I said.

"You will," he whispered. "Soon enough, you will."

Other wolves were gathering around the edge of the area where we sat. Their yellow-green eyes gleamed at me out of the night. A cub, small and fuzzy, came to nip at my father's foot. He poked the cub with his toe, and it rolled over to have its belly scratched. My father obliged, but only briefly. The cub's mother came and picked it up by the scruff of its neck, then carried it back to the circle that was forming around us.

"What do they want?" I asked, somewhat nervously.

"They are here to pay homage," said my father.

My puzzlement must have showed in my face. "I am their leader," he added, as if that explained everything.

I swallowed. "How can *you* be their leader?" I asked.

He smiled, a sad, wise kind of smile. "You know the answer," he said, "but you have tried to pretend that you were wrong. Now the time for games, for hiding, is over. Now you have to examine the truth."

A terrible thought had struck me when I first saw him sitting there. I had pushed it firmly aside. Now my father was forcing me to let it come forward again.

"You're one of them!" I whispered.

He nodded serenely. "I am one of them."

I stumbled over the questions that sprang into my mind. "I don't understand," I said at last.

"They need me," he said simply. "The pack always needs a man to keep it together, to make difficult decisions when times are hard."

I remembered the winter when the wolves invaded our town. "That was you in the henhouse!" I accused.

He nodded.

"Why did you kill my chicken?" I cried, remembering my childish grief and feeling doubly betrayed that it was my own father who had caused it.

He laughed, a short bark that bordered on contempt. "You sound as though you have never eaten a chicken yourself," he said.

He was right, of course, and I blushed at my question. Yet he went on to answer it.

"I protected you," he said. "As I tried to protect

everyone in the village." He sighed. "I brought the pack only because we were starving. Afterward, I wondered if it had been a mistake. I do not know. As for your hen—I thought you might as well learn early on that you were going to have to give up things you loved for the wolves."

Something in his words disturbed me. "What do you mean, give up things for the wolves?"

He leaned against Ragged Ear. Suddenly he looked old, and tired. "My time is almost up," he said. "The pack will need a new leader soon."

I recoiled from him in horror. "You want *me* to become a werewolf!" I cried.

He nodded. His dark eyes were locked on mine.

I was appalled. My own father was asking me to become one of the creatures of the night our priest had warned us about.

"It's evil!" I hissed.

My father's eyes flashed dangerously. "I am not evil," he snapped. "I made a choice a long time ago, a choice I have lived by, and honored—which is more than most men do. If that does not fit your little priest's petty idea of morality, it is no concern of mine." He spat on the ground in front of him, dismissing the priest. "You know you do not belong in that village. Do you want to try to become like them? Or do you have the courage to reach for your true destiny?"

I pressed my hands against my head, as if that

could keep out these frightening thoughts. It was true. I wasn't like the others. I had always known I didn't really belong there.

But did I belong here?

I looked at the pack that had assembled around us. *These are my father's people,* I thought. *They love him. He fits here. He . . . belongs.*

I remembered how it hurt to know I was not truly a part of my village, to feel that invisible wall against me. I wanted to belong, too. I wanted to fit in as he did.

But was this the place?

"Tell me more about it," I whispered at last.

He gave me a wolfish grin.

Hours later I sat in front of my cave, hoping the morning sun might somehow dissipate the chill that seemed to have settled into my soul. My father and I had talked long into the night. I understood better now how much he had given up to become the leader of the pack, and what he had gained. I understood, too, what I must give up to follow his path.

My shape was the first thing. If I agreed to his request, I would become a man only five times a year: on All Hallow's Eve, and on the nights of the solstices and the equinoxes. These were the nights my father had slipped into the village to visit my mother. It occurred to me that she must have loved him very much, to be so lonely for him.

My human shape was not the only price.

"I am young, for a man," my father had told me. "But my body has aged as though it were a wolf's. My time is short. I must pass the burden soon, or the pack will be left without a leader."

"And if I refuse?" I had asked.

He had shrugged and looked away, the only sign of his agitation the way his fingers worked in the scalp of the wolf he had been stroking. "I cannot force you."

But he could entice me. And he did, talking of the joy he felt when he ran through the forest with the pack at his side, and the richness he found in their community. Yet he did not hide the darker side of their life, and he told me, too, what it was like to catch a smaller animal and kill it in your jaws, and feel its warm blood trickling down your throat.

But mostly he spoke of the wolves and his deep love for them. He cared for them as if they were his children, making decisions, settling squabbles, keeping the pack away from the world of men where they would be hunted and killed.

I could tell he had been a good leader, wiser and far more compassionate than the village elders who had sentenced Wandis and me to death.

It was to be our only talk. He would not assume his human shape again for another month and a half, when the winter solstice came. And, one way or another, he would be dead before then.

I picked up a stick and threw it at Wild Eye, who was sitting several feet away. He blinked at me, as if he thought it an astonishing thing to do. But he didn't move. I hated him, hated all of them, for taking my father away from me. His life had been shortened by his wolfhood. Now he was like a candle whose wick was guttering in the last bits of wax. Even worse, he had made it clear that the effort of passing his power, which was what he wanted more than anything else in the world, would make this the last thing he would ever do. If I accepted it, he would die in giving it to me.

I thought of Wandis, led to some distant village by the wolves. Did she wonder what had become of me? What if I did this thing, and then came to her as a man on the first night of winter, to tell her what I had become? Would she still care for me? Would she wait for me, as my mother had waited for my father? Or would she draw away with the same horror that I was still trying to fight down in myself?

I looked at my hands and tried to imagine them as paws.

I shivered, and stood up.

At once Wild Eye and Ragged Ear were at my side.

"Not supposed to let me go anywhere, are you?" I asked.

They stared at me.

I wondered what it would be like to be able to

talk to them as my father could. I realized he was part of a whole world I was unaware of, a mysterious world of night and secrets. I was curious about it. I wished I could run with the pack for a night before I made my decision.

Another wolf came limping along the path. Though it was the first time I had seen him in this shape since I was five, I knew it was my father.

He made a motion with his head that I took as a command, then turned and headed back down the path. I rose to follow him. My guards made no move to stop me. When we had gone a way, my father dropped back to walk beside me. I looked at him and shivered. It was strange to see that dark, four-legged shape and know my father was inside it. And stranger still to think of inhabiting such a shape myself.

Passing through the quiet forest, we came at last to a rocky hillside where nearly two dozen wolves were gathered. Some were playing. Others lay dozing in the warm morning. Now and then their legs would twitch, and I knew that they were running in their sleep.

After a while I thought I understood why my father had brought me here. These were his people, the responsibility he wanted to pass on to me. He stepped into the clearing, and the others were instantly alert. I could sense their love for him. He came back and took my hand softly between his jaws, then drew me in beside him. He was introducing me.

The wolves crowded around us. I felt myself overwhelmed by their warmth, their musky odor.

"All right," I whispered. "I'll do it."

I opened my eyes. My father's naked body lay beside me, quiet and empty, but human once again.

I was still human, too.

Half relieved, half disappointed, I began to wonder if something had gone wrong. Then the moon slipped over the horizon and began pouring fire into my veins.

I cried out in agony. For all we had talked, my father had not warned me of the terror of the transformation, not spoken of the fear and the pain that strike as your skin begins to stretch, your bones wrench themselves into new shapes, and your teeth curve into deadly fangs.

I fell to the ground, writhing in pain.

And yet even in my pain, part of me watched in fascination as thick tufts of hair sprouted on my hands, my fingers curled into paws, and my nails thickened into strong, black claws. I began to rip at the clothing that seemed to bind me like a rope, shredding it in my torment.

As abruptly as it began, the change was complete. I stood on all fours, trembling with the wonder and the horror of what I had just experienced. Then I tipped back my head. Staring at the moon, I howled for the loss of my father, whom I had never had a chance to love.

Almost instantly Wild Eye and Ragged Ear detached themselves from the darkness and came to stand at my shoulders.

"Run with us," said Wild Eye, and I was not surprised when I understood him. "Run with us. It is good for sorrow."

I stretched my legs and headed into the night with them, and then stopped, almost dizzy with sensation. It was as if I had been blind and suddenly found that I could see. Except it was not only my eyes that were keener now, but my nose and my ears as well. I could hear the voles rustling in the soil beneath me, and smell where the weasel had passed an hour before. Stranger still was finding a man-scent and then recognizing it as my own, the path I had followed the day before. What a shock, to discover I had possessed such a rich and distinctive odor, and been so unaware of it.

But the biggest surprise was yet to come, as one by one the pack reached out to greet me.

"Welcome!" cried each voice in my head. "Welcome, welcome, and thrice welcome!"

How can I write of this thing that my father could not tell me, of this oneness that we share? For each of them is always with me now. And the pack is more than a pack, it is a being of its own, of which we are all a part. As they took me in and embraced me as their leader, I knew why my father had loved them so.

I knew, too, that I had found my community at last.

I am a wolf, and I will never be alone again.

Tonight is the night of the winter solstice. I have spent my precious time as a man writing all this down, while it is still fresh within me. When I have finished, I will also write a letter to Wandis. Because it is too soon for me to leave the pack, I will ask Wild Eye to carry it to her, tied around his neck.

But three months from now I will travel myself to the village where the wolves took her. And on the night of the equinox, when the change has come over me and I am a man once more, I will go to her, to learn her answer.

I think if anyone can accept this, it will be she.

I hope I am right.

After all, someday I too will need a son to whom I can pass the pack.

A BLAZE OF GLORY

I t was a house full of white bread and death. Silence grew beneath the chairs like balls of dust. Nothing was out of order, nothing seemed to breathe.

In the center of it sat an old woman, waiting to die.

That she had been full of life at one time I well knew, for she was my grandmother, and I had seen her eyes flash with a fire that seemed stolen from the stars; heard her laugh in the night with a clear joy that easily banished my terror when I was upstairs, lonely and moon-frightened.

Now that was gone, the fire and the clarity drowned in the muddy depths of an unyielding old age that, glacierlike, had crept across her and locked her in a grip of ice. Loss lay like dust in every room of the house: loss of husband; loss of friends; loss of strength, of sharpness of sight, keenness of ear, delicacy of touch. Loss, most of all, of memories, the most recent going first, so that if I entered the house and greeted her, then went to the kitchen to make her some tea, she would cry out in surprise when I re-entered the room five minutes later.

If I reminded her that she had said hello to me minutes earlier, she would shake her head, moaning that she was worthless.

Even that was not as painful as when she asked where my grandfather was, and I would have to remind her that he had died three years earlier. She could only remember him alive, and only knew he was dead when it was brought to her attention. Every day, sometimes more than once a day, she learned again that the man she had lived with for over fifty years was gone, endlessly repeating that horrible first moment of discovery.

Her memories peeled away like layers of an onion, each layer with the power to bring tears to the eye. I found myself growing younger in her eyes as she remembered me not as her youngest and most disgraceful grandchild, the high-school dropout with no prospects, but as the little boy I used to be. I wondered if her failing mind would finally carry her to a time before I was born, and if so, if she would then forget who I was and no longer recognize me when I came to visit.

This had been going on for some months before I began to suspect that as she lost memories she might not be simply moving away from the present, but might indeed be moving toward something else, something long lost that she wanted to regain.

"I can almost see it, Tommy," she moaned once, holding my hand, her eyes squeezed shut, something like tears but thicker oozing from their corners. "What was it? What *was* it?"

But the memory, and then the thought, eluded her.

By the next week she was confined to her bed. Being the only one in the family without a job, I began to visit daily to care for her.

It was during this time that she began to hint at her secret. "Did you ever see them?" she asked one afternoon while I was sitting beside her bed, working a crossword puzzle.

"See who, Gramma?"

"The fair ones," she replied impatiently, as if I were a stupid child not paying attention to something obvious.

"I don't think so," I said cautiously.

She sighed, then whispered, "Of course not." After a moment she added, "I wish you had."

"What are you talking about, Gran?" I asked, totally mystified.

She closed her eyes. Her face relaxed, and for a moment I thought she had fallen asleep. But when she spoke I realized that she was seeing something in her mind.

"Elves," she said. "I'm talking about the elves."

"I wish I had seen them," I answered with some conviction. I had the terrible feeling that she was finally losing her mind. Even so, it was a fact that I had wanted to meet an elf from the first time I had read about them.

"I helped them once, you know," she continued. "At least, I think I did. Do you think I helped them?"

"Of course," I said, squeezing her hand. It was the first note of whimsy I could remember hearing from her in many years, and I was amused. Amused, and oddly touched. I found something both sweet and very sad in the way we were exchanging roles, me becoming the grown-up, she the child.

"Didn't I ever tell you about it?" she asked. Before I could answer, she muttered, "Oh, of course not. I'm not supposed to talk about it. Never did, either, till now."

It was one of those moments she had when she suddenly seemed to lurch into the present.

"You can tell me about it," I said.

"Probably shouldn't," she muttered. Then she did sleep.

The next day she seemed stronger and more alert, and for a moment I wondered if her body was actually growing younger along with her mind. But the look in her eyes was almost feverish.

"I'm so glad you're here," she said. "I want to tell you about them. I think it will be all right."

It took me a moment to realize that she was talking about the elves again.

"I was nineteen," she said, leaning toward me and

whispering, even though there was no one else in the room. "And only recently married to your grampa. Falling through was an accident, actually, but they were desperate, and I was able to help them."

"How did you meet them?" I asked. I felt myself slipping easily back into a childhood mode where I had listened eagerly to her stories. Besides, there was no harm in humoring her.

"I fell through," she said softly. "I was walking across the field, the one between the house and the barn. One minute I was there, the next…*pfffft!*" She made a burring noise, almost a raspberry. It was quite funny, coming from that ancient, wrinkled face.

"Where did it happen?" I asked. "Where, specifically?"

"You know," she said slyly.

"The fairy circle?"

She nodded.

I felt a slight shiver. In the field between the house and the barn was a perfect circle about fifteen feet in diameter where the grass never grew quite right. My sister and I had always called it the fairy circle and said it was where the elves came to dance. I had had a lurking fear of the spot from the time I was in fifth grade and had bought a book of "strange but true" stories from our school book club. One story in particular had terrified me, a tale about a man who had vanished in full view of his wife and children while walking across a field. He was never seen again, but his children once heard his voice emanating from the exact spot where he had disappeared, calling faintly for help. Afterward, the grass around that place had never again grown quite the way it should.

The story and the "fairy circle" in my grandparents' field had merged in my mind, and I had usually given the spot a wide berth. Being of scientific mind, I had decided that the disappearing man had fallen into another dimension of some sort. Despite our name for it, I had never thought of our "fairy circle" as actually belonging to magical creatures. It was simply a place to watch out for. Now my grandmother's words were making me reconsider that position.

I shook my head and smiled at myself. What foolishness! I was being drawn in by her senile fantasies. But what harm in it? It seemed to make her feel better to tell the story. It certainly wouldn't hurt me to listen.

"What happened after you 'fell through'?" I asked.

Gramma closed her eyes and didn't answer for a long time. "So beautiful," she whispered at last. "So beautiful—and so sad."

"What was so beautiful?"

"The elves. Their world. I wish you could have seen it, sweetheart. It was more wonderful than I can tell you. But someone was dying." She paused, then added ruefully, "Like me."

I wanted to tell her she wasn't, but she had never appreciated that kind of comforting dishonesty. So I simply said, "Tell me more."

She sat up. It startled me, for she had not been able to do so on her own for several days. But it was as if the story she wanted to tell had overtaken her, was holding her in its grip.

"I was afraid when I first fell through," she said, her voice husky but strong. "Thank goodness I had read *Alice in Wonderland.* I don't know what would have happened to me if I hadn't. I think every child should read *Alice,* don't you, Tommy? It doesn't make any sense, but neither does the real world. It's a very educational book."

She shook her head. "Listen to me babble. I don't have much time; I have to stop going on so. Listen carefully. Otherwise you will forget. You can't count on memory. Memory can betray you." She paused, drew a breath, then said, "All right, here's what happened."

I listened carefully. That night, I wrote down what she said:

When I fell into the land of the elves, I was afraid; terrified. Not so Dyor, the elf who found me. He was tall, Tommy, tall and terribly beautiful—so beautiful that it made me ashamed to be seen by him. I felt like a little brown wren next to a magnificent cardinal.

I didn't see him right away, only the world into which I had fallen. The field was like our field, save that there were no fences or barns, the grass was somehow more lush, the flowers brighter, the sky more wildly blue. A sweet breeze blew through the grass. Floating on the breeze was an enormous lavender butterfly; it landed on my shoulder, as if it could not imagine being afraid of me.

Then Dyor stood, rising from the grass like a dream. He had been sleeping, he told me later, and my arrival had woken him.

"Thank the seventh star you are here," he said.

It's hard to tell you what his voice was like, Tommy, except to say that it wasn't simply beautiful; it was *thrilling*.

He must have seen that I was trembling. Or maybe he simply realized how I would feel. Anyway, he raised his hands, palms out, and said, "Please do not be afraid. We have been hoping someone would come. We need your help."

When I asked him what he meant, he shook his head and said, "Let me show you. It will be easier than trying to explain."

Taking my hand, he led me out of the field and into the woods. Such woods! Such *trees!* I felt that our trees were copied from them by some third-rate manufacturer.

Dyor led me to a grove filled with elves. They blinked and turned away when they saw me, as if something about me hurt their eyes. It made me sad.

At the far side of the grove stood two thrones, carved from burnished wood that had a strange grain. Sitting on the thrones were two elves, one male, one female. He was the most exquisite of all the elves, with silver hair that seemed to hold its own light. She should have been beautiful, but was not. Something had happened to her, weakened her somehow, so that she seemed to be wasting away.

The elf king stood and held out his hand to me. I crossed the grove. I was shaking. Not because I was afraid he would do anything to me, but simply because he was so wonderful. It was like meeting a god. At the same time, I was fretting inside over how I would ever get home to your grandfather. Of course, he wasn't your grandfather, yet; we had been married for less than six months at the time. But I knew I had to get home to him.

When I reached the elf king I knelt before him and bent my head to the ground. I had never met royalty before, but I had read my books, and it seemed like the right thing to do. After a moment he reached down and put his hand under my chin. His skin was warm and smooth. "Stand," he said in a voice even more wonderful than Dyor's.

I stood.

"What is your name?"

"Ivy," I said, hoping he wouldn't think it too foolish.

I was pleased when he smiled. "A beautiful name," he said. "For a beautiful young woman."

I began to blush. I knew I could not be beautiful in their eyes, but it pleased me that he said it.

He stared at me for a long moment, squinting a bit as he did, as if I hurt his eyes. "We need your help," he said at last. Even though Dyor had said the same thing, I found it astonishing. What could these people possibly need from me?

I started to say, "I will do anything I can," then stopped myself. These people were magical, after all. Who knew what they might ask of me? I wanted to help, but I didn't want to commit myself to something that would keep me from going home again. Choosing my words more carefully, I said, "How can someone like me help someone like you?"

The queen stirred then, moving as if it hurt to do so. "This is my fault," she said. "It is best that I explain."

Her voice sounded not like bells but like sand running between your fingers, and it was all I could do to make out her words.

The king paused, then nodded. I was aware of the elves all around me, staring at me. The queen held out her hand. I took it, wondering if I should kiss it, wishing Dyor would advise me. But the queen simply squeezed my fingers, then pulled her hand back. Unlike the king, her hand was cool, almost cold.

"I have made a serious error," she said softly.

The king was frowning.

I waited, but no one spoke. Finally I said, "What did you do?"

"I stayed too long at the fair."

I didn't know what to say to that, so I just stood and looked at her, waiting for her to go on.

"The goblin fair," she said at last.

The king looked away.

"There are rules," said the queen. "It is never wise to ignore them."

She straightened herself in her chair. I remember that specifically, because it was hard for me to imagine that someone so graceful could ever be uncomfortable. Finally she went on:

"Once a year the peoples of faerie gather at the goblin fair. It is a time of guaranteed peace, when dwarf and elf, goblin and sprite can freely meet and mingle, trade and talk, exchange everything from newts to news. I love the fair, love it too much, I suppose, for last year I broke the rules and stayed past midnight. When that happened, when I made that fool's mistake, the goblins took, as was their right, their penalty."

She closed her eyes and looked away.

"What was it?" I asked. "What was the penalty?"

"A part of me," she whispered. "They took a part of me and wrapped it in a stone, and now the stone is warm, but I am cold, and I am fading, and in time I simply will not be, unless the stone can be recovered."

I shivered at what she told me.

"It is part of the stone's enchantment that no elf can touch it," she continued, "nor no magical creature of any sort. Only a human can hold the stone. Would you do that for me, go and fetch the stone, bring it back so that I can be whole again?"

It would have taken a heart far harder than mine to say no to that, Tommy, though I did worry what your grandfather would say when I got home.

Well, getting that stone took longer than any of us imagined. What an adventure I had getting it back to the queen! Dyor and I met stranger creatures and saw wilder places than I can tell you about—giants and unicorns, and once I even saw a cave where a dragon lived, though I didn't see the dragon itself.

But with Dyor's help I did it, Tommy. We found the stone and carried it back to the queen. And when we did, when I placed it in the queen's hand, the most amazing thing happened. It was as if the stone dissolved, melted right into her palm. Something seemed to change and grow in her then, so that she was suddenly—oh, right somehow. Healthy again. Herself.

My grandmother began to cough at that point, as if the effort of telling the story had caught up with her all at once. "No more today, Tommy," she said. "I'm too tired."

To my shame, I tried to get her to tell me more, even though I could see that she was exhausted. Of course I realized the story was quite mad. But I was also enchanted by it.

The next day she went into the hospital.

I visited her daily. She told me more about the elf world when she could, though mostly she was too weak. A single strand ran through all the memories. "I have to get home," she muttered as she wandered through the back corridors of her mind. "I have to get home."

For three days I thought she was speaking about coming back from her adventure. It was almost too late when I realized that she meant she needed to go back to the farm.

"I have to go, Tommy," she cried, late one night, clutching my arm with a strength that astonished me. "Take me home!"

I wish I were stronger. I wish bureaucrats could be slain like dragons. But this was not an elven adventure, and I was not able to free her from the hospital.

She freed herself, I think. Through sheer effort of will she made herself well enough that they let her go home, on the condition that someone stayed with her around the clock.

That was all right. I had nothing else to do.

Three nights later I knew she was going to die. A trip back to the hospital might have squeezed out a few more days, but they were days that she didn't want, and that would have been spent in a place she hated.

She wanted to be home.

It was about three o'clock in the morning when the elves arrived.

I was sitting in my grandmother's room, holding her withered hand, wondering which labored breath would be her last. Suddenly I heard a rattling in her chest. Her hand tightened on mine.

"It's time, Tommy," she moaned.

Then the wall on the far side of the bed turned to liquid silver, and the elves stepped through.

There were eight of them. The first, I was quite sure, was Dyor. The king and the queen came last. I understood what my grandmother had said, about feeling like a wren next to a cardinal. The fact that all the elves blinked and averted their eyes, as if my plainness was painful to them, added to the feeling. I wanted to crawl under the bed and hide from their beauty, wanted to shake my grandmother and shout, "They're here!" But I could not, couldn't move at all. It was as though time had stopped, frozen at the moment of their arrival.

Dyor reached down and gently separated my grandmother's hand from mine. "Hello, Ivy," he whispered, and when she smiled I knew that she was still alive.

In that moment I felt a shift, as if I had moved from the place where time had stopped to their place, where time went on in its own way.

"We are here to redeem a promise," one of the elves said to me as they began to cluster around her bed.

"What promise?" I asked.

"A long time ago your grandmother did me a great service," said the queen, whose voice was not like sand now, but like breeze through leaves, like birdsong in spring, like rain on a window late at night.

"In return, we offered her a chance to stay in Elfland, where she would have been immortal. She refused."

The king took the queen's hand. "It was not that she didn't want to stay," he said. "She did. But she had made other promises."

I thought of my grandfather, and wondered if the old man ever knew what Gramma had given up for him.

"I offered her many things," said the queen. "But she had only one request. 'Let me be buried in Elfland,' she said to me, just before we sent her home. 'When it is all over, let me come back here to rest.'"

"So we have come to take her home," said the king.

Two of the elves were carrying a length of cloth, the color of the sky at midnight. Working gently, deftly, they slid it under my grandmother's frail body. She shifted slightly as they did, but was silent. I thought I saw a faint smile play over her lips.

Now the elves lined up, three to each side of her bed. Each took hold of the edge of the cloth. Together they lifted her from the bed.

Suddenly the liquid silver of the wall began to shift. It grew transparent, and I caught a heart-stopping glimpse of the world on the other side.

The king shifted his eyes so that he was looking right at me. He was squinting and frowning. It felt bad to be looked at that way.

"Would you like to see the Lady Ivy as we see her?" he asked.

"I don't know what you mean."

"You think we find you ugly, do you not?"

When I lowered my head in shame, the king laughed. "We see different things, you and I. Your senses observe the outside. Ours perceive what lies inside. Let me show you."

And so saying, he laid his hands upon my eyes. When he took them away I cried out in wonder. The elves were as beautiful as ever. But my grandmother— oh, my grandmother. What a blaze of glory she was.

Now I understood why the elves had averted their eyes.

Singing a song that broke my heart, they carried my grandmother through the silver portal, a small sun resting on the dark elven cloth.

"Your lives are short, Tommy," said the Elven king. "But, oh, how the best of you shine."

He reached for his queen's hand. Both of them nodded to me, then turned and followed my grand- mother's funeral procession, through the shimmering silver portal, back to the land of the elves.

The wall closed behind them. I stared at it for a long time, then turned, and began to straighten my grandmother's bed.

THE GOLDEN SAIL

His name was Jan. He was short for his thirteen years, and the sun had roasted his skin to a golden brown. His long, unruly hair was black as a moonless night, his heart hard as a sailor's knot. As for his eyes, they were mostly green but seemed to shift with his moods.

In this, they were much like the sea beside which he lived.

Jan loved the sea. But he also hated it, for it had taken his father when he'd set off to find the ship with the golden sail.

It was a story his father had always loved, the tale of a mysterious ship that fishermen and traders would see on the horizon, yet could never reach. Then one day word swept the coast that the ship had been seen again, and his father announced that he was going in search of it.

That was the last they had seen of him.

But Jan had not stopped waiting, not stopped hoping. Which is why he was squatting at the water's edge now, looking for a sign of his father's ship.

The gulls wheeled overhead, shrieking raucously. The waves rolled in to smash against the beach, splashing him with warm brine. The huge yellow eye of the merciless sun glared down at him. And the smooth line of sky and sea remained unbroken.

But still he watched, as he had always done when he was not busy on some task for his mother. Now that she was gone, too—a victim of the fever that had ravaged the coast the previous year—watching was what he did most of the time.

After an hour of squinting at the horizon without seeing any sign of a ship, the boy sighed heavily, stood, and stretched. He gave a final seaward glance, then began to wander down the beach. He moved slowly, enjoying the feel of the warm water as it foamed and bubbled over his toes.

A group of gulls that had gathered on the sand ahead began scolding for the sake of scolding. Jan tossed a pebble listlessly in their direction. They ignored him. He shrugged and continued down the beach, until he came to the hut of Samos, the blind net maker.

The old man paused in his work as the boy approached. After a moment he smiled and said, "Jan." It was both a greeting and a statement of pleasure. Even so, it made Jan shiver. The way Samos could tell who was standing nearby without being able to see made him uncomfortable. It was, however, the only thing about the man that Jan found disturbing.

In all other ways it felt good to be with him, for he would talk to Jan in ways that others would not, offering him advice, wisdom, lore of the sea, and most of all sympathy, which the other fisherfolk thought was a sign of softness, and would make him weak.

"No sign of your father?" asked the old man. His fingers, thick and twisted with age, yet amazingly supple, resumed work on the net he was repairing.

"No." The word was bitter in Jan's mouth. He felt like a fool, still waiting, still hoping, after all this time.

"Sometimes it is best to let go," said Samos. He held up the net to display the gaping hole. "If Markand had let go, instead of holding on to this net, he might be alive today. As it was, he saved the net, but lost his life. Not the best of trades, I think."

"My father is coming back," said Jan, fighting to ignore the knot of anger in his stomach.

"Ten years is a long time to be gone," replied the old man. Then he turned his attention back to the net. Jan stood in silence, gazing out at the sea once more. For a moment he thought he saw something. He blinked and shook his head, and it was gone.

No. There it was again.

The sun was halfway up the sky, and its fierce rays filled the water with flashes of gold and silver. Whatever Jan saw was blending with those flashes, barely distinguishable. He shaded his eyes, squinting for a better view.

A sail! He leaped to his feet, feeling a surge of hope and, at the same time, cursing himself for being fool enough to get excited by every sail that broke the horizon. It would be some time before he could see whether this one carried the family crest—a blue circle that held the image of a gull in flight, with a single star above it. Even if it didn't, the ship might carry his father. After all, the sea had its own ways of returning things. At least, that was what his mother had always said.

As the minutes wore on, Jan was troubled to see that the sail was the wrong color. It was not simply that it was not white, as his father's would have been. It was not any of the colors that were proper for a sail—not red, like the sails of the traders from the north, nor blue or green, like those from the south, nor even black, like those from the east.

At first Jan thought the sail was yellow. But it sparkled and shone in a way he had never seen before, and as it drew closer he took in a sharp breath.

The sail looked as if it was made of purest gold.

Could this be the ship his father had gone in search of? Could his father be on it, even now, sailing toward them?

Samos placed his hand on Jan's shoulder. "That is no ordinary ship," he whispered.

Jan trembled. The old man was blind. How did he know there was a ship at all?

They stood, waiting. The ship continued toward

them, its sail flashing in the sun. Jan's throat tightened. He could sense something powerful about the vessel, powerful and frightening. Something that was reaching out toward him.

"Samos, I'm frightened."

The hand on his shoulder tightened, but the old man said nothing. Part of Jan—a small voice inside—was urging him to run. He fought his fear and stood without moving.

As the ship drew closer, Jan saw that it was long and sleek, and rode low in the water. He was admiring its lines when he realized that rather than slowing as it approached the shore, the ship was moving faster.

"Samos! She's going to run aground!"

But he was wrong. Biting back a cry of astonishment, he watched the ship begin to rise in the water, floating higher and higher on the waves, as if being lifted by some marvelous dolphin. The water parted in white curls before its prow as it surged toward the shore. The ship continued to rise, until it seemed to be riding the air instead of the sea. It came to a halt a few feet from land, floating on a boiling cushion of white foam, its keel cleaving only the air.

Silently, the ship swung around until the starboard side was facing the shore. Silently, a gangplank appeared at the edge of the ship and extended itself onto the sand. The hair on Jan's neck stood up, but he was unable to resist the mystery. He stepped toward the ship. Samos reached for his arm—not to restrain him, but to join him.

Moving in silence, the old man and the boy ascended the plank.

The ship was silent. Silent, and empty.

Jan shivered. They should turn and run now, he thought, as fast and as far as they could, away from the sea and away from this witch ship. But whatever was calling to him was even stronger now, and the call was too powerful to ignore.

Samos started to speak, but a sound from behind interrupted him. They turned in unison, then Jan yelled and dived for the gangplank, which was sliding back into the ship.

He fell short in his jump. Lying on the deck, with the golden sun burning his back and the sound of the surf pounding in his ears, he felt the ship move away from the shore. His stomach clenched, and he yelled again, though yelling was obviously useless.

He looked at Samos. The old man's face wore a look of astonishment, and of fear. Yet lurking behind these was one thing more, thought Jan—a hint of burning, radiant joy.

"Back on the sea at last," Samos whispered.

Jan pulled himself to his feet and stood at the rail, watching as the shore faded from view. Despite his fear, he, too, felt a strange sense of elation. To be on the sea, with a friend like Samos and a ship that was as swift as the wind—this was a wonderful thing.

Terrible danger might be waiting. But for the moment, for this one golden moment, he felt wild and free, and close to the edge of a question that was worth answering.

Samos came to stand beside him. "Sea air," said the old man. "There's nothing like it. Even living right on the shore you don't get this. I've missed it."

"But what is this ship?" asked Jan.

"I don't know."

"But you're always telling me stories about the sea. You must have heard something about a ship like this."

"Oh, ghost ships, certainly," said the net maker. "But being empty and being a ghost ship are different things. I was on a ghost ship once. You could feel the death in the air—sense the dead men hovering around you. This is no ghost ship we're riding, Jan."

"Then what is it?"

Samos shook his head. "I wish I knew."

They stood at the rail for a long time. Then, with Jan leading the way, they went to explore the ship. It was tight and trim, clean and polished. Below decks they found three good-size cabins. One had a trunk filled with weapons. Jan, delighted, chose both a dagger and a sword for himself. He had never owned a blade before and had always wanted one.

As he began to strap the sword to his waist, he saw something that made his fingers tremble. On the hilt of the sword was a blue enamel circle. Inside the circle was a gull in flight. Above the gull was a single star.

"What is it?" asked Samos, when he heard Jan's gasp.

"This sword bears the sign of my family. What does it mean?"

He could not bring himself to ask the question that was really tearing at his heart: "Does it mean my father is dead?"

When Jan had recovered from his shock, they continued their exploration. They found a small galley. It was bare of food, which worried Jan until that night, when they entered again, planning to search for any crumb, and found a hot meal waiting for them.

Where the wine and cheese, the cool fruit and savory meat had come from they had no idea, and its strange arrival was almost as worrisome as the absence of food had been earlier. But they ate it anyway, and found it good indeed.

Later they went on deck, and Jan described the sky to Samos, who nodded and smiled as the boy talked in wonder of a darkness deeper than he had ever seen, and stars that twinkled more brightly than he had imagined possible.

Despite the fact that he had no idea where they were going, when (or even *if*) they would arrive, Jan slept peacefully that night, rocked by the gentle waves.

It did not take long for them to fall into a comfortable routine. Jan would rise early and meet Samos in the galley, where a breakfast of fruit and bread would be waiting. After eating, they would go on deck to check the wind and weather. They would discuss the sun and which way they were heading. Then Jan would climb the rigging, looking for any sign of land, or even of another ship. Often he saw distant islands, which he would describe to Samos, who seemed to recognize them all.

"South," the old man would mutter. "We're heading south."

The ship never went within shouting distance of any of the islands.

In the afternoon, at Samos's insistence, they would polish the ship's brass fittings, though to Jan's eye they seemed to gleam all on their own.

They searched for a ship's log but found none.

"Ah, well," said Samos. "It doesn't really matter, since neither of us can read. Even so, I would feel better if there were one."

When the wind was high, the ship raced across the water as if it were flying. When the air was still, the ship continued to move anyway. Once Samos told Jan to drop a piece of wood overboard, to check the current. The boy was troubled to see that even with no wind the ship was moving against the current, not with it.

On the fifth day, Jan was standing on the starboard

side of the ship, gazing into the water, when he saw a woman swimming alongside. Her long hair, gold streaked with green, trailed around her. When Jan called out to her she disappeared beneath the waves. It was only when her shining tail broke the surface that he realized her lower half was that of a fish.

The woman returned every day, usually in the late afternoon. Sometimes she would swim alongside the ship for hours, unless Jan tried to speak to her. Then she would immediately disappear beneath the water again.

On the eighth night, a gale swept down from the north, buffeting the ship with fierce gusts of cold wind. The waves grew higher and higher, until they were crashing over the bow. The ship was tossed across the water like a ball in the hands of the gods. Jan and Samos took refuge in the cabins below and finally tied themselves to their bunks to keep from being flung against the walls.

When morning came, they staggered up to the deck of the ship. Jan clutched Samos's arm in terror. "Look!" he whispered. And even when he remembered that the old man was blind and could not see what was ahead of them, he was too frightened to feel foolish.

Flying fish were leaping all around them. On the starboard side of the ship, a few hundred yards away, swam a pod of whales. They, too, were leaping out of the water, flinging themselves into the storm with abandon, creating enormous surges when they landed.

These things were strange, but not terrifying. What terrified Jan was the great waterspout that rose from the sea directly ahead, a whirling column that stretched so high he could not see its top.

"Drop the sail," ordered Samos, when Jan told him what he saw.

The ship was moving faster now, the sea peeling away from the prow in curls of foam. Jan raced to the mast and fumbled with the knots. They refused to budge. He drew his sword and sliced the rope.

It made no difference. The sail stayed proud and full.

They drew closer to the spout, which loomed above them like some living tower, dark and swirling. Jan grabbed a coil of rope. Taking Samos by the arm, he hurried him to the mast. Then he wrapped the rope around both of them and bound them to the wood.

The roar of the water was deafening, the headlong rush of the ship terrifying. The wind clutched at them, as if trying to pluck them from the deck.

Then they were part of the waterspout. The ship, snatched from the surface of the sea, swirled up and up, riding the dark column as helplessly as a leaf on the wind. Around and around they spun. Higher and higher they rose, sometimes on the surface of the spout, sometimes pulled into it. Water drenched them. At times they couldn't breathe.

And still up they went. The sea was appallingly far below now, so distant that the leaping whales looked like minnows. Looking straight ahead, Jan saw clouds swirling by. Twisting his neck, he saw the dark spout, and the strange sea creatures trapped within it. A moment later they were spun back inside the whirling wall of water themselves, and he could see nothing.

Then, like a cork bobbing to the surface, the ship burst out of the water spout. Jan shook his head, causing water to spatter from his long hair. He blinked to clear his vision, then cried out in astonishment.

"What is it?" gasped Samos. "Where are we?"

"I don't know," said Jan. "It looks as if we are on the sea again. But how can that be, when the spout carried us so high away from it? Is this a sea in the sky?"

"Perhaps the spout has taken us to another world," said Samos gravely.

Jan thought of the stories his mother used to tell, stories of worlds beyond worlds, and shuddered. He began to fumble with the rope that held them to the mast. At first the sea-soaked knots were hard to undo, but finally he managed to loosen them.

When he looked up again, he cried out in surprise.

"What is it?" asked Samos.

"An island. We're sailing straight toward it. Brace yourself. We may run aground."

And, indeed, moments later they ran right up onto the sand—crossing the line where the sea met the shore and continuing on for twice the length of the ship. Jan was still marveling at this when he realized something else.

"Come on!" he cried. Still holding Samos by the arm, he helped him climb over the edge. They dropped to the sand, which was warm and silky beneath their feet.

"What is happening?" asked Samos breathlessly.

"The ship is getting smaller," said Jan. His eyes widened. "And smaller still! Now it is no longer than you are tall. And still it shrinks. And now—"

He stopped, too surprised by what had happened to speak for a moment.

"What?" asked Samos. "What is it?"

"The ship has become a coin," said Jan. He plucked the shining disk from the sand. On one side the coin was engraved with a perfect replica of the ship. On the other the golden surface showed a gull in flight with a single star above it.

"What does it mean?" asked Jan.

"I'd say that it means we're supposed to take it with us," said Samos.

"Take it where?"

The old man shrugged. "Wherever we're going next."

Jan looked around. The beach ended at a jungle. It would have been too thick to walk through, save that directly ahead of them was a clear path. Taking Samos by the arm, Jan led him forward.

The jungle was so green and dark that Jan felt almost as if they were walking underwater. It was quiet, too—unnaturally quiet. No breeze stirred the leaves, which hung limp and still. No howl nor roar, no cry of bird, buzz of insect, hiss of snake, nor chatter of monkey disturbed the awful silence, which was so heavy it made Jan afraid to speak. The only sound was that of their own passing, and even that seemed oddly muted.

Jan stopped. A huge web blocked their path, its strands as thick as his thumbs. He turned aside, but the jungle was too dense for them to go around. Nervously, looking above and to the side for any sign of the creature that had woven it, Jan sliced at the sticky silk until he had made an opening through which they could pass.

And still all was silent. They walked on, Samos keeping one hand on Jan's shoulder.

Another web, and yet another. And then, a hundred paces past the last web, the jungle opened.

Jan caught his breath in wonder. In the center of the clearing stood a building of astonishing beauty. Made of shining white stone, with broad steps leading to a golden door, it stretched high above the trees. Ornate carvings of gods and monsters decorated the walls. Whether it was a temple or a palace, he could not say. He knew only that it was wonderful.

He thought he heard the murmur of voices as he and Samos climbed the steps. But he could see no one.

The golden door opened easily before he even touched it.

They entered the building and walked through long curving corridors until, finally, they came to another great door. Jan waited for a moment. When the door did not open, he reached forward and pushed on it.

It swung inward without a sound.

They entered a huge, high chamber, its painted blue ceiling so far above them that it seemed like a sky. Around the chamber, in niches carved in the walls, stood statues of men frozen in horrible postures, as if they had been turned to stone at the most awful moment of their lives.

A wide carpet, blood red, ran the length of the chamber, all the way to a platform mounted by a series of five broad steps. The carpet continued up the steps and stopped at the foot of a golden throne.

On the throne sat Jan's father.

It took a moment for Jan to realize who it was, for he had not seen his father's face in ten years, and he himself had been only three years old at the time. But soon enough he recognized the straight nose, the strong chin, and most of all the look in his father's eyes, which made it seem as if some part of him was always looking into the distance, looking for something he could never find. Then Jan was seized by a strange welter of emotions—joy at finding his father, but also sudden, unexpected anger at the man for having been gone so long with no word. Underneath all that, and equally unexpected, was a kind of terror. *What will he think of me?* Jan wondered. *Will he even know me?*

He started toward the throne. He walked for the first few paces. Then, unable to control himself, he bolted forward, racing along the carpet and hurling himself up the steps.

He expected his father to rise from the throne, to fling his arms around him. But he didn't, and Jan's joy withered into fear when he stood next to the throne and saw why his father remained sitting.

Hand and foot, arm and leg, he was bound to the throne by golden vines that seemed to grow directly from the throne and into his flesh.

The boy stood in silence, uncertain at first of what to say. Finally it was his father who spoke. "Is that you, Jan?" he asked, in a voice little more than a whisper.

Jan nodded. Then, as if the gesture had broken the cord that tied his tongue, he cried, "What has happened to you?"

Jan's father closed his eyes. "I have given my life to the crown and the throne."

Jan, his knees suddenly weak, slid to the floor. He leaned against his father's legs, which were clad in blue silk finer than any he had ever touched before. "I don't understand."

Straining against the vines, his father's fingers stretched forward just enough to touch Jan's hair. "When I went in search of the Golden Sail, I did not know I would be gone so long," he murmured.

"Why did you go?" asked Jan, holding back his tears.

"Like you, my heart was restless. I longed for adventure."

"My heart longed for you," whispered his son.

His father drew in a sharp breath and didn't speak for a moment. At last he said, "As you know, I went in search of the Golden Sail. When I found it, when I boarded the ship that carries it, the ship sped off on its own, bearing me to this land. Here I was greeted as hero, and king. Can you understand what that means, Jan? I was a fisherman, a sailor."

"A father, too," put in Samos.

Jan's father groaned. "A father, too. But suddenly I was called 'king.' Little was it in me to resist, even though I understood what was being asked of me." He sighed heavily, then shuddered. "I could have refused. They would not have forced me."

"Who?" asked Jan. "Who would not have forced you?"

"The golden people," said his father. "The

people of this land. The golden land must have a king, Jan, or it withers and dies. But the land devours the king, as it has devoured me. Now I am withering, too; used up."

"No!"

His father gave him a weary smile. "No sense in trying to hide from what is. I sent the ship to search for you, to bring you back, so that I could say farewell."

"And who will be king when you are gone?" asked Samos, who had come slowly down the carpet to join them.

"Whoever will take the task," replied Jan's father.

"Not Jan!" said Samos protectively.

The king, Jan's father, shook his head. "I did not bring Jan here to ask him to take my place. I brought him to say farewell, and to ask him to set me free. Could he be king? If he wants."

"Why would I want such a thing?" asked Jan, drawing back.

"Because it is beautiful," said his father, looking past him, as if he was seeing some other place, some other world. "The first years are more wonderful than I can tell you, Jan. You are beloved of the people. Feasting and dancing are the order of the day. But there comes a time when you grow tired, when what you are giving is more than what you have been given. Then the people grow petulant, like little children who have gone too long without a nap. And, eventually, you are empty, and it is time for a new king."

"I'll set you free," said Jan, drawing the sword he had claimed on the ship.

His father shook his head. "Not that way. It's too late for that. I want you to do something much more difficult."

Jan felt his grip on the blade begin to falter. Fear blossomed in his heart. "What?" he asked softly. "What do you want me to do?"

His father looked directly into his eyes. "Forgive me," he whispered.

Jan felt a deep heaviness inside him, a weight on his heart that threatened to sink it in the heaving sea of his sorrow and anger. To wait so long, to come so far, aching for his father, for what he had never received from him—and now, after all that, to find not that his father was going to come home with him, nor that he had become a great ruler and wanted to share his kingdom, nor that he had a treasure to enrich their lives, but rather that he wanted something more from his son, and the hardest thing of all at that, this was a bitter discovery indeed.

"Jan," said his father softly. "Look at me."

The boy stared into his father's eyes. They were like the sea during a storm, dark and troubled, and strange currents ran beneath their surface.

"I brought you here because it was the last thing I could do for you," said his father.

"For *me*?" cried Jan.

His father stretched his fingers toward Jan. The boy hesitated, then reached out and took his hand.

"Forgive me and you will be free," whispered the king. "You can go on to grow and live as you must. But forgive me not and I will haunt you as long as you live. You will carry me like a stone in your heart for all your days, and everything you do will be twisted out of shape."

"You brought the boy here to threaten him?" growled Samos.

Jan's father closed his eyes. "This is not a threat," he said wearily. "It is a warning. I have sat in this chair for many years now, and as the vines grew deeper into my flesh, and then my veins, binding me to both the throne and the people, I came to know their lives, and their hearts. This has brought me great wisdom." He gave his son a sad smile. "Alas, the wisdom comes far too late for me. But not for you, Jan. Not for you. I tell you only what I have learned. Forgive me, or carry me like a stone for all the days of your life."

Kneeling, clutching his father's hand, Jan gazed up into the eyes he knew so well, though it had been so long since he last had seen them. Hurt boiled within him, acid in his veins. So much lost. So much lost.

"I am more sorry than I can tell you," whispered his father.

"Biscuits, biscuits of glory,
   This is my story,
   Biscuits of glory..."

By now the hair was standing up on the back of my neck. Yet somehow I didn't think anyone who sounded so sad and sweet could hurt me.

Clutching my Louisville Slugger, I tiptoed down the rest of the steps and stopped outside the kitchen door.

"Biscuits, biscuits of glory," sang the voice, sounding so sad I almost started to cry myself.

Pushing lightly on the kitchen door, I swung it open just a crack. When I peeked through, I let out a little squeak of fright. There was no one in sight, not a person to be seen.

What I did see was a bag of flour, which wouldn't have been that unusual, except for the fact that this bag was *floating* through the air.

"Biscuits of glory," sang the voice, as the bag of flour opened, seemingly by itself. "Lighter than lovin', floatin' to heaven, straight from my oven..."

A measuring cup drifted into the air, then dipped into the flour bag. As the cup came out of the bag, a little thrill ran down my spine. Suddenly I could see the hand that was holding it! That was because the hand was now covered with flour.

The hand repeated the action. It was an eerie

Jan blinked, then nodded. He tightened his grip on his father's hand. "I forgive you," he whispered.

Then he dropped his head against his father's knees and wept, until the knot of his anger had turned to water as salty as the sea and flowed its way out of his heart.

"Now go," whispered his father at last. "Go out into the world. The ship is yours. It will take you anywhere you want to go. But one thing I beg of you, Jan. When you find what you love...stop looking."

An hour later Jan and Samos stood on the beach where they had landed. Jan took the golden coin from his pocket and flung it into the air. It spun high in a glittering arc. As it passed the peak, began to move away from the sky and back toward the sea, it changed into a ship, tiny but growing.

"Where shall we go?" asked Samos, as they climbed aboard.

Jan started to answer, but the words caught in his throat. He closed his eyes, took a deep breath, tried again. "Where shall we go? Anywhere we want! After all...I'm a free man."

The Golden Sail caught the wind. The sea air was fresh and sweet in their nostrils. A gull cawed and wheeled above them. Beyond the gull they saw a single bright star, the first star of evening.

A mermaid sang in the distance.

And the ship sailed on.

BISCUITS OF GLORY

I am haunted by biscuits—Elvira Thistledown's biscuits, to be more precise. But I don't have any regrets. If I had it to do over again, I would still eat one, if only to free that poor woman from her curse. I'd do it even knowing how it was going to affect the rest of my life.

I was ten when it happened. We had just moved into a new house. Well, new to us; it was really a very old one—the fifth we had been in that I could remember. That was how my parents made their living: buying old houses, fixing them up, then selling them for a bundle of money. It was sort of neat, except it meant we never stayed in any one place very long, the places we moved into were always sort of crummy, and just when they got good, we had to move on.

Anyway, on our third night in the house, I heard a clatter in the kitchen. Now all old houses have their noises, their own personal creaks and groans, and I was still getting used to the sounds of this house. But something about this particular noise didn't sound

right to me. So I grabbed my baseball bat and headed for the stairs.

I grabbed the bat instead of waking my parents because I had been through this before. I was tired of embarrassing myself, so I generally investigated night noises on my own. But I always carried my trusty Louisville Slugger when I did. Just in case, you know?

The floor was cold against my feet.

My door squeaked as I opened it.

Trying not to wake my parents, I tiptoed along the hall, past the peeling wallpaper (roses the size of cabbages floating against gray stripes—truly ugly), past the bathroom with its leaky faucets (I had already gotten used to *that* noise), on to the head of the stairs.

I paused and listened.

Something was definitely moving in the kitchen. I could hear scrapes and thumps, soft and gentle, but no less real for all that. I was about to go wake my parents after all when I heard something else—something totally unexpected.

I heard a woman singing.

I leaned forward and closed my eyes (I d
know what good that was supposed to do, but
know how it is), straining to hear. The voice w
sweet and sad—almost like someone singing
I had to go halfway down the steps to mak
words:

sight: a floating hand, seemingly unattached to any-thing else, dumping flour into a big ceramic bowl.

Next came the baking powder. *Lots* of baking powder.

"Biscuits, biscuits of glory...," sang the ghost. Her voice caught as she choked back a sob.

I couldn't help myself. Stepping through the door into the kitchen I asked, "What is it? What's wrong?"

The flour-covered hand jerked sideways, knock-ing over the container of baking powder. "Who are you?" asked the ghost in a soft voice, almost as if *she* was frightened of *me*.

"I'm Benjie Perkins. I live here. Who are you?"

"Elvira Thistledown," whispered the voice, so lightly it was as if the words were floating. "I died here."

I shivered. "What are you doing?" I asked.

"Making biscuits," she replied, setting the baking powder upright once more. "I make biscuits every Saturday night. Saturday at midnight. It's my curse."

"Sort of a strange curse."

"It was a strange death," whispered the ghost of Elvira Thistledown, as her one visible hand picked up a fork and began to stir the flour.

"Care to talk about it?" I asked.

My mother always said I was a good listener.

"I can talk while I work," she said.

Taking that to be a yes, I pulled up a stool and sat next to the counter. Soon I was so involved in her story, I stopped paying much attention to what she was doing. Oh, how I wish now that I had watched more carefully!

"I always loved to make biscuits," said Elvira Thistledown. "My mother taught me when I was only seven years old, and soon my daddy was saying that he thought I was the best biscuit maker in the county."

"You must have liked that."

"I did," she said, sounding happy for the first time since we had begun to talk.

"I hate to interrupt," I said, "but is it possible for you to become visible? I might feel less nervous if you did."

"Well, it's not easy. But you seem like a nice boy. Just a minute and I'll see what I can do."

Soon a milky light began to glow in front of me. It started out kind of blobby, almost like a cloud that had floated into the kitchen, but after a minute or two it condensed into the form of a woman. She was younger and prettier than I had expected, with a turned-up nose and a long neck. I don't know what color her hair or eyes were; she had no color. She wore old-fashioned clothes.

"Better?"

"I think so."

She returned to her work. "It was vanity did me

in," she said, measuring baking powder into the mix. "I was so proud of my biscuits that I just couldn't stand it when that awful Dan McCarty moved into town and started bragging that *he* made the best biscuits in the state. 'Why, my biscuits are lighter than dandelion fluff,' he used to say. 'Apt to float away on the first stiff breeze.' After a while his proud talk got to me, and I challenged him to a contest."

"What kind of a contest?"

"A biscuit bake-off," she said, dumping milk into the bowl. I realized with a start that I had no idea where she was getting her ingredients from. "Both of us to make biscuits, results to be judged by Reverend Zephyr of the Baptist Church."

"Did you win?"

She was busy working on her biscuits, so she didn't answer right away. She had turned the dough out onto the counter and was kneading it lightly. After a few minutes she began to pat it out to an even thickness. When it was about half an inch thick, she turned to me and said in a bitter voice, "I lost. I lost, and that was the beginning of my downfall. I became obsessed with biscuits. I swore I would make a better biscuit than Dan McCarty or die trying."

Using the top of the baking powder can, she began to cut the dough into rounds, flipping them off the counter and onto a baking sheet as she spoke.

"We began to have a weekly contest, Dan and I. Every Sunday morning we'd take our biscuits to church, and after the service Reverend Zephyr would try them out. He'd measure them. He'd weigh them. Finally he'd taste them, first plain, then with butter, then with honey. And every Sunday he'd turn to me and say, 'I'm sorry, Elvira, but Dan's biscuits are just lighter and fluffier than yours.'"

She popped the tray into the oven. "I was like a madwoman. I worked day and night, night and day, trying every combination I could think of to make my biscuits lighter, fluffier, more wonderful than any that had ever been made. I wanted biscuits that would float out of the oven and melt in your mouth. I wanted biscuits that would make a kiss seem heavy. I wanted biscuits that would make the angels weep with envy. I tried adding whipped egg whites, baking soda and vinegar, even yeast. But do too much of that and you don't really have a biscuit anymore. No, the key is in the baking powder."

Her eyes were getting wild now, and I was beginning to be frightened again. I wondered if she really was crazy—and if she was, just what a crazy ghost might do.

"One Sunday I was sure I had it; I came to church with a basket of biscuits that were like a stack of tiny featherbeds. But after the judging, Reverend Zephyr shook his head sadly and said, 'I'm sorry, Elvira, but Dan's biscuits are just lighter and fluffier than yours.'

"By the next Saturday night I was wild, desperate, half insane. In a fit of desperation, I dumped an entire can of baking powder into my dough."

"What happened?" I asked breathlessly.

"The oven door blew off and killed me on the spot. And ever since, I've been doomed to bake a batch of biscuits every Saturday at midnight, as punishment for my pride. What's worse, I finally know the secret. Learned it on the other side. These biscuits are the lightest, fluffiest ever made, Benjie. Just plain heavenly. But no one has ever tasted them, and I can't rest until someone does."

"How come no one has ever tasted them?"

"How can they? My biscuits of glory are so light and fluffy they float right out of the oven and disappear through the ceiling. If I could leave them on the counter overnight, someone might have tried them by now. But they're always gone before anyone gets a chance."

She sounded like she was going to cry. "I'm so weary of biscuits," she sighed, "so everlastingly weary of baking biscuits..."

"These biscuits of yours—they wouldn't hurt someone who ate them, would they?"

"Of course not!" she cried, and I could tell that I had offended her. "These are biscuits of glory. One bite and you'll never be the same."

"What if I grabbed one as it came out of the oven?"

"You'd burn your hand."

"Wait here!" I said.

Scooting out of the kitchen, I scurried up the stairs and rummaged through my room until I found what I was looking for—not easy when you've just moved. Finally I located it. I went down the stairs two at a time, hoping to make it to the kitchen before Elvira's biscuits came out of the oven.

She was standing by the big old oven as I slipped through the swinging door.

"What's that?" she asked as I came in.

"My catcher's mitt. Are the biscuits ready?"

"They can't wait any longer," she replied. "They're done to perfection."

As she spoke, she opened the oven door. Out floated a dozen of the most perfect biscuits I had ever seen—light, golden brown, high and fluffy, crusty around the edges. They escaped in sets of three, rising like the hot-air balloons at the state fair.

Reaching out with the mitt, I snagged a biscuit from the third set.

"Careful," said Elvira. "They're hot!"

Ignoring her warning, I took the biscuit from the glove. "Ow!" I cried as it slipped through my fingers and headed for the ceiling.

The last row of biscuits had already left the oven. I scrambled onto the counter and snagged one just as it was heading out of reach. I was more careful this time, cupping the glove over it and holding it tenderly while it cooled. I could feel the heat, but the leather protected me.

Finally I thought it was safe to try a bite. Elvira Thistledown watched with wide eyes as I took her work from my glove and lifted it to my lips.

It was astonishing, the most incredible biscuit I have ever tasted.

Suddenly I realized something even more astonishing: *I* was floating! I had lifted right off the counter and was hovering in midair. I worried about getting down, but as I chewed and swallowed, I drifted gently to the floor.

"What an amazing biscuit," I cried. "I feel like I've died and gone to heaven!"

"So do I!" said Elvira Thistledown. Only the last word was dragged out into an *eyeeeeeeee...*, as if she were being snatched into the sky.

That was the last I ever saw of Elvira Thistledown.

Her biscuits, however, haunt me still. It's not just the memory of their taste, though I have never again tasted anything so fine. It's the effect of the darned things. See, whenever I get too happy, or too excited, or begin thinking about those biscuits too much, I start to float. If I dream of them—and I often do— I may wake to find myself drifting a foot or two above the bed.

It gets a little embarrassing sometimes.

I'll tell you this, though. Unlike some people, I'm not afraid of what happens after you die.

I know what I'll find waiting on the other side....

Biscuits.

Biscuits of glory.

I, EARTHLING

It's not easy being the only kid in your class who doesn't have six arms and an extra eye in the middle of your forehead. But that's the way it's been for me since my father dragged me here to Kwarkis.

It's all supposed to be a great honor, of course. Dad is a career diplomat, and being chosen as the first ambassador to another planet was (as he has told me more times than I can count) the crowning achievement of his career.

Me, I just want to go home—though to hear Dad tell it, Kwarkis *is* home. I'm afraid he's fallen in love with the place. I guess I can't blame him for that. What with the singing purple forests, the water and air being sparkling clean (which *really* makes me feel like I'm on another planet), and those famous nights with three full moons, this truly is a beautiful place.

But it's not home. The people aren't *my* people. Most of the time I just feel lonely and stupid.

According to Dad, the first feeling is reasonable, the second silly. "You've got cause to feel lonely,

Jacob," he'll say, standing over me. "And I'm sorry for that. But you have *no* reason to feel stupid."

A fat lot he knows. He doesn't have to go to school with kids who can do things three times as fast as he can because they have three times as many hands. Even worse, they're just basically smarter than I am. *All* of them. I am the dumbest one in the class—which isn't easy to cope with, since I was always one of the smartest kids back home.

I'll never forget my first day at school here. My father led me in and stood me next to Darva Preet, the teacher. She smiled that strange Kwarkissian smile, reached down one of her six arms to take my hand, then turned to the room and cried: "Class! Class! Come to order! I want you to meet our new student—the alien you've all heard so much about!"

I began to blush. It was still hard to think of myself as an alien. But, of course, that's what I was: the only kid from Earth on a planet full of people that *I* had considered aliens until I got here. Now that I was on Kwarkis, the situation was reversed. Now *I* was the alien.

The kids all turned toward me and stared, blinking their middle eyes the way they do when they are really examining something. I stared back, which is what I had been taught to do on the trip here. After a moment one of them dug a finger into his nose, pulled out an enormous booger, then popped it into his mouth and began to chew. The sight made my stomach lurch, but I tried not to let my disgust show on my face. Fior Langis, the Kwarkissian diplomat who had been in charge of preparing me for this day, had taught me that Kwarkissians feel very differently about bodily functions than we do.

"Greetings," I said in Kwarkissian, which I had learned through sleep-tapes on my way here. "I am glad to be part of the class. I hope we will have good times together."

Everyone smiled in delight, surprised that I knew their language. Then they all farted in unison. The sound was incredible—a rumbling so massive that for a moment I thought a small bomb had gone off. I jumped, even though Fior Langis had warned me that this was the way Kwarkissians show their approval. What she *hadn't* told me about, prepared me for, was the tremendous odor.

My eyes began to water.

I had a hard time breathing.

I fell over in a dead faint.

When I woke, I was in the hospital.

Since then the kids have referred to me as *Kilugwan,* which means "The Delicate One." I find this pretty embarrassing, since I was one of the toughest kids in class back on Earth. It doesn't really make that much difference here on Kwarkis, where no one fights. But I don't plan to live here forever, and I'll need to be tough when I get home to Earth. Back there you have to be tough to survive.

The only one who doesn't call me *Kilu-gwan* is Fifka Dworkis, who is the closest thing I have to a friend here. Fifka was the first one who talked to me after my embarrassing introduction to the class.

"Do not worry about it, Jay-cobe," he said, pronouncing my Earth name as well as he could with his strange oval mouth and snakelike green tongue. "The others will not hold your oversensitive olfactory organ against you."

He put his arm around my shoulder. Then he put another arm around my ribs, and another one around my waist!

I tried not to squirm, because I knew he was just being friendly. But it sure felt *weird*.

To tell the truth, it wasn't just the weirdness that bothered me. It was also that I felt pretty inadequate having only one arm to offer back. Kwarkissian friends are always walking down the street arm in arm in arm in arm in arm in arm, and I wondered if Fifka felt cheated, only getting one arm back.

Whether or not he felt cheated, he doesn't spend a lot of time with me. He's always kind when he sees me, but he has never stayed overnight or anything like that. Sometimes I suspect that the reason Fifka is nice to me is that his mother has told him to be. She's part of the Kwarkissian diplomatic team that works with Dad.

The only *real* friend I have here is my double miniature panda, Ralph J. Bear, whom I brought with me from Earth. In case you've been living on another planet (ha-ha) the new double miniature breeds are only about six inches long. Ralph can easily fit right in my hand.

I like to watch him strolling around my desk while I do my homework. (Yes, I still have homework; I guess some things are the same no matter where you go!) And he's so neat and clean that Dad doesn't object to my letting him eat off my plate at the table. I love him so much I can hardly stand it.

The Chinese ambassador gave me Ralph at the big going-away party the United Nations threw for Dad and me. The gift was a surprise to everyone, since the Chinese are still pretty much holding on to the miniatures.

(Of course, between the fact that there are so few of them available, and the fact that they are so devastatingly cute, there is an enormous demand for them. People were wildly jealous of me for having Ralph, but I figure I ought to get *some* benefit from being a diplomat's son. I mean, none of those people who were so jealous about Ralph was being dragged off to live on another planet!)

As it turns out, Ralph is one reason that the Kwarkissians made contact with Earth in the first place. Well, not Ralph J. Bear himself. But the breeding program he came from was part of a major last-ditch effort to save the pandas. According to Dad, the Kwarkissians had been monitoring us for a long time. His contacts say that one thing that made them decide we were worth meeting was that we had started taking our biosphere seriously enough to really work at saving endangered species, such as pandas.

Anyway, Ralph is the only real friend I have here. So you can imagine how horrified I was when I was asked to give him away.

"What am I going to do, Ralph?" I said, trying not to cry.

The genetic engineers who created the miniatures have enhanced their intelligence, too. Ralph J. Bear is very bright, and he always knows when something is bothering me. Waddling across my desk, he stood on his hind legs and lifted his arms for me to pick him up.

I set him on my shoulder, and he nestled into my neck. Normally that would have made me feel a lot better. Now it had the reverse effect, because it only made me more aware of how much I would miss him if I had to give him away.

I've been avoiding talking about how I got into this mess because it is so embarrassing, but I suppose I had better explain it if any of the rest of this is going to make sense.

It started while we were having a diplomatic dinner here at the house.

According to my father, diplomatic dinners are very important. He says much of the major work in his profession happens around dinner tables, rather than at office desks.

The big thing he is working on right now is a treaty that has to do with who gets to deal with Earth. See, what most people back home don't know yet is the Kwarkissians aren't the only ones out here. But since they were the first to make contact with us, according to the rules of the OSFR (Organization of Space-Faring Races), they get to *control* contact with us for the next fifty years.

My father was not amused when he found this out. He thinks the Kwarkissians shouldn't be able to do that. He feels they're treating Earth like a colony, and that it should be *our* choice who has contact with us. But he doesn't want to make the Kwarkissians angry. For one thing, they've been very good to us. For another, we suspect they could probably turn us (by "us," I mean the entire planet) into cosmic dust without much trouble.

So the situation is very touchy.

Dad had been dealing with this other planet, called—well, I can't actually write down what it's called because no one ever says the name; it's against their religion or something. Anyway, this planet that shall remain nameless was interested in making contact with us. But to do so they had to go through the Kwarkissians.

Dad was all in favor of it; he says the more trading partners Earth has, the better. So he was throwing this dinner, where we were going to get together with a bunch of Kwarkissians, including Fifka's mom, and a bunch of dudes from the nameless planet, including their head guy, whose name is Nnnnnn.

Dad asked me to be part of the dinner group because (a) people usually want to meet your kids, no matter what planet you come from, and (b) it's good diplomacy, because it usually softens people up. I know Dad felt a little guilty about using me like that, but I told him not to, since I was glad to be of some help—especially here on Kwarkis, where I felt like such a doof.

Diplomatic dinners are always a little tricky because you want to keep from offending anyone, which is not so easy when you have people from three different cultures sitting down to eat together. This is true even on Earth, so you can imagine what it was like for us to have representatives from not three countries, but three *planets*.

"Look, this is going to be a delicate situation," said Dad. "The Kwarkissians want to have you around tonight. They were quite insistent on it, in fact; they're very fond of you, you know. But Nnnnnn and his group don't like children—partly because in their culture childhood barely exists."

"What do you mean, 'Childhood barely exists'?"

Dad frowned. "On Nnnnnn's planet, children are hatched. They come out of the egg looking much like two-year-olds do on Earth, and mature very rapidly thereafter. Even with that, they're pretty much kept out of sight by their nurses and teachers until they're ready to join adult society. On Nnnnnn's world someone who looks as old as you do might well have gained adult status, which is a thing they take very seriously. They are going to consider you not as a child, but as an equal—so for heaven's sake be careful."

He handed me a computer printout on their culture and told me to read it. "There's a lot here you should know," he said. "Study it. The main thing to remember is, whatever else you do, don't compliment them on anything they show you."

He got up to leave the room. Stopping at the door, he added, "You'd better keep Ralph locked up for the night, too."

Then he told me how he wanted me to dress and hurried off to tend to some details for the dinner.

I don't know about you, but when someone hands me something and tells me to read it, my mind immediately starts thinking of other things I need to do instead. It's not that I didn't want to learn about the new aliens; it's just that my brain rebels at being told what to do. So I put the printout aside and started to do something else.

A few minutes later my message receptor beeped. I pushed the receive button, and a holographic image of Fifka, about four inches tall, appeared in the center of my desk. Ralph skittled away in surprise—he still hadn't gotten used to the Kwarkissian version of a phone call. I pushed the send button, so that Fifka could see me as well.

We started to talk about the dinner. He was excited because his mom was coming. I almost got the feeling he was jealous of her. That surprised me. When I thought about it, I realized that I had never actually invited Fifka to come visit; I had only thought about it and waited for a good opportunity. Maybe he was more genuinely friendly than I had thought.

We got talking about something that had happened at school, and then about a game we were both working on, and by the time we were done I had pretty much forgotten about the printout Dad had given me. Next I did a little homework. Then I spent some time fooling around with Ralph J. Bear.

Before I knew it, it was time to get dressed.

That was when I noticed the printout lying on my bed.

I sighed. The thing had to be twenty pages long. No time to read that much before dinner. I would just have to be on my best behavior.

The flaw in that plan, of course, was that what

one culture considers good behavior can get you in a lot of trouble somewhere else....

The dinner party consisted of Dad, me, three Kwarkissians (including Fifka's mother), and three beings from the planet that shall remain nameless. These guys only had two arms, which was sort of a relief, but they were bright green and seven feet tall.

The first part of the dinner went pretty well, I thought, if you set aside the fact that eating dinner with a bunch of Kwarkissians is like going to a symphony in gas-minor.

I had had a long talk about this with Fifka one day.

"Biology is biology," he'd said. "What is it that you people find so bad about it, anyway? Good heavens, think what life would be like if your bodies *didn't* process all the stuff you take in, if your bodies *didn't* do their jobs! I hope this won't offend you, Jay-cube, but most of us feel that if your people paid more attention to ideas and less to biological by-products, you would all be better off. The important choices have to do with the mind and the heart, not the stomach and the intestines."

When he put it that way, it was hard to answer.

Still, it was a strange thing to sit down to dinner with some of the most important people on the planet and have them punctuate their conversation with gaseous emissions.

I had no idea how the guys from the planet whose people dare not speak its name were taking all this, since they barely talked at all. But they've been dealing with the Kwarkissians for centuries, so presumably they cope with it just fine.

The real trouble started *after* dinner, when we all went into the water room for dessert.

Every home on Kwarkis has a water room. It's one of my favorite things about living here. Basically it's a huge room with a multilevel stone floor. Clear water runs down one wall, then flows through streambeds into pools and ponds that dot the floor. There are even a few small waterfalls. Some of the ponds have fish—well, they're not really fish, but that's close enough for you to understand. Also, there are a lot of plants and a few flying things that are sort of like birds.

The Kwarkissians spend a lot of their free time in the water rooms; they're a great place to chat and relax.

Well, we went there for dessert—at least, Dad and I were having dessert (gooey chocolate pie, to be precise). The Kwarkissians were chewing purple leaves, which is what they like to do after dinner. The guys from Planet X were just sort of watching us. I got the impression they don't do much of anything for fun on their planet.

While we were sitting there, Ralph J. Bear wandered in. I flinched, remembering that Dad had told me to keep Ralph in my room that night. I glanced at Dad. He didn't seem upset, but this didn't give me any useful information; Dad's training as a diplomat makes him *very* good at masking his real feelings. Certainly his face gave me no clue as to the kind of trouble I was about to get myself into.

When our guests saw Ralph they all wanted to pick him up—which seems to be an almost universal reaction to the little guy. At Dad's suggestion, I showed him around. Everyone liked him. Even the guys from the planet with a secret name seemed to lighten up at the sight of him.

A little while later Nnnnnn tucked one long green hand under his robe and pulled out something that looked like a picture frame, the kind that you can open like a book. He opened it, looked inside, nodded, smiled in a sad kind of way, then started to pass it around. Each person who looked into it first appeared startled, and then—well, a strange look would cross his or her face. Sometimes it was happy, sometimes sad, but in all cases it was intense.

I couldn't wait for it to come to me.

I was sitting next to Fifka's mother. I had taken off my shoes, and we both had our legs dangling in the water. (Kwarkissians don't wear shoes, since the soles of their two-toed feet are like leather.)

When the thing the nameless-planet guys were passing around came to Fifka's mom, she looked into it and sighed. Then she passed it on to me.

Dad moved forward, as if to stop me from taking it, then settled back against the mossy stone on which he was sitting. He looked worried, a slight slip in his diplomatic mask. That should have been a warning to me. But I was too eager to see what was inside the frame, so I ignored the expression on his face.

Big mistake.

Taking the frame, I opened it, and cried out in shock when I saw my mother looking out at me. Mom had died six years earlier, in a small war in Asia she had been covering for the *New York Times,* and I mostly tried not to think about her, because it hurt too much. Now she was smiling at me as if she had never been gone.

I closed my eyes.

"The heartmirror sends a signal that generates an image from the brain," said Nnnnnn. "It pulls from the mind that which is deeply buried—that which you love, or fear, or wish most to see. What you see in the frame comes from yourself."

I opened my eyes again. My mother's face was still there, smiling at me. "It's wonderful," I said.

Nnnnnn's eyes narrowed in his green face. He made a sharp gesture, almost as if he were angry. "It is yours," he said gruffly.

My stomach tightened as I remembered Dad's warning: "Don't compliment them on anything they show you."

Suddenly I wished I had read that printout. What had I just done?

The room was silent, a heavy kind of silence that I found very frightening.

"Thank you," I said at last, nodding toward Nnnnnn.

More silence. Then Nnnnnn said, "Your pet is wonderful, as well."

"Thank you," I said again.

For a time the only sound in the water room was that of the water rolling down the wall, across the floor. The tension among the beings who sat around me was distinctly uncomfortable. I got the sense that they were waiting for something. I also had an idea *what,* but I tried to convince myself that I was wrong.

Finally Fifka's mother leaned over and whispered, "Nnnnnn is waiting for you to offer him your pet."

I felt as if she had hit me in the stomach.

Nnnnnn just sat there, staring at me.

Jumping up, I grabbed Ralph and ran from the room.

I was lying on my bed, holding Ralph and staring up through my ceiling—which I had set on "clear"—when my father came in. His face was dark with anger.

I ignored him and continued to stare at the moons. They were all out, one at full, one at the half, and one no more than a tiny crescent.

"Jacob, did you read that printout?" he asked.

I shook my head. A tear escaped from the corner of my eye. I was half-embarrassed at crying, half-hopeful that it might get me out of this mess.

Dad sighed.

"Why can't we just give Nnnnnn back the heart-mirror?" I asked, trying to fight down the lump in my throat.

"If we do that, it will mark us as unworthy trading partners. Jacob, we have to follow through on this. It is a matter of honor for Nnnnnn and his people."

"So you want me to give Ralph to this guy just because he thinks I'm an adult and I got caught in some weird ritual that I didn't even know was going on? Forget it!"

I had overplayed my hand.

"If you had read the information I gave you, you would have been well aware of the custom," Dad snapped back. "Even ignoring that, you knew you were supposed to keep Ralph in your room. If you had done as I asked, none of this would have happened!"

He had me. I decided the best tactic was to ignore that fact and move on.

"Well, they can just go back to the nameless place they came from," I said defiantly. "I'm not giving Ralph to Nnnnnn. For all I know the guy just wants to eat him!"

Ralph whined and snuggled closer, and I felt a

twinge of guilt. No one is sure just how much human language the little guys can understand. I hoped I hadn't scared him.

"Jacob, listen to me. Forging a good relationship with Nnnnnn and his group is—well, it could be a matter of life and death. The implications for Earth are overwhelming, and we simply can't afford a diplomatic incident right now. I'm sorry, but I have to insist…"

I knew he meant it.

I also knew that I was not going to give Ralph to some weirdo from a nameless planet.

Which meant I also knew what I *was* going to do.

I remembered what Fifka had said about the important choices, that they had to do with the mind and the heart.

My mind and my heart were both telling me the same thing right now. I didn't like what they were saying, but when I thought about it, it wasn't a choice at all. Running away was my only option.

The trees were singing their night song as I slipped into the forest. The sky was darker now because the full moon had set, leaving only the two partial moons.

A buttersnake slithered around the base of one of the trees and stared at me in astonishment. (It wasn't really a snake, of course—that's just what Dad and I call them. They're bright yellow and can spread themselves out so flat they look like melted butter.

They can go from flat to round in half a second when they are startled or angry. I tried not to make this one angry.)

Ralph J. Bear clung to my neck, looking around with bright eyes and whimpering once or twice when shadows moved too close to us.

"It's all right, Ralph," I whispered. "We'll find someplace where we can hide until this blows over. Or maybe we'll hide out forever," I added, thinking that I couldn't see any good reason to go back at this point. I was tired of being the alien, the weird one, the outcast.

I remembered Toby, and wondered if this was how he had felt.

Toby had been the dumbest kid in my class, back in the last school I had been in before Dad and I moved to Kwarkis. He was okay, but he just wasn't with it. Some of the kids were mean to him, which I thought was stupid. Most of us pretty much ignored him.

I felt bad about that now. I wanted to go back and put an arm around him, like Fifka had put three arms around me, and tell him that I liked him. Which was true, now that I thought about it. He was a nice kid and never did anything to hurt anyone. I had always figured that he didn't add anything to the class, but now that I thought about it, I realized that just his being there had been important. He was part of who we were, and we would have been different without him.

I wondered how the kids in Darva Preet's class felt about me. Did they think about me at all? Would they miss me, now that I was gone—or would they just be relieved that they didn't have a two-armed gimp around to deal with anymore? Did I make the class more or less than it had been when I came to it?

I was so wound up in my thoughts that I hardly noticed where I was going, hardly noticed Nnnnnn standing in my path until I almost bumped into him.

"Do you think this is wise?" he asked, his voice deep and solemn. He didn't sound mean, but there was something very frightening about him. I think it was simply that he was so sure of himself.

I stared at him, unable to speak.

He knelt in front of me and looked directly into my eyes.

"Are you an adult, or are you a child?" he asked.

My throat was dry, my stomach tightening into a knot of fear and despair. I remembered what my father had told me about the way Nnnnnn and his people felt about kids. Running away was one thing— without me around, Dad might have been able to skinny his way out of the mess I had created. (Though when I stopped to think about it, I realized he would have turned that forest inside out to find me, no matter what it meant to the deal.) But face-to-face defiance of the diplomat from another planet was something else altogether.

The silence lay thick between us. Nnnnnn continued to stare into my eyes. I realized that there was no way I could lie to him.

"Are you an adult, or are you a child?" he repeated.

I swallowed hard, then told him the truth.

"I'm both."

Nnnnnn nodded, which seemed to mean the same thing on his planet as on ours. "I suspected as much. Come with me."

He turned and walked away. I could have run in the other direction, but I didn't. I followed him.

We left the forest. The purple trees were singing the song they sing when the sky is clear. I cradled Ralph in my arms.

Nnnnnn led me to the bank of a stream. We sat and looked up at the stars.

I knew what he was showing me, or at least I thought I did. He was showing me the community that Earth was being invited to join—or might be invited to join, if I didn't screw things up.

Are you an adult, or are you a child?

The question burned in my ears. My father had given me the printout. He had told me to keep Ralph in my room. He had warned me not to compliment our guests on anything they showed us.

Every bit of the trouble I was in was my own fault.

"Will you take good care of Ralph?" I asked, my voice thin and whispery, like dry leaves sliding against one another.

Nnnnnn was silent for a moment. At first I thought he was trying to decide how to answer the question. Later, I realized that what he was debating was whether to answer it at all.

Finally he nodded.

"I will," he said.

Trying hard not to cry, to keep the part of me that was an adult in charge, I lifted Ralph from my neck. Pressing him to my cheek, I wiped my tears against his fur, then passed him to Nnnnnn.

I wanted to say, "You don't know what this means." I wanted to say, "I am so lonely, and he is my closest friend." I wanted to say, "I hate you."

I said nothing.

Nnnnnn took Ralph from my hands. He placed him in his lap and stroked his fur. The water rippled past Nnnnnn's green feet. The stars filled the sky, the clear sky of Kwarkis, in an abundance we never see through the soiled air of Earth.

"Over there, that way, is my home," said Nnnnnn. "It is a sacred place of great beauty. I do not like to be away from it."

I wondered why he was telling me this, then

realized that it was a kind of gift. In saying this he was speaking to me as one adult to another.

He turned to look directly at me. "We have things that will bring your world much benefit, Jacob—things of beauty, things of value. We have medical technology, for example, that will mean that many who might have died in the next year will live, instead."

I thought for a moment. "If I had known that, I would have given you Ralph without so much fuss. I would have hated you for it, but I would have given him to you."

"Of course you would have. That was not the issue. We are a trading race. It was not your compassion for your own kind that mattered to us; it was your honor. Can we trust you? That was what we needed to know."

"Can you?" I asked, my voice small. "I had to be pushed."

He stopped me. "Your impulses are good," he said softly.

We sat in silence for a moment. Finally Nnnnnn moved his green hand in a circle, indicating the stream, the forest, the city. "I know you feel like an alien here," he said softly. "But that is because you are thinking too small. Yes, you are from another world. So am I. If we think of ourselves only as citizens of those worlds, then here we are indeed the aliens. But think in larger terms, Jacob." He swept his hand in a half circle across the sky. "Look at the grandness of it. You are a part of that, as well. Your planet, my planet, Kwarkis—they are all a part of something bigger. If you think in terms of planets, then here you will always be an alien. But you and your people can be more, if you choose. You can be citizens of the universe. If you see yourself that way, you will never be an alien, no matter where you go. You will simply be—one of us."

Lifting Ralph from his lap, he handed him back to me.

I looked at him.

"It was not necessary that I *have* the animal," he said. "What was important was that you fulfill your responsibility to me. I am glad that you did. It will mean much for your world."

He put his hand on my shoulder.

Ralph snuggled into the crook of my arm and went to sleep.

The stars shimmered above us.

I stared out at them, wondering how many I would visit.

THE GIANT'S TOOTH

Edgar Twonky had no intention of getting eaten by a giant the morning he left for Cottleston Fair.

Sometimes these things just happen.

He was ambling along, humming tunelessly while he dreamed of what he might buy for Melisande with the money he hoped to make from his eggs that day, when an enormous hand swept down from the sky, scooped him up, and deposited him in a mouth the size of a cave.

The tongue on which he landed was coarse and soggy, like a bed of rain-soaked ferns. It flung him toward the back of the mouth, where a vast bulb of red flesh dangled above the gaping black hole that would, Edgar presumed, be the last thing he ever saw. With a leap, Edgar grabbed the dangling piece of flesh. It was moist and slick, and far too wide for him to put his arms around. Digging his fingers into the soft surface, he hung on for dear life.

"*Gunnarrrgh!*" said the giant, causing Edgar's fleshy perch to swing back and forth in a dizzying way.

When the giant's mouth was open, Edgar could see. When it closed, he found himself in a darkness deeper than any he had ever known.

"Gunnarrrgh!" repeated the giant.

Edgar's grip was loosening, and he was expecting to fall into the waiting hole at any second, when he heard a creaky voice call, "Over here! Hurry!"

Twisting toward the voice, he was astonished to see a flash of light—a torch!

"Hurry!" repeated the voice.

"Gunnarrrgh!" said the giant for a third time. Edgar flung himself forward, landing on the giant's tongue once more. The great pad of flesh rippled alarmingly as the giant tried to swallow him. Digging his hands into the tongue's surface, which consisted of pulpy red fibers thick as his wrists and long as his arms, Edgar clung to it like a barnacle to a ship's bottom.

"Come on, come on!" cried the voice behind the torch. "I can't hold this out here forever. It'll make him sneeze, which will almost certainly kill you!"

Reaching forward, Edgar grabbed another handful of tongue and pulled himself along the rough surface. Fighting the motion of the tongue (which was accompanied by disgusting gagging sounds from the giant), he dragged himself hand over hand toward the beckoning torch, which was yards away. He had just reached a wart, wider than a tree stump, when the giant made a last desperate attempt to swallow him.

Edgar managed to get himself on the forward side of the wart—toward the teeth and away from the throat—and braced himself against it.

"Gak gak gak!" hacked the giant.

Edgar leaped forward, landing within a foot of the torch. A withered hand reached out to him. He grabbed it thankfully and was pulled into the most astonishing room he had ever seen.

Well, it wasn't a room, exactly.

It was the inside of one of the giant's back teeth. But the flickering light of the torch showed that it had been hollowed out to make an area large enough to hold a table and two chairs. The back wall—back being the side toward the giant's throat—had a niche about six feet long and two feet wide carved into it. The ceiling was low—too low for Edgar to stand at full height—and everything was too close together, giving the room a cramped feeling. That feeling was made worse by the clutter of items that covered both floor and table: cups, plates, knives, pitchforks, shovels, coils of rope, chunks of wood, and an old wagon wheel, among other things.

"Salvage," wheezed a voice behind him.

Edgar turned and received yet another surprise. His rescuer was a woman. Half a head shorter than Edgar, she had long, stringy gray hair and eyes that burned with fever brightness. Her clothing, of which she had several layers, was an odd mix, some of it coarse homespun, some costly velvet. Nearly all of it was tattered and worn. It hung heavy on her body, as if it was slightly damp.

"By salvage," said the old woman, "I mean the stuff in the room, not you—though I suppose you might qualify as well. First time since I've been here that I've actually been able to save someone. Silly things all panic and slide down his gullet before I can do a thing to help them. That was very good, the way you managed to grab on to something. Quick thinking. I like that in a man."

"Thank you," said Edgar nervously. He looked around. "How long have you lived here?"

The woman shrugged. "Can't really say. It's hard to keep track of the time in here. There's no sunrise or sunset, no full moon or new, no summer or spring, winter or fall. I keep a calendar now—that's it, carved in the wall over there. But I don't know how long I had been here before I started it." She stroked her hair. "I do know I was young when he took me." A slightly mournful note colored her voice. "Young and pretty, some thought. And my hair was black as a raven's wing. At least, that's what all the boys said. Now come on, ducky. Sit down, sit down. I haven't had a visitor in…well, ever, actually."

"Then why two chairs?" asked Edgar.

"I live on hope," replied the woman as she thrust the torch into a bracket carved into the yellow wall.

She returned to the table and cleared it with a sweep of her arm. "Sit," she said, gesturing to the seat opposite her. "Sit."

Edgar crossed to the table—it took only two steps to reach it—and joined her. He tried to pull the chair away from the table, but found that it was solidly joined to the floor. Only then did he realize it had been carved from the tooth itself.

"It was something to do," said the woman with a shrug. She flipped her gray hair back over her shoulders and said, "My name is Meagan."

"And I'm Edgar."

"Good name," Meagan replied, nodding in approval.

Edgar smiled. "I seem to owe you my life."

Meagan arched an eyebrow. "I hadn't really thought about it that way. But now that you mention it, I suppose you do. Not that it's much of a life here in the giant's mouth."

"How do you live here, anyway?" asked Edgar, glancing around the room once more. "Where do you get your food?"

Meagan shrugged. "I scavenge."

"Scavenge what?"

"Anything that comes along that doesn't go down his gullet." She gestured toward a pickax that leaned against the enamel wall. "I've dug bits of meat out of his teeth that would feed a family of ten."

Edgar shuddered, and decided not to ask what

she did for water. He was afraid he already knew the answer. He leaped ahead to the bigger, more important question.

"Have you ever tried to get out?"

"What do I look like?" she asked bitterly. "Of course I've tried to get out. I tried every way I could think of. Finally, when it became clear I wasn't going to make it, I gave up and accepted my fate." She narrowed her eyes. "You, you come in here and find me waiting to help you—you have no idea what it was like for me when I first got here. No light, no one to explain, no one to talk to, weep with, hold. Just me, alone, in the dark, trying to find a way to survive. Just me in this hole, which back then was barely big enough to hold me, just big enough to keep from getting swallowed. I thought I would die of loneliness. I thought I would die of fear. More than once I considered just flinging myself down the big oaf's gullet. But that's not my way, Edgar. I cling to life—cling to it like a leech if I have to. So with every flash of light that came when the giant opened his mouth, I took stock of where I was. With every flash of light, I learned a little more. Many was the hour I spent huddled in this tooth, weeping to myself, wondering what was to become of me. But I didn't give up. I never gave up. I drank from pools of spit. I snatched passing food. And when I found my first tool, I began to dig, to make myself a home. Chip, chip, chip, I picked away at this tooth."

She paused, and actually chuckled. "He didn't like that, I can tell you. Oh, the roars of pain! I thought I would go deaf. And the shaking of his head. First time it nearly killed me. I would have had to give up if I hadn't managed to grab a piece of leather harness that was tied to an ox he snatched up. Used it to lash myself down. Then it didn't matter how he shook his head, I was safe."

She leaned across the table, fixing her glittering, half-mad eyes on Edgar. "Did I try to get out? Of course I tried to get out. But in the end, I made myself a home here. And I'm alive while all the others he swallowed before and after are gone. But even so, it's lonely here, Edgar. At least, it was. Now you're here, that will be different."

"But I've got to get out!" cried Edgar.

"Well, be my guest," she said, gesturing toward the hole through which she had dragged him. "The door is open. Don't let me stop you."

"You don't understand," groaned Edgar. "I'm supposed to be married next week."

"That's very unfortunate," said Meagan sharply. "But it doesn't really change things. This is your new home—or, at least it is as long as I choose to share it with you." Her eyes glittered in the torchlight, and Edgar caught just a hint of menace in her tone. "Don't forget, *I* built this place. And it's barely large enough for one. You could throw me out, I suppose, and take the place for yourself. But you don't seem the type. Besides, after all the years I've survived in here, I'm about as tough and nasty as they come. So I wouldn't advise you mess with me, Mr. Edgar. You might be surprised at what a woman can do."

Edgar, who had no intention of messing with this strange, repellent woman, put up his hands and said, "I'm not going to do anything to hurt you. I owe you my life."

"Interesting point," said Meagan.

Night inside the giant's tooth came in two stages. The first was when the giant himself lay down to rest, which changed the floor into a wall, and the rear wall into the floor. Everything not locked in place— including Edgar—tumbled to the back of the tooth when this happened.

Meagan laughed, not unkindly. "Sorry," she said. "I should have warned you."

Stage two came when Meagan decided to put out the torch, which she did only after first checking to make sure that she had her flint and steel for re-lighting it tucked securely in her pocket. Prior to this she had gathered some soggy fabric and piled it in the carved niche Edgar had noticed earlier. He under-stood now that this was her bed.

Edgar took his rest on the opposite side of a bar-rier she had erected between them, huddled on a col-lection of tattered pieces of damp cloth that she offered him—everything from a lace tablecloth to a single shirtsleeve. ("Almost managed to save that fellow," she had muttered as she handed him that particular item.)

As he lay in the dark, wrapped in misery, Edgar thought of Melisande, wondering if he would ever find his way back to her, and what she would do if he did not. He had a horrible few moments when he imagined her giving up on him and marrying Martin Plellman, but beat the idea from his mind so fiercely that it was nearly ten minutes before it came creeping back.

After several hours he finally did drift into a fitful slumber—only to be jolted back into wakefulness by a deep rumble, something like a cross between a thunderstorm and an avalanche. It eventually tapered off to a high-pitched keening—which Edgar thought for a moment must be the wail of a lost soul—and ended with three short peeps.

"What was that?" cried Edgar in horror.

"What was what?" asked Meagan groggily. It was clear from the sound of her voice that she had slept through the appalling sound.

Before Edgar could answer, it started again.

"That!" he cried, once the last of the peeps was over.

"You woke me up for that?" snarled Meagan incredulously. "It's just the giant, snoring. Forget it and go back to sleep."

The snoring started again. When it was over,

Edgar wanted to ask Meagan how long it had taken her to learn to sleep through the horrible racket. But she was already snoring herself, and he dared not wake her again.

He was still wide awake, though completely exhausted, when Meagan lit the torch again. Only a few moments later the giant groaned and lurched to his feet, causing everything that had fallen to the wall the night before to return to the floor.

"I've been thinking," said Meagan, as she kicked the loose fabrics against the wall, "and I've decided that you're going to have to build a home of your own. This place really is too small for the two of us. Odds are good I'd end up killing you."

Though she sounded genuinely regretful, she was also firm on the point.

Edgar, who was still determined to think of this as a temporary situation, felt that digging out his own home would be a waste of time and energy. On the other hand, he was not the sort to impose—certainly not the type to force himself into the abode of a woman who did not want him there.

"Where do you suggest I make this home?" he asked, trying to keep both the snarl and the whine out of his voice.

"Well, he has nearly thirty more teeth to choose from!" snapped Meagan. "However, I'd suggest you stick with the molars. They're roomier." Then, as if the idea of being pleasant was still new to her, she patted back her hair and said, "It might be nice if you built nearby. More neighborly, if you know what I mean. Best thing to do is start with a tooth that already has the beginnings of a hole. I'll help you look, if you want."

"Thank you," said Edgar. "I'd appreciate that."

And so, after a breakfast so gray that Edgar decided he didn't really want to know what it consisted of, they left Meagan's home to search for a tooth where he could live. Meagan carried the torch, and they both had picks and knives and coils of rope strapped about them. Before they left, Meagan anchored another rope to one of the chairs inside her tooth and tied it around them both.

Edgar understood why when they stepped down onto the giant's gums. A narrow trench between gum line and teeth provided a good foothold. Even so, the flesh was moist and slippery, and without the anchor rope it would have been all too easy to slide into the damp cavern of the giant's throat. The giant's tongue, pulsating beside them like a pink and fleshy whale, was a constant danger. Even worse, when they first started out they had to dodge into the gap between Meagan's tooth and the next one while the giant poked at their hiding spot with the tip of his tongue, as if he was trying to dislodge an irritating bit of food that had become stuck there.

It was a humbling thought for Edgar to realize

that "an irritating bit of food" was, in fact, precisely what he had become.

"Does he ever use toothpicks?" he asked Meagan nervously.

"Too stupid," replied the woman. "Come on, he's done now. Let's go."

The tooth directly next to Meagan's was strong and solid, with no obvious place for Edgar to begin excavating a home. The one next to that, however— the tooth farthest back in the giant's mouth—had a hole twice the size of Edgar's fist. The odor of decay hung rank about it, but Meagan said that would disappear when Edgar had cut away the rot.

It had taken a while to find the hole, since they had had to crawl all over the tooth looking for it. Unlike the opening to Meagan's home, it was on the tooth's outer side, facing the cheek rather than the tongue. They had reached that side by crawling on their bellies through the same gap between the teeth where they had taken shelter earlier.

"Nice location," said Meagan, when they found the opening. "Safer than mine, though not quite so convenient for snagging food. I suppose you might give yourself a door on the other side of the tooth as well, once you've dug through it. Need to be careful, though, not to weaken it too much."

Before Meagan would let him start to work, she bound them both to the tooth with a combination of ropes and leather straps. When she had driven Edgar nearly mad with checking and rechecking to make sure they were secure, she nodded and said, "Dig in."

Edgar swung the pick and knocked away a chunk of the yellowed enamel.

The outraged roar of pain that rose from deep within the giant nearly deafened him. At the same time, the giant slapped his hand against his cheek. The mushy cheek wall pressed Edgar and Meagan against the tooth. The torch went out with a sizzle.

"Meagan!" cried Edgar. "Are you all right?"

The question—and her answer—were lost in the giant's reverberating *"Owwwwwwieeee!"*

Despite the horrifying darkness, the awful squishiness of the cheek pressed against him, and the fact that he could scarcely breathe, Edgar almost felt sorry for the giant. Then he reminded himself that the only reason the creature was suffering this way was because it had tried to eat him.

"Now you see why I strapped us down," gasped Meagan, after the bellowing had died away. "I'm afraid you'll have to work in the dark for now. I won't be able to light the torch again out here."

Edgar located the hole by touch, then began chipping away at it. Without light the work was excruciatingly slow, since he could not take mighty swings with the pick. Instead he began tap-tap-tapping at the tooth, and in this way painstakingly enlarged the hole. This method was clearly safer, since the giant merely moaned, rather than howling in pain, and did not again slap his hand to his cheek. Edgar and Meagan did have one bad moment, when the giant began digging at the back of his mouth with his fingertip, trying to dislodge whatever was bothering him. But Meagan had tied them down with slipknots, and as soon as she saw the light at the front of the giant's mouth, she loosened the ropes so they could again take shelter in the gap between the teeth.

The giant's blunt and dirty fingertip prodded against their hiding place but was far too wide to get at them. He did try his fingernail a couple of times. It came somewhat farther into the gap between the teeth, but by cowering back they were able to avoid it. Edgar longed to attack the probing nail with his pick, but Meagan held him back.

By the time they decided to rest, Edgar had managed to enlarge the hole to the point where he could get his head and shoulders into it. His arms ached, and he longed for light. But he reminded himself that Meagan had done the same thing all on her own, with no company and no hope of light for relief, with nothing but her own will to survive driving her on.

When they had returned to the tooth where Meagan made her home and she had lit a fresh torch, Edgar found himself looking at her with new respect.

The outer coating of the tooth was hard but brittle, and broke away fairly easily. After about four feet, the material changed to something dense and yellow, and tougher to work with the pick.

It took five days—which is to say, five of the times between when they slept—to reach this inner material. Two days before that, the hole had been big enough that Edgar could crawl completely inside. Though it was big enough for him to fit in comfortably—if you consider being curled in a tight ball comfortable—Meagan did not make him move there immediately, as he had once feared she would. This pleased him, and not merely for the obvious reasons. They had grown more easy in their companionship as the work on Edgar's home had continued, and he had come to think of her not merely as someone sharing a disaster, but as a genuine, if somewhat irascible, friend.

Finally the time came when the excavation in the tooth was big enough for Edgar to take up his home in it. He moved his things—that is, the two or three items Meagan had given him, as well as a pitchfork (the single thing he had managed to snag on his own)—to his new abode.

After a day, he was surprised to find Meagan knocking at the edge of the hole he had made.

"I missed you," she growled. Then she showed him a bottle of wine she had recovered from a wagon the giant had swallowed two years earlier, which she had been saving for a special event.

Edgar invited her in and they had a small party,

sitting in the darkness and discussing what he should do next to make his tooth more homey.

The following day they ran a rope from Meagan's home through the gap between it and the next tooth, and then along the outer wall of the teeth to Edgar's door, which made it easier for them to visit each other whenever they wanted.

While he continued work on his new dwelling, Meagan taught him how to snatch things from the tide of food and rubble that poured down the giant's throat three times a day. When she "went fishing," as she called it, she first secured a safety rope about her waist, anchoring the other end of the rope to one of the chairs inside her tooth. Normally she pulled things in with the help of a long pole that had a hook on one end. But if something particularly good came rushing past that was too far out on the tongue for her to snag simply by leaning for it, she would fling her whole body onto the surface of the tongue, then use the rope to haul herself back.

Once they saw an old man go past, but he was all the way in the center of the mouth and they were not able to reach him, despite their best efforts.

His cry of despair as he disappeared down the giant's gullet echoed in Edgar's dreams for many nights afterward.

Once Edgar was truly settled, he began to explore the giant's mouth in search of a way out. Though he did not tell Meagan this was what he was doing, he suspected she was able to guess. Not that it made any difference. He could find no way of escape. His greatest hope had been to climb out of the giant's mouth while he was sleeping. But the moist walls of his lips were too slick to climb easily. Twice Edgar tried using the pickax to help him make the climb, but both times this caused the giant to rub his mouth, with results that were nearly fatal. (The second time, he barely made it back to Meagan's tooth, where she set his broken bones but gave him no sympathy for the pain that kept him awake for seven nights running.)

It was like being at the bottom of a well: easy enough to fall in, impossible to climb out.

Despite his misadventures at the front of the giant's mouth, Edgar continued his explorations, until he had at last reached the most distant of the giant's molars. He carried a torch with him, which he lit and waved to Meagan when he reached the far side.

When he returned from that trip, he was burning with a new idea. "If we string a rope directly across the center of his mouth, we might have better luck snagging things as they go by," he said.

"The giant would rip it out," replied Meagan.

"Well, what if we didn't make it permanent? We could put in a couple of hooks or pegs or something, one on each side of his mouth, and run the rope between them when we wanted to use it."

"Might work," said Meagan dubiously. "We'd have to put the pegs in the upper teeth, though; if we try it with the lower ones he's sure to snap it with his tongue right away."

The next day Edgar again made his way to the far side of the giant's mouth. As he traveled, he tucked a rope into the narrow trench that ran along the edge of the teeth.

He made the trip without incident, except for one frightening moment when he was at the front of the mouth and the giant happened to make a clucking sound. The violent forward movement of his whalelike tongue had almost flattened Edgar.

After some searching, Edgar found an upper tooth with a small hole, into which he pounded a peg. Then he waved his torch to Meagan to let her know he was going to take up the slack on the rope.

Once they had the rope tight, he swung himself onto it. Then, moving hand over hand, he inched his way toward the center of the giant's mouth.

His ambition was rewarded when the giant tossed a cart full of melons into his mouth. Though it went directly down the center, Edgar was able to retrieve not only a pair of the melons but one of the wagon wheels, which he thought would look nice in his new home.

When he returned to the other side, Meagan grudgingly admitted that the rope had been a good idea. Just how good an idea became clear as the weeks rolled on and they were able to retrieve more and more items.

The most unexpected of these items was a young man named Charles, whom Edgar snatched from certain doom by hanging upside down from the rope and reaching out to him.

When he escorted Charles home with him, Meagan muttered about things getting too crowded in the giant's mouth. But when Edgar said that Charles could live with him until they were able to excavate another tooth, she settled down.

Charles turned out to be clever with his hands, and it was not long before they were hard at work making a home for him in the tooth between the two they had already hollowed out.

Many hands making lighter work, the home took less time to complete than Edgar's had, and soon they were turning their energies to new and better ways to salvage things.

During Edgar's second year in the giant's mouth, they rescued Farley. His arrival upset Meagan even more than Charles's had, and she began muttering that she didn't like having so many men around. On the other hand, she seemed to find Farley attractive, and once it became clear that he returned the compliment, she stopped fussing. They hollowed a home for him in the tooth above hers—the first in an upper tooth—and soon the two of them were visiting each other several times a day to consult on various ideas and projects.

Their masterpiece was a system of buckets for collecting fresh water whenever the giant took a drink. This freed them from reliance on the giant's saliva, which was a great relief to everyone. Even better was when they could save some of the occasional flood of beer. Such a catch was always a signal for a party—which helped make up for the dangerous (not to mention putrid) belches that the giant inevitably unleashed an hour or so later.

Next to be pulled to safety, about six months later, were a pair of sisters, named Babette and Cleo, and their dim-witted brother, Herbert. The time had come to begin building homes in the teeth on the other side of the mouth. Babette and Cleo chose to live together. Herbert took the tooth above them.

Once their homes were complete, Edgar began thinking about doing some bridgework.

Before too many more years had passed, a thriving community had risen in the giant's mouth. The people got on well enough, though there were occasional conflicts—as there always will be when you have people locked together in a crowded space.

To the surprise of no one save Edgar, he turned out to be the one who usually solved these conflicts, and eventually he was elected mayor of Giant's Mouth

Township. They gave him a jeweled scepter, which they had managed to retrieve one afternoon when the giant swallowed a king. (They had tried to save the king, too, of course, but his grip was weak and flabby, and he had not been able to hold on when Herbert reached out to him.) Many was the night Edgar sat in his tooth and looked out the window he had carved on the tongueward side, feeling warm and cozy at the sight of the lights twinkling on the other side of the giant's mouth.

In this way, the years rolled on.

And then, one afternoon while he was setting a rope, Edgar was suddenly yanked from the giant's mouth.

It happened because the giant, who was in a foul mood that day, became particularly irritated by the feeling of things moving in his mouth. Edgar was stringing a rope across the roof of the giant's mouth in order to do some salvage work when the giant reached in and began to scratch at the roof of his mouth. Though the rope was less to him than a silk thread would be to a human, it caught on his fingernail. When he pulled his hand out, one end of the rope came free—and with it, still clinging to the end, came Edgar.

As he hurtled out of the giant's mouth, two things caused Edgar to blink. The first was the unexpected brightness of the sun, which he had not seen except at a distance for so many years. The second was the horrifying distance that separated him from the ground.

Knowing he could not keep his grip on the saliva-slick rope, Edgar made a desperate leap and landed on the giant's collar. The giant swatted at him, as one would at an annoying insect, but Edgar quickly scrambled under the giant's collar, where he held as still as he could, scarcely breathing.

All through the long hot day he stayed there, peering sideways at the world below, longing for it, thinking of how he had missed it.

Finally night darkened the sky, bringing with it the stars that he had not seen in so many years. Their beauty made him weep.

The giant lay down, and after a time began to snore.

Edgar climbed out onto his chest. He stood, staring out at the rising moon, the river on whose water it was reflected, the dark ridge of the distant mountains, and the road that led back to his village, back to Melisande.

He wondered if she had waited for him, or if she had married Martin Plellman after all.

The giant's clothing was so coarsely woven that the threads were almost like the rungs of a ladder. Now that the giant was lying down, it was only a few hundred feet to the ground.

Edgar took a deep breath of the clean, clear air, and released it with a sigh.

Then he began to climb the giant's shirt—not down, but up—onto the giant's chin, where the stubble grew so thick it was like a grove of small pine trees. Across the loose and pendulous lip Edgar climbed.

Then he lowered himself back into the moist cavern of the giant's mouth, where his home and friends lay waiting.

THERE'S NOTHING UNDER THE BED

I suppose I can't really blame my parents for not believing me when I told them about the weirdness under my bed. After all, adults never believe a kid when he or she talks about that kind of thing. Oh, they'll believe you're *afraid*, of course. But they never believe you've actually got a good reason to feel that way. They'll certainly never believe you if you tell them something horrible is lurking under the bed, waiting to take you away.

But you and I know they should. You and I know that there *are* terrible things that hide there, waiting to catch you, snatch you, steal you.

At least, I know. Because now I'm one of them.

I'm not sure when I first realized there was something wrong under my bed. I must have been fairly young, because I can remember that one night, when I was about five or six, I rolled a ball under the bed by accident. I heard a popping sound and started to cry because I knew I would never get my ball back from the weird gray nothingness down there.

So clearly I knew about the nothingness by then, and understood that things disappeared into it. But at the time I was upset simply because I had lost my ball. Like a kid who needs glasses but doesn't know it, and just assumes things look fuzzy to everyone else, too, I figured that was just the way the world was.

Besides, everyone loses things in their bedroom—socks, pencils, yo-yos, homework you're certain you did. It wasn't until I began staying overnight at friends' houses and saw the incredible messes under their beds—messes that *didn't disappear*—that I realized something was truly wrong at my house.

My second clue came when I tried to tell my parents about this and they thought I was playing a silly game. "For heaven's sake, David," said my mother. "Don't be ridiculous!"

I remember these words well because I heard them so many times in the months that followed. The few times I actually did manage to drag Mom and Dad up to look under my bed, the weird gray nothingness wasn't there, and all they saw was solid floor. That happened sometimes. Finally I realized that the nothingness disappeared whenever grown-ups were around.

As you can imagine, this was very frustrating.

After a while Mom and Dad decided to get me some "special help"—which is to say they sent me to a shrink. Unfortunately the nothingness under my bed wasn't something that could be fixed by a shrink. All I learned from the experience was that I had better keep my mouth shut if I didn't want to get sent away for even more intense treatment.

Personally, I thought Mom should have figured out that a kid as sloppy as I was could never naturally have a bed that didn't even have dust bunnies under it! But Weztix has taught me that people will believe really stupid things in order to avoid having to believe something else that they think is just plain impossible. I guess Mom just assumed that my losing so much stuff simply indicated I was even lazier, sloppier, or more addle-brained than most kids.

Maybe I was. That didn't mean that the area under my bed wasn't weird and scary.

Even so, I managed to live with it—until the day it swallowed Fluffy.

Yeah, I know: Fluffy is a disgustingly cute name for a cat. But when we got Fluffy she was a disgustingly cute kitten. And according to my parents I was a disgustingly cute toddler. So when I wanted to call the kitten Fluffy, they were happy to oblige.

As you get older, you discover certain things you wish your parents had done differently, maybe even been a little stricter about. Letting me name our cat Fluffy was one of them. By fifth grade I had earned at least two black eyes from fights that started with people teasing me about my "sissy" cat.

Not that Fluffy cared what anyone called her, as long as we fed her on time. She was pretty aloof. But she was mine, and I loved her.

Fortunately Fluffy seemed to have figured out on her own that she should avoid the area under my bed. Maybe it was some instinctive awareness of danger. Whatever the reason, I never had to worry about losing her there. She just naturally avoided the area.

If it hadn't been for my rotten cousin Harold, I doubt she would ever have gone under there.

When I was little and got upset, my mother used to say, "Well, David, into every life a little rain must fall."

If that's true, then Harold was my own personal thunderstorm. Two years older than me and about forty pounds of solid muscle heavier, Harold projected all the friendly charm of a porcupine having a bad hair day.

Even so, his mother adored him—a fact probably worth a scientific study all by itself.

Harold and his mother came to visit more often than I would have liked. Well, once in a hundred years was really more often than I would have liked, but Harold and Aunt Marguerite actually showed up almost once a month—including the day that I was stolen.

I had already had a rough week, and when I found out that they were coming that afternoon I threw myself to the floor and screamed, "Just kill me now and get it over with!"

"That's not funny, David," said my mother.

"I'm not trying to be funny," I replied.

They came anyway.

As usual, Aunt Marguerite had "private things" to discuss with my mother—meaning that she was having trouble with her latest boyfriend and wanted Mom's advice. In my opinion, Aunt Marguerite's endless string of boyfriends was one source of Harold's problems. But no one asked me. Anyway, the fact that she wanted to talk to Mom meant that I got to entertain Harold.

It was a wretched, rainy day, so the two of us had to play up in my room. After a while Harold grabbed Fluffy and said, "How about a game of Kitty Elephant?"

Kitty Elephant is something Harold invented, and it will tell you a lot about him. Basically it consists of putting a sock over a cat's face so that the cat looks like it has a long trunk, then laughing hysterically while you watch the cat try to get out of the sock.

I had learned to stay out of the way when Harold was doing something rotten, but when I saw Fluffy getting too close to the bed I tried to grab her. Harold grabbed me first. Twisting my arm behind my back, he hissed, "Don't interfere with the game, Beanbrain."

"Harold, you don't understand!"

"I understand that you're a wuss," he said. "I'm embarrassed to have you for a cousin."

I thought about telling him that I was *disgusted* to have him as a cousin but decided against it, since he had already twisted my arm so far behind my back it felt like it was coming out of the socket.

Fluffy got closer to the edge of the bed.

"Let me *go*!" I screamed.

To my surprise, Harold did let go—mostly, I think, to keep our mothers from coming up to see what was going on. It was too late. In her efforts to get the sock off her head, Fluffy had rolled under the bed.

A bolt of lightning sizzled through the rainy sky.

For an instant I had dared to hope that this was one of the times when the floor was in its solid state. The lightning told me that it was not. And when I heard a *pop* like someone pulling his finger out of a bottle, I knew Fluffy was gone.

The popping sound drew Harold to the edge of the bed. "Come on out, Fluffy," he said, reaching under to grab her.

When he couldn't find her, he bent and lifted the edge of the bedspread. Then he scrambled over the bed and looked down the other side.

"What happened?" he asked nervously. "Where did she go?"

"Why don't you crawl under there and find

out?" I said bitterly, feeling so wretched I thought I might throw up.

Having Harold as a witness did not, of course, mean that our mothers were going to believe us. Nor did it help that when we finally did convince Mom and Aunt Marguerite to come upstairs we found Fluffy sitting on my bed, licking her paws. Glad as I was to see her, the sight gave me a shiver. Nothing had ever come back from underneath my bed before.

Nothing.

"Harold, you know that David has been playing this foolish game for years," said Aunt Marguerite sharply. "I don't want you to encourage it. His poor mother has enough trouble with him as it is."

"Just look under the bed," insisted Harold. "Look at the floor!"

I could have told him what would happen. In fact now that I think of it, I *had* told him—several times—when we were younger. He just never believed me. So he was actually surprised that when he finally convinced Aunt Marguerite to get down on her knees and raise the edge of the bedspread all she saw was bare floor.

Harold and my aunt didn't stay much longer. After they left, Mom yelled at me for "dragging up that stupid fantasy again."

And that was the end of things—until later that night, when Fluffy began talking to me.

She had come and curled up on my pillow when I climbed into bed, the way she often did. This had made me a little nervous. But she had seemed perfectly normal since her reappearance, so I had let her stay.

It was storming again when the big clock downstairs struck midnight. As the last chime faded, Fluffy opened her eyes.

They were red.

Now, sometimes a cat's eyes will catch the light just the right way to reflect off the back of them or something, and they look red. I've seen that. I know what it looks like.

This was different. Fluffy's eyes were fire red, blazing with their own light. Before I could move she nuzzled her face close to my ear and whispered, "Weztix wants you, David. He wants you to come to the other side."

I screamed and yanked up the covers, sending Fluffy flying off the bed.

"What's going on up there?" shouted my father.

"It's Fluffy!" I cried. "She's…she's…"

My voice trailed off as I realized that Dad would never believe me.

"She's *what?*" he yelled.

"Nothing!" I shouted. "Never mind. Forget it."

Why did I give up so easily? Because I had been through this a hundred times before. Because I had barely avoided being sent to a mental institution after

I had insisted on clinging to the "delusion" that there was something strange under my bed. And most of all because I didn't know that being sent to an institution would have been infinitely preferable to what lay in store for me.

Fluffy clawed her way back onto the bed. Her eyes blazed in the darkness.

"Go away!" I hissed. "Get out of here!"

Instead of leaving, she slunk onto my chest. "Go under the bed, David," she hissed. "Weztix wants you under the bed."

I jumped to my feet, scooped up Fluffy, and threw her out the door. Then I took a flying leap back onto my bed, avoiding at least six feet of the floor. I lay there shaking with terror, wishing I could sleep downstairs for the night. But my parents had put a stop to that one angry night years before.

After I caught my breath, I hung my head over the bed and lifted the edge of the sheet, hoping not to find anything too strange. And what I saw wasn't that strange, really. Just that familiar shimmering grayness. But it scared me then in a way it never had before.

I rolled back onto the bed and stared up into the darkness, wondering if I would make it until morning.

Suddenly I felt something pounce onto the bed. I cut short my scream when I realized it was Fluffy again.

I glanced sideways. The door was still closed.

"How did you get in here?" I whispered.

I know people talk to their pets all the time, but I realized with a kind of terrible fascination that I expected her to answer me.

"The same way I got back from the other side," she purred. "Once you've been there, doors don't mean that much. But you'd better go soon, David. They're waiting for you."

"Who?" I asked desperately. "What do they want?"

Instead of answering, Fluffy jumped to the floor and scooted under the bed. I rolled over and stuck my head down again. Heart pounding, I lifted the bedspread. My cat was gone. But the shimmering gray nothingness that had replaced my floor now had a small blue circle in the middle of it.

From the circle came a new voice. "We're waiting for you, David. Come to us. *Come to us!*"

I rolled back onto the bed, pulled the covers over my head, and tucked the sheets tightly around me, trying to convince myself I would be safe if I just stayed wrapped up that way. I have no idea why I thought that; desperation, probably. Who knows? Maybe it would even have worked if I hadn't fallen asleep.

I tried hard not to sleep. But when everything is dark and silent, and sleep starts tugging at the edges of your mind, even terror can keep you awake only so long. I might have been able to stay awake if I could have gotten off the bed to move around. But I didn't dare do that. I could only lie there, wrapped in the sheets, still and silent, hoping I would survive until morning. I fought sleep, fought it hard. But finally it claimed me.

Even then, things might have been all right if only I hadn't been such a restless sleeper. But I was, a real tosser and turner, and it probably wasn't long after I fell asleep that I flopped out of my protective cocoon. It probably wasn't much longer before my arm was dangling over the edge of the bed, my fingertips brushing the floor.

I was woken by another hand, cold and damp, grabbing mine.

"Who's there?" I cried, trying to push myself up from the bed.

The cold hand linked with mine gripped me tighter, holding me in place. I screamed, loudly, not caring what my parents thought this time, not caring if I got sent away for special treatment, as long as it got me out of this room, away from this house.

I heard my parents pounding up the stairs, my father cursing as he ran. I continued to scream as loudly as I could. "Let go!" I shrieked. "*Let go!*"

The hand began pulling harder.

"David, what's going on in there?" cried Dad. He tried to open the door—I could hear him rattling the knob—but it wouldn't budge, despite the fact that it had no lock. "David? *David!*"

"It's got me!" I screamed. "It won't let go!"

"What has you?" cried my mother. "David, what is it? What's wrong? Harvey, can't you get that door down?"

The door shuddered as my father threw himself against it, but it held solid.

Another hand grabbed my wrist, adding its strength to the first. Thrashing, twisting, fighting every inch of the way, I was drawn over the edge of the bed. I hit the floor with a thump. The hands continued to pull. Soon my arm was under the bed up to my elbow. With nothing on the floor to hold on to, nothing to give me traction, the rest of my body would soon follow.

"No!" I screamed, pushing my free hand against the side of the bed. "No! No! Let me go!"

I heard my father throw himself against the door again.

The cold hands kept pulling and pulling. I swung myself around, jamming my shoulder against the side of the bed, deciding I would rather let them pull my arm out of its socket than let them pull me under the bed.

A third time my father slammed against the door. It splintered and burst open. Too late. My bed slid across the floor to reveal the swirling gray nothingness that lay waiting beneath it. A horrible crackling filled the air as the nothingness sucked me in.

Somewhere above me, I heard my parents shouting my name.

"Now do you believe me?" I cried.

I was sinking into something like a thick, foul-smelling pudding. It was colder than anything I had ever experienced—a cold that worked its way into the deepest parts of me, penetrating to the center of my bones.

Then, suddenly, I was through the coldness and falling into dark.

The fall lasted only an instant. I landed with a dull thump against something that felt like a mattress but turned out to be a huge fungus. Above me swirled a cool gray circle with a spot of blue in the center—the place through which I had fallen.

I could still hear my parents shouting my name.

Four torches, mounted on poles, formed a square around me. I heard an evil chuckle to my right. I turned toward it, and the flickering light provided my first sight of the creature who had dragged me here. He was foul looking, with long hair that hung around his shoulders in greasy strings. When he beckoned to me, I saw that he had long yellowed fingernails; when he smiled, he showed sharp, rotting teeth. His eyes glittered with malice from their deep sockets. Yet for all that, I could tell that he had once been human, which may have been the scariest thing of all.

That, and the fact that he looked oddly familiar. With a shudder, I realized I had seen him in my dreams—or, to be more accurate, in my nightmares.

"Got you at lasssst," he said in a hissing voice that was filled with deep satisfaction. "Got you at lasssst."

My terror was so deep that at first I was unable to speak. When I finally realized that he wasn't going to kill me on the spot, I asked in a trembling voice, "Who are you?"

"You mean you don't know?" he replied, sounding genuinely astonished.

I shook my head.

He laughed. "Weztix will tell you," he said, making an odd little leap. "Weztix will tell you!"

He reached for my hand. When I drew back, his eyes blazed. "Stand up!" he snapped. "We're going to ssssee Weztix."

"I want to go home," I whimpered.

"Don't be sssstupid! Now come along. I don't want to have to hurt you."

He said this last with such feeling that I actually believed him—though if I had understood just *why* he didn't want to hurt me, I might have been even more terrified than I already was.

It was a terrible journey. The place into which I had fallen was a sort of living nightmare, darkened by strange shadows that stretched and twisted around us, though I could see no source of light, nor anything to block it and cause the shadows. It was as if the darkness had a life and a mind of its own.

I could hear unpleasant noises in the distance: desperate, cackling laughter; sighs so deep they could have been made by a mountain; an odd rumbling; an occasional scream. The dank air smelled so weird I was almost afraid to breathe it.

Eyes peered out at us from the darkness. I was terrified that they might belong to some new creature that would reach out to snatch me away. (Though what could be worse than the situation I was in already is hard to imagine.) Later, unseen hands *did* pluck at me, but my captor shouted and drove them away. In several places spiderwebs stretched across our path, and since I was forced to walk in the lead, they continually wrapped themselves across my face. I shuddered each time they did. Other things, less familiar, seemed to brush over my face as well, which was even more frightening.

"Are we in hell?" I asked at one point.

The creature behind me hissed and said, "Don't be ssssilly."

We entered a cave and began to follow a series of tunnels through other caves, some small, some enormous. The tunnels were pitch-black in places, lit by torches in others. At one point we walked along a narrow path that had a rock wall on one side, an immeasurable drop on the other. Though I'm used to that path now, I was terrified at the time.

Sharp stones cut my bare feet, and they began to bleed.

Eventually I spotted a red glow ahead of us. As we drew closer, I saw that the glow came from a large cave. We walked toward it, splashing through a wide patch of muddy water where slimy things slithered over my feet. When something began nibbling on my bloody toes I cried out in fear, but my captor just pushed me forward.

We stopped at the mouth of an enormous cavern. A stone path, about three feet wide and lined with torches, led across a stretch of black water to a tall rocky island that looked like a giant skull rising from the water.

Carved into the island's side, curving up the jaw and around the back of the head, was a slender stairway.

On top of the skull stood Weztix.

Fluffy was sitting on his shoulder.

Weztix was far taller than a man, and unbelievably beautiful, like some statue of a Greek god come to life. Light seemed to pour from his face when he looked down at me.

"Welcome, David," he said in a voice that was as

beautiful as he was. "Welcome. We have been waiting for you for such a long time."

Though I had felt a surge of relief at seeing this beautiful creature, his words made me nervous again.

"Waiting for me?" I asked.

He chuckled. "Surely you knew *something* was waiting for you under your bed."

"I just know it scared me," I replied.

He smiled, which made his face even more beautiful. "Good. That's what this place is all about."

"What *is* this place?" I asked.

"The land of nightmares, of course," he said, spreading his arms in welcome. "And I am the Lord of Nightmares. My name is Weztix, and I am the source of all your worst dreams."

My blood felt cold in my veins. "Why...why have you brought me here?"

"Because we need you," he said. "And because we could."

"I don't understand."

He spread his arms, then rose into the air and began to float in my direction. I cringed as he came down, fearing that he would land on top of me and crush me. But he touched down about three feet away.

My head came up to about his kneecap.

Looking down at me, Weztix said, "There aren't many places where the border between nightmare and reality is frail enough for someone to pass through it to our side. *We* can go through, of course; we have to, in order to do our job."

As he spoke, I began to have flashbacks of old nightmares, terrifying dreams that had vanished from my conscious memory but turned out to have been lurking at the back of my mind, waiting to spring out again. Nightmares, I now understand, that had been meant to prepare me for this moment.

"The thing is," continued Weztix, "bringing new people to *this* side is a bit of a problem. Sometimes I actually run short on help. After all, the way the world is these days there are often more nightmares than I can deliver! Anyway, we've known for some time that there was a weakness under your bed—which meant that you were a candidate for a job here."

More old nightmare images came surging to the surface. I felt hot tears running down my face.

"Why?" I asked. "Is this punishment for something bad I did?"

Weztix threw back his head and laughed. "Don't give yourself airs, David! It is completely and utterly random. There's not a thing you could have done to make it happen, not a thing you could have done to avoid it. It has nothing to do with you as a person. You just happened to have the wrong bedroom."

He smiled again. "I think it's scarier that way, don't you?"

I nodded solemnly.

"Anyway, weak as the boundary was beneath your bed, we still couldn't bring you through until some other living thing from your side had made the final break. When your cat came through the floor today, Timothy knew that his long wait had been rewarded."

"Timothy?"

Weztix nodded toward the evil-looking creature who had pulled me into the nightmare world. With a sick feeling, I realized that my captor was—or at least had been—a kid.

"Timothy is one of my delivery boys," said Weztix. "Same as you will be. After all, *someone* has to pass out the nightmares."

"I don't want to!" I cried.

Weztix shook his head. "Look at it this way, David. Most people your age don't have any idea what they want to be when they grow up. They muddle their way through school then thrash around, trying this, trying that, wondering what to do with themselves. You don't have to worry about any of that. Your life's work has been chosen for you!"

He began to laugh again. This time the sound was not so beautiful. Pushing my hands against my ears, I threw myself to the ground and began to sob.

It did no good. Nothing did any good. I was a prisoner in the land of nightmares.

————

I don't know how much longer it was before my training began. Back then I found it hard to measure time in this place where reality shifts so easily that not only can one day slide into the next, but one place can slide into another as well. Here in the land of nightmares, boundaries merge and break the way they do in dreams. You might walk into a small house and go through dozens or hundreds of rooms before you find your way out. Or you might walk through a door and find yourself in a forest—or sit down under a tree and find yourself having dinner with an army of the dead.

After a while you begin to learn to look past those things. You can move fast down here once you know the shortcuts. And you do have to move fast to do your job.

I hate my job. It works like this: Weztix calls me and I go to sit with him inside the stone skull, in a dark chamber that smells of loss and suffering, and sometimes of death. He closes one huge hand over my head and fills my brain with images.

Sometimes when he takes his hand away I realize that I've been screaming. So I won't talk about those images right now. But maybe you've seen them anyway; maybe you've *dreamed* them. Because what I do when Weztix is finished with me is carry the things he's poured in my head back to the real world.

Which is to say, I climb the ladders of nightmare and come up underneath your bed. Now that I'm one of Weztix's messengers, I can cross the barrier easily. And once I've risen up beneath your bed, I lie there in the darkness beneath you and whisper to you while you sleep, spinning back the images that Weztix has planted in my brain.

Why don't I try to run away one of those nights?

If I told you, you might never sleep again.

And I need you to sleep.

After all, if you don't sleep, how can I do my job?

The only good thing about all this is the nightmares I got to take to Harold. Hch. The truth is, I took him a lot that weren't meant for him, which is sort of against the rules. But I don't do it anymore. I pretty much stopped after they took him away for special treatment.

I used to be a good boy. I want to be good again, but I don't know if that's possible anymore. Because the only way out is for me to do what Timothy did, what all the others do eventually, and find someone to take my place.

Of course, Timothy didn't get to leave right away. As Weztix said, there's a labor shortage down here. But his reward for recruiting me was to be allowed to go back to the land of the living about ten years after I got here.

That's what I'd like to do someday. After all, I've been down here delivering nightmares for nearly thirty years now. The thing is, being a messenger of darkness and fear is the kind of work that twists a guy.

I'm not the person I used to be.

Even so, I dream of going back to the other side to stay.

It won't be long now. I've found a weakness in the boundary between the worlds. It's not as good as the one under my bed was, at least not yet. But it will be when I'm done with it. A place where some-one real, someone living, could pass through into this world.

It's under a bed, of course.

Maybe yours.

The thing is, I'll feel funny about pulling another kid down here to take my place. After all, he or she won't be any happier doing this than I am.

That's why I sent this dream to the person who's writing this story. I figure if I send a warning, if I give kids a fighting chance to save themselves, I won't have to feel so bad when I finally do bring one of them down here.

Well, there it is. Now you know what might be waiting under your bed. You know what can happen if you don't get out.

Whether you do anything about it or not—well, that's up to you. But I've done my time. Sooner or later someone is going to take my place down here. Sooner or later someone—maybe you—is going to have my job.

Sleep well, friend.

I'll see you in your dreams.

THE STINKY PRINCESS

O nce there was a princess named Violet who didn't smell very good.

This was an unnatural condition for a princess, of course, and it did not reflect well on her parents. On the other hand, it had nothing to do with either her birth or her upbringing. In fact, she had started out smelling just fine. When she was born, she had smelled as a rosebud does when it is just beginning to open on a misty morning in early June. When she was a little girl, she had smelled of mischief and mud pies (it was a small kingdom, and she had an understanding nurse), as well as cinnamon, apples, and sunny afternoons. And when she was just becoming a young lady, she smelled of clear mountain streams a moment before the rain comes, of lilacs, and of a small red blossom called dear-to-my-heart that grew on the castle grounds and nowhere else.

So, all in all, she smelled just as a princess should, and her parents were pretty well satisfied. More satisfied than the princess herself, certainly. Violet found her own smell boring, and often declared that there must be many far more interesting scents in the world, a statement that always gave her mother a bad case of the quivering vapors.

It did not improve matters any when Bindlepod the goblin came to visit.

If it had been up to him, the king never would have allowed the goblin into the court to begin with. Alas for him, Bindlepod was not merely a goblin, but an ambassador from Goblinland, with which the kingdom had recently been at war. So the king was obliged not merely to let him in, but to offer him hospitality.

Bindlepod's skin was the color of rotting toadstools. His bare feet slapped on the stone floors of the castle like dirty dishrags. The pupils of his oversize yellow eyes did not stay still, but instead swam about like tadpoles—which made it very distracting to try to hold a conversation with him.

But the most distressing thing about him was his smell. While nobody could say exactly *what* it was Bindlepod smelled of, everybody agreed that it was distinctly unpleasant, and somehow made them think of dark and distant places.

Everybody, that is, except the princess.

She thought Bindlepod smelled quite interesting.

"You must be joking, darling," said the queen, speaking through the handkerchief she was holding over her mouth and nose.

"Of course I'm not joking," said Violet.

"But he's...he's *revolting*," sputtered the king.

"I don't think so," said the princess calmly.

"I can't stand this!" cried the queen, and she fled the room, shedding copious tears as she went.

"There," said the king. "Now see what you've done?"

"What?" asked Violet, who was totally baffled. "What have I done?"

"As if you didn't know," sniffed her father bitterly.

Later that day, the princess was walking in the castle garden when she spotted Bindlepod's frog, which was nearly as tall as she was. It was wearing its saddle, as if Bindlepod had just returned from a ride, or was about to leave on one.

A little farther on she spotted the goblin himself. He was perched on the stone wall, gnawing a raw fish.

Violet walked over and looked at him for a few moments. He nodded at her but said nothing, preferring to give his attention to the fish.

"My parents don't like you," she said, partly because she was annoyed, but mostly to see how he would respond.

The goblin took another bite of the fish, smacking his lips as he did. Then he said, "I'm not surprised. Are you?"

"I think they're pains," said the princess, surprising herself with her bitterness.

"That doesn't surprise me, either," said Bindlepod. He cleaned the last of the flesh from the fish's spine, sucked out its eyes, then tossed the skeleton over his shoulder. It landed in the moat with a tiny splash.

"My parents are not merely pains," said the princess, warming to her topic. "They're royal pains."

"That's appropriate," said the goblin, who privately thought of Violet as sweet, but dangerous.

Violet climbed onto the wall and took a seat next to Bindlepod. "What's it like in Goblinland?" she asked.

Bindlepod shrugged. "Nice enough, if you're a goblin. It's a bit darker than here, but that's mostly because it's underground. It's damp, too. We call it Nilbog, by the way, not Goblinland. That's rude. It would be like calling your kingdom Peopleland."

"Is Nilbog smelly?"

Bindlepod closed his eyes and seemed to be remembering something. "Yes," he said at last, with just a hint of a smile. "Very."

"Let's go there," said the princess.

"You," said the goblin, "are walking trouble, a danger zone with feet."

"Does that mean no?" asked Violet.

"It means never in a million years!"

Then he hopped down from the wall, whistled for his frog, and rode away.

———

Every day for the next two years Violet asked Bindle-pod to take her to Nilbog, and every day the goblin told her no. This was not because he did not like her. Actually, he had come to find the princess fairly interesting. He had even begun to like her odor, which was not nearly as boring as that of her parents. But much as Bindlepod liked the princess, he liked his own skin even better. More specifically, he liked his skin exactly where it was and preferred to keep it there rather than have it peeled from his bones while he was still living—an event he was fairly sure would occur were he to run off with the king's daughter.

At the end of the second year, it was time for Bindlepod to return to his own land. As he saddled his frog to leave, the princess once again asked if he would take her along.

"Not for all the jewels in your father's treasury," said the goblin. "Nor all the fish in his moat," he added, hoping to make the point more clearly.

Princess Violet wrinkled her nose at him. "You're not very nice!"

"I never claimed to be," replied the goblin. "And you're something of a stinker yourself, when it comes right down to it."

Then he went to say good-bye to her parents.

Late in the first morning of the trip back to Nilbog, Bindlepod's frog stopped in the middle of the road and said, "I am not taking another hop until you get that princess out of the saddlebag."

"What are you talking about?" cried Bindlepod in alarm.

"The princess," said the frog patiently. "She's in the saddlebag, and I'm getting tired of carrying her."

"Why didn't you say something before now?" asked Bindlepod, torn between exasperation and despair.

"She bribed me," said the frog. "With june bugs. You know I can't resist june bugs."

Bindlepod groaned and climbed down from his steed's spotted green back. Poking the saddlebag, he said, "Princess, are you in there?"

No one answered.

Even so, the shape of the saddlebag was distinctly suspicious. So Bindlepod unstrapped it from the frog, loosened the top, and turned it over.

Out tumbled the princess.

Bindlepod sighed. "What are you doing here?"

"Going to Nilbog," said Princess Violet, picking herself up from the road and brushing the dust from her backside.

"You most certainly are not," said Bindlepod.

For a moment Violet considered telling him that if he tried to take her back she would claim he had kidnapped her to begin with, then had a change of heart, but only after he had done unspeakable things to her, and so on. She decided against this tactic, mostly because she had always hated the girls who acted that way in stories. It was a cheap way to get what you wanted.

"Well, if it's not Nilbog, it will be somewhere else," she said. "I'm not going back, and you can't make me."

"She's got a point," put in the frog. "Even if you took her back, they probably wouldn't let her in on account of…well, you know."

"I know," said Bindlepod. "The smell."

This conversation alarmed Violet considerably. Despite her wish to escape from the palace, she had done so assuming that she could return any time she wanted. "What are you talking about?" she demanded.

"The smell," said Bindlepod again. "You've been in my saddlebag for three hours already. By now the smell will have worn deep into your skin. Your parents may have put up with goblin smell on me, but they certainly aren't going to accept it on their daughter."

"Well, I'll just wash," said Princess Violet indignantly.

"Goblin smell doesn't come off with mere soap and water," said Bindlepod. He sounded offended at the thought.

"What does it take?" asked the princess, indignation turning to alarm.

"A dip in Fire Lake, if I remember correctly," said the frog.

"Good grief!" cried Bindlepod. "We can't expect her to do *that*! There's no telling how she might come out."

"What does that mean?" asked Violet, more alarmed than ever.

"Never mind," said Bindlepod. "Be quiet. I have to think."

"Never an easy task for him," put in the frog with a smirk.

"Shut up!" snapped the goblin.

The frog winked one melon-size eye at Violet but said nothing more.

An hour later Bindlepod stood, stretched (a movement that created an odd symphony of pops, clicks, and crackles), and said, "We're turning back. Even if the princess's parents don't let her in, we have to let them know what's happened. If we don't, they're going to assume I stole her, and before you know it we'll be at war all over again."

He climbed onto the frog. "Come on, Princess, hop up here behind me. And no complaints from *you* about the extra load," he added, digging his heels into the frog's side to get him moving again. "If you'd said something to begin with, we wouldn't be in this mess."

————

They had traveled only about a third of the way back to the castle when they found the king coming in their direction. His brow was dark, he was dressed for war, and he had a hundred knights riding behind him.

Violet, who had not expected this, was both frightened and thrilled.

"Hail, King Vitril!" said Bindlepod, springing down from the frog.

The king said nothing.

"I have your daughter," said Bindlepod, gesturing to where Violet was perched atop the frog. "I was just bringing her home."

"Why did you take her to begin with?" demanded the king.

"He didn't!" cried Violet, scrambling down from the frog's back. "He didn't, Papa! I snuck into his saddlebag, because I wanted to see the world. I longed for new sights and sounds and smells. I'm sorry if I caused you any worry."

She raced to her father's side. But when the king dismounted to embrace her, he made a terrible face.

"*Euuuw!*" he cried. "You stink of goblin!"

And, indeed, the princess—who had once smelled of apple blossoms and spiced muffins—now had a distinctly strange odor about her. A quick sniff was more apt to remind you of wind-wild October nights and distant caverns than of dew on the grass and freshly washed laundry. A deeper inhalation of the scent was likely to bring to mind secrets better left unspoken.

The king looked at his daughter sadly. "I can't take you home like this. It would never do, not at all."

Violet's eyes widened in astonishment. "You can't be serious, Papa!"

"Alas, I am utterly serious," said her father. "What do you think your mother would say if she got a whiff of you now? The smell would break her heart quite in half." He turned toward Bindlepod. "Had you taken my daughter against her will, I would have cleft you in two, fed both parts to my dogs, then ridden in vengeance against your people. As she chose to go with you, I leave her to you."

With that he bade his daughter farewell, told her to be wise and good, and to write as often as she was able, apologized for not embracing her, then climbed onto his horse and rode for home.

The astonished princess stood in the road, blinking back tears as she watched her father gallop away. It is, after all, one thing to run away from home. It is another thing entirely to run away and discover that they don't want you back.

She stood watching until the army had galloped completely out of sight, and neither Bindlepod nor the frog said a word to disturb her. Finally, when she could no longer see even the smallest cloud of dust from beneath the horses' hooves, she sighed and turned her face toward Nilbog.

Bindlepod still said nothing, simply held out one clammy hand and helped her onto the frog's back.

Toward evening on the third day of their journey, they came to an opening in the side of a hill.

"This is the path to Nilbog," said the goblin. "Are you still sure you want to go with us?"

Violet looked at the dark hole, then glanced back toward her old home. After a while she nodded. "I'll go in."

Bindlepod and Violet dismounted, for the entrance was too low for the frog to carry them through. Bindlepod took the princess by the hand and led the way into the cavern.

It was darker than Violet had imagined possible.

"How can you see?" she asked, as she picked her way forward on the stony path. She was holding tight to the goblin's hand and was secretly terrified that if he let go of her she would never find her way to the light again.

"There's enough light," replied Bindlepod. "It's just that your eyes are too small."

"It gets better soon, anyway," added the frog.

And, indeed, after another five or ten minutes, she could see a dim glow ahead of them, which was like food to her light-starved eyes.

The glow turned out to be coming from some greenish mushrooms that grew along the cavern walls. It was sufficiently bright to let her walk with confidence, though not bright enough to cast shadows. Violet noticed that it gave an odd tinge to Bindlepod and his frog. Then she held up her hand and realized that the light made her look strange, too.

Narrow stone bridges took them across dark chasms. Winding passages with many tunnels branching to the sides carried them deeper into the earth. And at last they arrived at the entrance to Nilbog— or, at least, *one* of the entrances.

It was carved in the shape of a great mouth. Within that mouth, barring their path forward, were dozens of spiky stone teeth.

An enormously fat creature who looked something like a goblin, though not entirely, was leaning against one side of the entrance, cleaning his navel with a sharpened bone. When he saw them coming, he opened his yellow eyes a little wider but made no movement.

Bindlepod stopped a respectful distance away. He stuck out his long tongue by way of salute, then said, "Greetings, Frelg. I return from the land above."

"Not alone, I notice," said Frelg, shifting his huge bulk to the side just a bit.

"Princess Violet wished to see our world," said Bindlepod, not referring to the fact that her father had banned her from returning home.

"Come here," said Frelg. "Not you, Princess! Just Bindlepod."

The goblin stepped forward. Frelg lurched to his

feet, and the princess shuddered to see that he was twice the height of Bindlepod. Bending forward—not easy, given his enormous bulk—he began to sniff.

Sniff. Sniff sniff.

Frelg frowned in disgust. *"Whooie!"* he cried. "You stink, Bindlepod! You smell of quiet rooms and cramped hearts, tiny minds and tiny places. You smell small and nasty."

Hearing this, the princess grew nervous. "Does that mean he's not going to let us in?" she whispered to the frog in a quivering voice.

"If I sent you away, then I would have a tiny little mind, too, wouldn't I?" asked Frelg, who had heard her in spite of her caution. (No surprise, really, given the size of his ears.) "You may enter. Just don't be surprised if people are not particularly happy to smell you."

With that he wobbled his way from in front of the gate and gestured for them to enter. At the same time the stone teeth slid out of sight, leaving the path clear.

With Bindlepod leading the way, they passed through the gate into a long dark tunnel that led down at a steep angle. After about an hour the tunnel widened and they came out on a ledge overlooking a stone city. It was lit all about by that same glowing fungus.

Bindlepod sighed with pleasure. "Home."

Not for me, thought the princess sadly, wondering what was to become of her.

They followed the stone path, which was sometimes dry, sometimes slimy, down to the level of the city. As they drew closer to the city, the path widened into a road, and Bindlepod and Violet climbed back onto the frog. As they hopped toward the city, they occasionally saw other travelers, goblins all. Some of them merely waved. Others, recognizing Bindlepod, greeted them with respectful bows. But all of them, even the goblins who bowed, stayed at the far side of the road, sniffing suspiciously.

Their reception at the court of the goblin king was no more encouraging than Violet's last interview with her father had been. The goblin king—a huge creature with leering eyes, fantastical warts in several colors, and a tongue as long as his arm—was sympathetic, but disturbed. "I am glad to have you back, Bindlepod," he said. "And your young lady friend is welcome to stay as well, of course. But really..."

With that, his voice trailed off, and his eyes rolled around, as if he was searching for exactly the right word.

The goblin queen, who had been plucking out a tune on the back of a strangely scaled creature, looked up and said, "Your father is troubled, son, on account of the princess's smell."

"Son?" asked Violet in surprise. "You didn't tell me you were the *prince* of Nilbog!"

Bindlepod shrugged.

"And what's wrong with my smell, anyway?" continued Violet indignantly. "My father thought I smelled too much like a goblin to go home. So I would think I would smell just fine for you."

"You do smell of goblin," said the king wearily. "But you also smell of the world above, of something lost and distant that it pains us to remember. We will give you shelter, of course. But I fear my people will not be jolly in your presence."

"I fear not," said the queen, striking a particularly melancholy chord on the back of the lizard-thing.

Time proved the queen to be correct. Though everyone in Nilbog was polite to Violet and Bindlepod—at least, polite by goblin standards—no one seemed terribly *comfortable* in the presence of either of them.

The result, not surprisingly, was that Violet and Bindlepod spent more and more time alone together.

The result of that situation *was* surprising, at least to those who think goblins and humans are more different than they really are.

Bindlepod and Violet fell in love.

It happened—or, at least, they became aware it had happened—one afternoon when they were sitting beside an underground river, basking in the gentle light of the glowing fungus. Bindlepod had just caught a fish and was trying to convince the princess to try a bite.

"Princesses don't eat raw fish!" she said tartly.

"You have done many things princesses are not supposed to do," replied Bindlepod, speaking a little tartly himself.

Violet pursed her lips in exasperation but couldn't think of a good answer for this. "All right," she said at last. "I'll try a bite. One. A small one."

Bindlepod cut a bit of flesh from the fish with his knife, then took it between his fingers and held it out to the princess. As she bent forward to take it in her mouth, Bindlepod found himself, much to his own surprise, running his finger gently along her lower lip. Though he drew his hand back in shock, the bigger shock was the one that had passed between them, a jolt of recognition that made it impossible for them to ignore what their hearts had known for a long time.

From that moment on they knew that they were in love.

"I can't say we were made for each other," said Bindlepod, later that same afternoon. Violet was reclining in his arms, dreamily gazing at the waterfall. "Even so," he continued, "I am glad we found each other."

"And why weren't we made for each other?" she asked, reaching up to pat his sallow cheek.

"Well, my stinky little sweetie, our smells are, to say the least, incompatible."

"Oh, fiddle," said Violet. "You smell fine to me."

"And I've grown quite fond of your odor as well," he replied—which was not what you would call a ringing endorsement, but it satisfied the princess nonetheless.

As the days and weeks wore on, Violet began to realize that Bindlepod was right. Though they were utterly happy in each other's company, the world around them—or, to be more specific, the other goblins—were most uneasy with their relationship. And though Bindlepod claimed this did not bother him, Violet was perceptive enough to see that he missed the company of other goblins, missed their easy teasing, their wild energy, their bizarre games.

Finally she decided to seek help for their situation, and, after a bit of asking around, learned the whereabouts of the wisest of goblins, an incredibly ugly female of astonishing age. Her name was Flegmire, and she lived in a cave at the edge of Nilbog.

Violet did not tell Bindlepod where she was going, simply asked if she could borrow the frog for a time.

Bindlepod agreed, on the condition that she not be gone for long.

Violet and the frog hopped away.

———

Flegmire's cave was deep and dank and hung about with moss. Snakes lounged around the entrance, as well as some other creatures that were like snakes, only stranger.

Standing at the front of the cave, Violet called, "May I enter, O Wisest of the Wise?"

"Yeah, yeah, come on in," replied a gravelly voice.

Picking her way around assorted slimy creatures, Violet entered the cave.

Flegmire sat on the floor, which meant that her knees were considerably higher than her ears. She was playing with a collection of colored rocks that had been carved into various shapes. Violet recognized the game—she had seen the goblin children playing it fairly often—and wondered if coming to see Flegmire had been such a good idea after all.

Her doubts increased when the ancient gobliness held up her hands, cried, "Wait! Wait!" and then farted with such violence that it raised her several inches off the floor.

The smell caused Violet to gasp in shock, and she grabbed a nearby stalactite to keep from falling over. Flegmire, however, sighed in contentment and said, "Well, now that I can think again, tell me what it is you want."

Eyes watering, the princess explained her difficulty.

"A sad story," said the gobliness. "But I still do not know what you want of me."

"You are the wisest of your kind," said Violet. "Don't you know anything I could do to rid myself of this smell?"

Flegmire hooked a curved green fingernail over her enormous lower lip. "You can't think of anything yourself? No hints you've had along the way?"

The princess started to say no, then stopped. She swallowed nervously. "Well, Bindlepod's frog did mention something about...Fire Lake."

Flegmire spread her arms as if the whole thing had been the essence of simplicity. "Well, there you go! If you already knew about that, why did you come here to bother me? I've got games to play, you know."

"But the frog said the lake would change me," said the princess.

"There are worse things that can happen," said Flegmire. "Not changing isn't so good, either."

"But *how* will it change me?"

"What do I look like?" asked Flegmire. "A prophet? You want to get rid of your smell, you go in the lake. How you come out, that's no concern of mine."

"Well, can you at least tell me how to get there?" asked Violet.

Flegmire smiled. "Sure," she said. "That's easy."

That night—night and day being pretty much the same in Nilbog—Violet rose from her bed in the little stone cottage behind the palace grounds that the goblin king had given her to live in. She put on her riding clothes, then slipped out the door, intending to saddle up the frog and ride to Fire Lake. But she hadn't gone more than ten paces from her door when Bindlepod stepped from behind an enormous mushroom and said, "Going somewhere, my darling?"

Violet jumped and gasped. "What are you doing here?" she cried. Then, spotting the frog, who was crouched on the far side of the mushroom, she hissed, "Blabbermouth!"

The frog merely shrugged.

"He does have his loyalties," said Bindlepod. "As do I. If you are going to do this thing, then so am I."

"You can't!" cried the princess.

"Piffle," said Bindlepod. "There's no point in only one of us taking the risk. If we're going to change, we might as well change together."

And nothing the princess could say would dissuade him.

So together they rode to Fire Lake, a journey that took them ever deeper into the earth.

At the end of the second day, they crossed a field of bubbling hot springs, and the frog narrowly escaped scalding his rear quarters when a geyser erupted behind him. "You're going to owe me a lot of june bugs when this is over," he said bitterly.

At the end of the third day, the horizon began to glow. Nervously, they climbed to the top of a slippery hill. Ahead lay Fire Lake, its flaming waves lapping idly against its scorched shore.

Violet tightened her hand on Bindlepod's arm. "I'm frightened," she whispered.

"You should be," croaked the frog, who was standing next to them.

"Whatever happens, we're in this together," said Bindlepod.

They started forward again.

In a few hours they were standing at the edge of Fire Lake. The blazing waves hissed and crackled as they rolled against the shore.

Bindlepod took Violet in his arms. He held her close, burying his nose in her neck.

"You know," he murmured, "I like the way you smell."

"And I like the way you smell," she replied.

"Then what are you going to do this for?" cried the frog, who had been growing more alarmed as they approached the lake. "Are you out of your minds? What do you care what the others think? It's none of their damn business! You love each other the way you are. Who are you going to change for?"

Violet blinked. Bindlepod stared at her. "Do you care if they think we stink?" he asked gently.

"I don't care if you don't care," said the princess.

And they both laughed.

———

Princess Violet and Prince Bindlepod never did step into Fire Lake.

What they did do was build a home for themselves in a giant oak tree halfway between the gates of her father's kingdom and the entrance to Nilbog. Part of the home was in the branches, and part beneath the roots. It smelled of sky and leaves, of stone and soil, and they loved it nearly as much as they loved each other.

Though they never went back to either kingdom, their home was always open to anyone who cared to visit, and who would take them as they were.

As the years passed Violet and Bindlepod had seven children, who brought a great deal of jolliness to the home in the tree. They were an odd group: goggle-eyed, pale-skinned, and full of mischief. They adored the frog, who taught them to swim, and always called him uncle.

The frog adored the children, too, and often said to visitors, "They're really sweet." Then he would chuckle deep in his throat and add, "For a bunch of little stinkers."

THE JAPANESE MIRROR

I was bleeding the first time I saw the Japanese mirror. I had been cleaning the side counter in Mr. Colella's Curio Shoppe, and an unexpected piece of metal had sliced open my fingertip.

Crying out in rage, I threw my rag to the counter, stuck my bleeding finger into my mouth, and stamped my foot. I probably would have stamped again, except I noticed Mr. Colella giving me a warning stare.

I took a deep breath and tried to get my temper under control. I knew I might lose my job if I didn't watch myself, and I didn't want that to happen. Not only did I really need the money, I actually liked working with the strange junk the old man kept in his antique shop.

I took my finger from my mouth to look at the cut. It went straight across my fingertip. And it hurt like crazy. All those nerves so close to the surface, I guess.

Scanning the countertop, I found what had snagged me—the top of a screw Mr. Colella had used to make a repair and hadn't wound deeply enough into the wood.

I was still hunting for a Band-Aid when Mr. Colella shouted, "Jonathan, come here. I need your help."

Pressing thumb against fingertip to stem the bleeding, I went to the back room.

Mr. Colella was standing in front of a large wooden crate. "Open this," he said, handing me a crowbar. *"Gently."*

The mirror inside the crate—a Japanese mirror, according to Mr. Colella—was nearly eight feet tall. The glass was surrounded by a wooden frame carved with interlocking designs and finished in black lacquer. I couldn't help but imagine strange messages hidden among those whorling symbols. Though the silvering behind the glass had worn thin in two or three places, for the most part the reflection it gave was clean and pure.

"Not bad, eh?" said Mr. Colella, once I had all the packing pulled away. He pulled at the ends of his gray mustache, always a sign that he was pleased with an item.

"What do you think you'll get for it?" I asked.

He shrugged. "It's in good condition; it's a little unusual. Given its age, it could go for maybe three thousand. Maybe a little more, if I find the right buyer."

My heart sank. For a moment I had considered trying to buy the mirror myself.

Either Mr. Colella didn't see my disappointment or he chose to ignore it. "Here," he said, handing me one of his seemingly endless supply of rags. "Polish."

"Probably wouldn't have fit in my room anyway," I muttered as I went to fetch a stepladder so I could reach the top.

Half an hour later I stood back to admire my work but got caught up examining my reflection instead. You could have talked to me all you wanted about inner beauty; I preferred having it outside, where it counted. Not so handsome it scared people off, but definitely good-looking. A little too much like my father, though. Sometimes it startled me when I glanced in a mirror and found myself staring at someone who looked just like the guy in the old army photo on our mantelpiece.

Suddenly I noticed a small streak of blood on the mirror. Glancing down at my finger, I saw that the cut had reopened while I was working. I rubbed the rag over the blood, but the mirror wouldn't come clean. I spit on a different finger and tried to rub the blood away. No luck.

I was starting to get angry when the tinkle of the bell above the door announced a customer.

When I came back an hour later, the stain was gone.

Guess Mr. Colella took care of it, I thought, hoping he wouldn't be angry with me for doing an incomplete job. It wouldn't be fair, of course. But like my late father, Mr. Colella tended to yell at me for things that weren't my fault.

I could hardly complain, given my own temper. The thought caused me to scowl at my reflection. Big brown eyes and a try-to-catch-me smile might make it easy to get girls; my sudden bursts of anger sure made it hard to keep them. I rolled my eyes as I remembered yesterday's argument with Gina, which had ended with her slapping me and shouting, "I don't care how cute you are, Jonathan Rawson, I won't be treated this way!"

I put my fingers to my cheek, remembering the slap. Last night I had figured it was time to move on. But Gina was special. Maybe *I* should apologize for a change.

Looking in the mirror to practice my rueful expression, I noticed the beginnings of a pimple beside my nose. I prodded the spot with my fingertips but couldn't feel any bump. Maybe if I was careful it would go away without blossoming into a full-fledged zit.

That seemed to be the case, for when I checked myself in the bathroom mirror at home that night, my skin was smooth and clear.

Whoa! I thought. *Could this be the beginning of the end for zitosis? What a relief that would be!*

I called Gina to apologize. She was cautious but finally agreed to go out with me on Saturday. I don't know who was more surprised by my apology: Gina, or me.

Humming contentedly, I returned to my desk, where I was building a miniature room for my little sister, Mindy. It was mostly for her birthday. But it was also a way of apologizing to her for all the times I had yelled at her over the last year.

The project had turned out to be a bigger time-sink than I expected. But Mindy had been wanting one of these rooms for years. Our father had promised to make her one several times, but (as usual) he hadn't come through. And now he was gone.

Despite how tricky it was, I found I actually enjoyed the work. And I was really proud of it. I loved seeing each piece come to its final polished perfection. That was one good thing about my job at Mr. Colella's: I had learned a lot about working with wood.

I spent an hour carefully sanding and staining the chair I had finished assembling the night before. When I finally grew so tired I was afraid I would botch the work, I threw Beau, our golden retriever, off the bed and climbed between the sheets.

The next morning my mother overcooked the eggs.

"Sorry, Jon," she said, as she placed the rubbery

henfruit in front of me, "I'm not functioning on all cylinders yet. I don't think they're making the coffee as strong as they used to."

"No problem," I said, kissing her on the cheek. "I can manage a tough yolk every now and then."

"Is this *my* kid?" she asked, widening her eyes and putting a hand on my forehead. "The one who used to have a tantrum if his eggs weren't runny enough to use up all his toast?"

"For Pete's sake, Ma," I said, ducking away from her hand.

School went well, and I had a good time with Gina during art. So I was in a good mood when I got to Mr. Colella's shop.

Mr. Colella, unfortunately, was not. He was standing in front of the Japanese mirror—which was now in the display area—rubbing a rag almost violently over the glass.

A touch of coldness seized my chest when I saw the red streak that marred the surface of the mirror.

"I would have sworn I wiped this off yesterday," said Mr. Colella. He turned and handed me the rag. "Here. You take care of it. And do it right this time!"

He stomped off, banging his leg on an old oak dresser.

I studied the mirror. The red streak was longer than I remembered.

As I reached forward to rub it with the rag, the stain disappeared.

I flinched back as if I had been burned. I stared at the mirror, then focused on my own reflection. The spot I had noticed the day before had erupted into an ugly pimple after all.

I put my finger to my face.

The skin was smooth.

I dropped the rag and grabbed both edges of the mirror, as if I could anchor it into reality. I don't know how long I stood there.

Mr. Colella's voice wrenched me from my trance. "Come on, glamour boy. That mirror's not the only thing in the shop. Get to work!"

I turned away from the mirror. I thought about quickly turning back, to see if it still showed the pimple, and realized I was afraid to do so. I hurried over to Mr. Colella, grateful for an excuse not to have to face myself again.

I avoided the mirror throughout the afternoon.

But if I could avoid it physically, I couldn't keep it out of my thoughts. I tried and discarded a dozen different explanations for the altered reflection: a flaw in the glass, a trick of light, a momentary daydream. Finally I told myself it had simply been an unlikely combination of all of those things, and that I was getting myself wound up over nothing.

———

My mother met me at the door with a worried look on her face. "Jon, I'm sorry..."

I knew that tone. Something had happened that was going to make me angry, and she was trying to avert the explosion.

"What is it?" I asked tensely.

"Beau..." She waved her hands helplessly. "Well, you should have put it away when you were done last night!"

A sick feeling grabbed me. Pushing past my mother, I ran to my room. I saw the mess with my eyes, but I felt it with my stomach, as solidly as if someone had landed a punch right below my ribs. The miniature room—the five pieces of oak furniture I'd so lovingly crafted, the walls I'd so carefully measured and papered—lay in the center of the rug, reduced to nothing more than a pile of wet splinters and dog slobber.

Beau slunk in, drooping his tail and looking guilty.

"You stupid dog!" I shrieked, raising my hand.

"Jonathan!" cried my mother, as Beau whimpered and cowered away.

To my surprise, the storm of anger passed as quickly as it had come. I lowered my hand. Filled with sorrow, I knelt to gather the sodden remains of three months of work. They felt slimy in my hands.

"I'd like to be alone for a little while," I said softly.

Looking at me in astonishment, my mother grabbed Beau by the collar. "I'll call you when supper is ready." But instead of leaving the room, she pushed Beau out, closed the door, and put her arms around me. "It's just that you look so much like your father when you get mad," she whispered.

I laid my head on her shoulder. We both cried.

Monday afternoon Mr. Colella asked if I could stay late to close the shop while he went to an auction. I said I would have to check with my mother. I called, half hoping she would say no. But she okayed the extra hours, and even said she would pick me up after work.

After Mr. Colella left, I found myself glancing uneasily toward the mirror. I shook my head and busied myself with other chores. It was a quiet night; I didn't have a single customer until nearly eight, when Mrs. Hubbard hobbled in. She was one of Mr. Colella's best customers, and it was a relief to see her—though at that point I would have been glad to see *anyone*.

"Hi, Mrs. Hubbard," I said cheerfully. "Can I help you?"

"Just looking tonight, Jonathan," she replied. But a few minutes later she called me over to the mirror.

Reluctantly I crossed to join her.

"This is an interesting piece," she said. "What can you tell me about it?"

"It was made in Japan, about three hundred years ago," I said, trying to remember everything Mr. Colella had told me. "We don't know the name of the craftsman, but from the style it appears to have been made in…"

I caught my breath. Couldn't she see it?

"Made in Kyoto?" Mrs. Hubbard prompted, obviously thinking I had forgotten the name of the city.

I hadn't forgotten anything. I was simply too frightened to speak. An inch-wide streak of red had slashed its way across the center of the mirror. That would have been bad enough. But it was the image in the glass that truly terrified me. Two people looked out at me, one a kindly looking elderly woman, the other a strangely altered version of myself. A scattering of open sores stretched from my nose across my right cheek to my hairy, pointed ear.

I glanced at Mrs. Hubbard. She was staring at me expectantly.

I looked back at the mirror.

My reflection smiled at me.

Mrs. Hubbard shook my arm. "Jonathan, are you all right?"

"Don't you see?" I whispered, my voice trembling.

"See what?" she asked, taking a step away from me.

"Nothing. I'm sorry!"

I put my hands over my eyes and pressed them into my face.

She took another step back. "I'll come to see Mr. Colella about the mirror tomorrow." She paused, then looked at me with concern. "Listen to an old woman, Jonathan. I've had my time with mirrors. Don't let them get to you. They're useful, but the truth is, they always lie. Everything is backwards in a mirror. And whatever you see is never more than just a part of you."

I nodded, unable to speak.

She looked at me more closely, then furrowed her brow and said again, "I'll talk to Mr. Colella about the mirror tomorrow."

"No, wait!" But it was too late. She had scurried from the shop, leaving me alone with the mirror.

I sidled back to the counter, unwilling to turn my back on the mirror, equally unwilling to look at it. I considered calling my mother and asking her to pick me up early, but couldn't figure out what to give as a reason.

When nine o'clock came I was standing by the door with my hand on the light switch, ready to scoot out as soon as I saw Mom's car.

Tuesday was a good day. Not having to go to the shop, I found myself at peace with the world. Things seemed to be on track with Gina, and the minor annoyances that normally would have made my temper flare seemed unable to affect my good mood.

Wednesday afternoon I went to work determined to confront the mirror.

It was gone.

"Mrs. Hubbard bought it yesterday morning," said Mr. Colella. "Said she was going to put it in her front hall. She has a lot of oriental stuff, you know. She and her husband used to live in Japan, before he died. Anyway, I thought you'd be glad it was gone, since it seemed to make you nervous." He paused and looked at me quizzically. "Don't know why. You're a good-looking kid. You shouldn't worry about that kind of thing."

I nodded and set to work, uncertain whether I was relieved or disappointed that the mirror was gone.

Over the next few months I forced myself to forget the mirror. The forgetting was made easier by the fact that my life was taking a turn for the better, as Jonathan the Wild and Temperamental was slowly replaced by Jonathan the Calm and Strong.

"A pleasure to be with" was the way people spoke of me now—the same people who had once avoided me because of my temper. I felt more able to focus on things. My schoolwork improved, and my grades went up. I had more friends.

When I started volunteering at the hospital Gina nicknamed me Saint Jonathan. At first it was a joke, but after a while she began saying it seriously, and I sensed that my unswerving calm was actually beginning to worry her.

A month later she broke up with me. Though she wouldn't say why, I had a feeling that I was boring her. I should have been upset, but I wasn't. For one thing, half a dozen girls had made it obvious that they would be available if Gina dropped out of the picture. I didn't call any of them, though. Somehow I wasn't that interested.

The horror started in school, oddly enough, where normality seemed to be embedded in the very walls. I was looking in the rest room mirror to adjust my hair when I saw a twisted, evil version of my own face staring back at me.

The image lasted for only a moment. But it left me gasping. Had I really seen it? Or was I having a nervous breakdown?

When I was preparing to go to upstairs to bed that night, my mother put a hand on my shoulder and said, "I see such a change in you, Jonathan."

I flinched. Had the evil I had seen in the mirror started to show on my face? My mother misread my reaction. "Don't be upset. I was trying to tell you how pleased I am. I used to worry you were going to turn out like your father."

I twisted away, started up the stairs.

"Jonathan, I'm sorry! That wasn't fair. Your father had his good qualities. What I meant...What I was trying to say...was that I was afraid you would have his temper. That it would do to your life what it did to his."

I paused on the stairs but didn't speak.

"Anyway, you seem to be getting a handle on that. I'm pleased. And very proud." She was silent for a moment. "Well, I just wanted to let you know I noticed," she said at last. "Good night, son."

"Good night," I whispered.

Upstairs, I lay staring into the darkness, shaking with terror as I remembered what had happened earlier that day. Finally I climbed out of bed and turned on the light. Whirling around, I saw it again in the mirror over my dresser: a horrifying version of my own face. Though it disappeared almost instantly, I no longer had any doubt that it was real.

Mirrors became my enemy. Though most of the time they were safe, I never knew when I would look into one and see the horrible face that was so much like my own, yet so filled with evil, leering out at me.

It grew worse—uglier and angrier—each time I saw it.

I prayed someone else would see it, so I would know I was not going mad. I also prayed that no one else would see it, for it was far too humiliating.

I stayed away from mirrors as much as possible, even cut my hair short so I wouldn't have to worry about combing it.

"I'm worried about you, Jonathan," said my mother, late that spring. "You seem a little...I don't know, a little thin around the edges. Maybe you're working too hard."

"I'm fine," I said, kissing her on the forehead.

It was a lie, and we both knew it.

"We've got a big house sale," Mr. Colella told me one Friday afternoon. "Former customer passed away and left a huge collection of stuff. No kids. The nieces and nephews live a thousand miles away and all they want is the money. Anyway, I'll need some extra help for the next few days. I want you to come with me."

So the following morning Mr. Colella picked me up in the shop truck and we drove to a large old house. When I saw the mailbox, I caught my breath.

Mrs. Hubbard had lived there.

The Japanese mirror stood in the foyer, right where the old woman had told Mr. Colella she was planning to put it all those months ago.

I averted my head as we walked past.

Though I kept myself busy in other parts of the house, the mirror was on my mind all morning. When Mr. Colella left me to continue the inventory while he went to pick up lunch, I found myself drawn irresistibly back to the foyer. I hesitated to enter, but finally a curiosity stronger than terror drove me on—curiosity... and the hope that perhaps here I could find the answer to the strangeness that had overtaken my life.

I walked slowly toward the mirror. From the angle of my approach I could see the opposite wall reflected in its smooth surface. Everything seemed normal.

I stopped and took a deep breath, then stepped forward and planted myself in front of the mirror.

I screamed.

The wall in the mirror was the same wall that stood behind me. The pictures, the coat rack, and the umbrella stand were all the same. But where I should have seen myself crouched a creature more hideous than anything I had ever imagined.

Blood began to seep down from the top of the mirror. The creature raised its hands and reached forward, reached *toward* me, as if it wanted to snatch me through the glass.

I ran.

In the garden behind the house I threw myself to the ground and sobbed. What made the thing in the mirror so horrible was not horns or scales or anything demonic. What made it horrible was the smoldering rage twisting the features that were all too clearly my own. That, and the understanding that the anger I thought I had escaped for the last six months had been coming here. All my darkness—every vile thought, every angry moment, every instant since October when I had been less than my best—had collected in the mirror, slowly creating a beast that was now nearly strong enough to break out. It was a repository for all that was bad about myself, and what I had seen there was not merely terrifying, it was disgusting.

My mother had said I looked "thin around the edges." Now I understood why: Too much of me had gone into the mirror.

I thought back to the bits of information Mr. Colella had dropped in his usual terse way as we were working. "She died of a heart attack," he had said at one point, for no reason that I could make out. "They found her body in the foyer," he had commented later.

A chill ran over me as I concluded that my other self had scared Mrs. Hubbard to death.

I sat up and wiped my face.

"All right, Saint Jonathan. Now what do you do?"

The answer was simple. The creature had to be destroyed.

But what would that mean to me? The creature was part of me, *was* me, in a way. If I killed it, would I die, too?

Well, saints never hesitated to die for a good cause. Or would this be like committing suicide?

"Jonathan?"

It was Mr. Colella, back with lunch. I took a breath and forced myself to be calm. "Be right there," I called.

I found a hose and washed the tears and dirt from my face.

"What were you doing?" asked Mr. Colella sharply, when I appeared at the door of the kitchen.

I felt an instant of anger at Mr. Colella's tone, then felt the anger disappear. This was a sensation I had experienced often over the last several months. At first I had welcomed it. After a while the feeling had become so familiar that I usually ignored it. Now, though, it horrified me, for I finally understood that it meant I had just fed my terrible alter ego.

No more free ride, I thought. *I've got to teach myself to be calm for real.*

Doing so took most of my energy for the rest of the day. By the time I went to bed I was exhausted from trying to control my anger. Even so, sleep would not come, and when the alarm I had set to go off at two began to beep, I was still wide awake.

I reached out and snapped it off. Moving slowly, I climbed from my bed and dressed.

Half an hour later I pulled my bike to a halt in front of the Hubbard house. A cool wind whispered around me, making leaves rustle in the darkness. As I traveled up the sidewalk, the nearly full moon sent a long shadow stretching ahead of me.

I fumbled in my pocket for the key Mr. Colella had given me earlier that day. Once I had it, I paused. It wasn't too late to turn back.

But the thing waiting inside belonged to me.

So I unlocked the door and stepped into the foyer.

"Hello, *brother.*"

I caught my breath. The voice came from the mirror. Had the creature known I was coming? Could it read my mind?

I turned on the light and it appeared immediately, a ravaged parody of my own face staring out from the mirror.

"I've been waiting for you, *Saint* Jonathan," it hissed.

I took a step backward.

The image should have moved back as well, away from me. It didn't. It stayed exactly where it was.

"It's too late for that kind of game, Saint Jonathan. I have a life of my own now. Your mother was right, you know. You *are* getting thinner. Soon there won't be anything left of you. All that goodness will vanish like a puff of smoke in the wind." It laughed. "That's when I'll come back and take over your body. It won't be like dying, not at all like dying. I'm too much a part of you for that, the biggest part of you. Just a few more days—a few more days and we'll be together again."

The eyes looking out at me glowed with an unholy fire.

"Oh, the things we'll do then, Jonathan! We'll start with your sister, probably. Or maybe your mother. Yes, maybe your mother. That would be nice, don't you think?"

"Stop!" I shouted. I felt the surge of my anger flow into the thing in the mirror and suddenly realized it was goading me, pushing me to give it more strength, more power.

I did the only thing I could think of. Moving as slowly and calmly as I could manage, I turned to the umbrella stand behind me.

I picked it up.

Then I threw it into the mirror.

The glass shattered. The pieces crashed and tinkled to the floor.

My sense of triumph lasted only a second. With a sudden hiss a flare of blue light crackled around the black lacquer frame.

A moment later my other self came crawling over the edge.

"How kind of you to set me free. Earlier than I expected. But not unwelcome. No, not unwelcome at all."

It lunged at me. I screamed and jumped back as my own face, burning with hatred, riddled with oozing sores, surged up at me. I dodged to the right, racing around the creature. It clutched at me. I jumped forward, tripped over the black lacquer frame—and fell into the world of the mirror.

The creature followed close behind me. I could hear it scrabbling on the floor, panting, not from exertion, but from a lust to possess me.

"I don't want you!" I cried as I ran through the mirror version of Mrs. Hubbard's house. "I don't want you. You're not part of me anymore!"

"I've always been part of you," laughed the creature. "And now *you* will be part of *me*...Saint Jonathan."

The last words were spit out with such contempt that I felt my fear double. If this thing that hated me so much were to catch me, what would it do to me? *What would it do to those I loved?*

I stumbled around a corner, regained my balance, saw a door and a stairwell. I took the stairs rather than the door, because to lead this thing out of the house and into the world—even the mirror world—was too awful.

I was halfway up the stairs when I heard my mother's voice call, "Jonathan! Jonathan, wait for me!"

I turned back. But the voice had come from the creature. It was standing at the base of the stairs, leering up at me. A string of drool dangled from its pendulous lower lip.

I turned to run, and gasped. Above me, floating at the top of the stairs, was Mrs. Hubbard. A pale glow surrounded her translucent figure.

"I'm sorry, Mrs. Hubbard!" I cried. "I didn't know what was happening. I didn't mean for you to die!"

"Don't be foolish!" she snapped. "Listen to me, Jonathan. Remember what I told you. Mirrors always lie. Everything is backwards here. Now you have to want him more than he wants you."

"What do you mean?"

But her image vanished, shimmering out of sight like a reflection in a pond when the water is disturbed.

A snarl from behind sent me bolting the rest of the way up the stairs.

You have to want him more than he wants you.

I stumbled along a hallway.

"Jonathan, you're mine. Stop running."

Stop running. That wouldn't be good enough. I had to stop being afraid. The creature was feeding on my fear, growing stronger every moment.

You have to want him more than he wants you.

I stopped. Heart pounding, I turned to face the creature.

It paused, looking wary.

Summoning every ounce of courage I possessed, I spread my arms and whispered, "Come back."

The creature's eyes widened. It hissed in alarm.

I took a step toward it.

It backed away, still hissing.

I took another step. It turned and ran. I raced after it, caught it with a flying tackle at the head of the stairs.

"No!" it screamed, struggling to escape my grasp. "Get back!"

I was too sure to let go now. I clutched it to me, for it was my own. Screaming, it clawed its way forward until it managed to pull both itself and me over the edge of the stairs.

We tumbled down, rolling over and over, thumping and bouncing. It felt as if I were trapped in a cement mixer, but I didn't let go. When we hit the bottom, I was on top. Wrapping my arms around the creature, I pulled it to me and whispered, "You're mine. You're mine, and I claim you."

I could feel it wavering, growing thinner in my arms. But it was still struggling, still real and solid.

Stronger now, I pinned it to the floor. I stared at that fierce and horrid face—my own face, twisted and ravaged by all my anger. Pushing past my disgust, my revulsion, I pressed my cheek to the creature's.

"You're mine," I whispered in its ear. "Welcome home."

Then I held it as close to my heart as I could, and howled in sorrow and triumph as my lost anger seared its way back into my soul.

The beast vanished from beneath me.

I collapsed to the floor, where I lay for a long time, weeping but whole, Saint Jonathan no longer.

"Not bad, kid," said a deep, dear voice, once so familiar, now nearly forgotten. "Not bad at all."

I looked up and saw my father smiling down at me, translucent and shimmering as Mrs. Hubbard had been.

I reached toward him, but he shook his head sadly and began to fade from sight. "Can't do it, kid. I'm breaking the rules as it is. But I wanted to let you know you did good."

"Don't go! I need you!"

"I know. You always did. And I was never there."

He shimmered back into view and stepped closer. Fearful, I started to draw back but forced myself to stay.

My father lifted his hand. I whimpered at the sight. How often when I was five, six, seven had I seen that hand rise like this to strike me? But there was no anger now, only deep, enduring sorrow as the memory of flesh came down to brush against my cheek.

I swiped at a tear, trying to hide it, too aware of how my tears had always stirred my father's wrath.

"I always loved you, Jonathan," he whispered, his voice cracking. "I was just too dumb to say it."

He put his arms around me, embracing me as I had embraced the creature, and though no touch could be felt it was as real as salt and as deep as love itself.

Then, before I could say a word, he was gone.

———

After a time I got to my feet.

Moving slowly, I walked toward the mirror's frame. I glanced back only once.

There was nothing behind me.

Turning, I stepped through the black lacquer frame, back to where my own sweet, harsh world lay waiting.

AM I BLUE?

It started the day Butch Carrigan decided I was interested in jumping his bones.

"You little fruit," he snarled. "I'll teach you to look at *me*!"

A moment or two later, he had given me my lesson.

I was still lying facedown in the puddle into which Butch had slammed me, as the culminating exercise of my learning experience, when I heard a clear voice exclaim, "Oh, my dear! That *was* nasty. Are you all right, Vince?"

Turning my head to my left, I saw a pair of brown Top-Siders topped by khaki pants. Given the muddy condition of the sidewalks, pants and shoes were both ridiculously clean.

I rolled onto my side and looked up. The loafers belonged to a tall, slender man. He had dark hair, a neat mustache, and a sweater slung over his shoulders. He was kind of handsome—almost pretty. He wore a gold ring in his left ear. He looked to be about thirty.

"Who are you?" I asked suspiciously.

"Your fairy godfather. My name is Melvin. Come on, stand up and let's see if we can't do something with you."

"Are you making fun of me?" I asked. After Butch's last attack, I had had about enough of people calling me a fruit for one day.

"*Moi?*" cried the man, arching his eyebrows and laying a hand on his chest. "Listen, honey, I have nothing but sympathy for you. I had to deal with my share of troglodytes when I was your age, and I *know* it's no fun. I'm here to help."

"What the hell are you talking about?"

"I told you, I'm your fairy godfather."

He waited for me to say something, but I just sat in the puddle, glaring at him. (It was uncomfortable, but I was already soaked right through my undershorts, so it didn't make that much difference.)

"*You* know," he said encouragingly, "like in *Cinderella*?"

"Go away and let me suffer in peace," I growled, splashing muddy water at him.

He flinched, and frowned, but it was a reflex action; the water that struck his pants vanished without a trace.

I blinked, and splashed at him again, this time spattering a double handful of dirty water across his legs.

"Are you angry, or just making a fashion statement?" he asked.

I felt a little chill. No spot of mud nor mark of moisture could be seen on the perfectly pressed khakis. "How did you do that?" I asked.

He just smiled and said, "Do you want your three wishes or not, Vincent?"

I climbed out of the puddle. "What's going on here?" I asked.

He made a *tsk*ing sound. "I think it's pretty obvious," he said, rolling his eyes. "Come on, let's go get a cup of coffee and talk. All your questions will be answered in good time."

The first question I thought of was "How much trouble is it going to give me to be seen with this guy?" With Butch and his crowd already calling me "faggot" and "fruit," walking around with a guy who moved the way Melvin did wasn't going to do anything to improve the situation.

The first question I actually *asked* was "Do you have to walk like that?"

"Like what?"

"You know," I said, blushing a little. "So swishy."

Melvin stopped. "Honey, I gave my life to be able to walk like this. Don't you dare try to stop me now."

"Don't call me honey!" I snapped.

He sighed and rolled his eyes toward the sky. "I can't say you didn't warn me," he said, clearly not speaking to me.

———

We went to a little café on Morton Street called Pete's. It's mostly frequented by kids from the university, but some of the high school kids hang out there as well, especially kids from the theater group.

"Not bad," said Melvin, as we entered. "Brings back memories."

Things were slow, and we found a corner table where we could talk in private.

"Okay," I said, "what's going on?"

I won't relate the first part of the conversation, because you've probably read a lot of things like it before. I couldn't believe what he was saying was real, so I kept trying to figure out what this was really about—*Candid Camera,* an elaborate practical joke, that kind of thing. But after he instantly dried my puddle-soaked pants by snapping his fingers, I had to accept it: Whether or not he was actually my fairy godfather, this guy was doing real magic left and right.

"Okay, if you're real," I said, lifting my coffee (which had changed from plain coffee to Swiss double mocha *while* I was drinking it), "then tell me how come I never heard of fairy godfathers before."

"Because I'm the first."

"Care to explain that?"

"Certainly. Once you buy the farm, you get some choices on the other side. What kind of choices depends on the usual stuff—how good you've been and so on. Well, I was going up and not down, and it was pretty much expected that I would just opt to be an angel; they've got these things all planned out for you. But I said I didn't want to be anyone's guardian angel. I wanted to be a fairy godfather."

He took a sip of coffee and rolled his eyes. "Let me tell you, *that* caused a hullabaloo! But I said people had been calling me a fairy all my life, and now that I was dead, that was what I wanted to be. Then I told them that if they didn't let me be a fairy godfather, I was going to bring charges of sexism against them. So they let me in. You're my first case."

"Does that have any significance?" I asked nervously.

"What do you mean?"

"Me being your first case. Does that mean I'm gay?"

I didn't mention that I had been trying to figure out the same thing myself for about a year.

He got that look in his eye that meant he was about to make another wisecrack. But suddenly his face got serious. Voice soft, he said, "You may be, you may not. The point is, you're getting picked on because people *think* you are—which is why I've been sent to work with you. Gay bashing is a special issue for me."

"How come?"

"It's how I met my maker, so to speak. I was walking down the street one day last year, minding my own business, when three bruisers dragged me into an alley, shouting, 'We'll teach you, faggot!' They never did explain exactly what it was they were going to teach me. Last thing I remember from life on earth was coming face-to-face with a tire iron. Next thing I knew, I was knocking at the Pearly Gates."

We were both silent for a moment. Then he shrugged and took another sip of his coffee.

"You're taking this awfully casually," I said, still stunned by the awfulness of what he had told me.

"Honey, I did a lot of screaming and shouting while it was happening. Afterward, too, for that matter. Didn't do me a bit of good—I was still dead. Once you've been on the other side for a while, you get a little more Zen about this kind of thing."

"But don't you want to go get those guys or something?"

He shook his head. "I prefer reform to vengeance. Besides, it's against the rules. Why don't we just concentrate on your case for the time being?"

"Okay, do I really get three wishes?"

"Sure do. Well, two, now."

"What do you mean?"

"You used up the first one on that coffee."

"I didn't tell you to change it into Swiss double mocha!" I yelped.

"You didn't have to. You wished for it."

"I'm glad I didn't wish I was dead!" I muttered.

"Oh!" he cried. "Getting personal, are we?

Don't you think that remark was a little tasteless under the circumstances?"

"Are you here to help me or to drive me nuts?"

"It hurts me that you could even ask. Anyway, the three wishes are only part of the service, even though that's what people always focus on. I'm really here to watch over you, advise you, guide you, till we get things on track."

He leaned back in his chair, glanced around the room, then winked at a nice-looking college student sitting about five tables away from us.

"Will you stop that!" I hissed.

"What's the matter, afraid of guilt by association?"

"No, I'm afraid he'll come over here and beat us up. Only he probably can't beat you up, so he'll have to settle for me."

Melvin waved his hand. "I guarantee you he wasn't offended. He's one of the gang."

"What gang?"

Melvin pursed his lips and raised his eyebrows, as if he couldn't believe I could be so dense.

I blinked. "How can you tell something like that just from looking at him?"

"Gaydar," said Melvin, stirring his coffee. "Automatic sensing system that lets you spot people of similar persuasion. A lot of gay guys have it to some degree or other. If it was more reliable, it would make life easier on us—"

I interrupted. "Speak for yourself."

Melvin sighed. "I wasn't necessarily including *you* in that particular 'us.' I was just pointing out that it's harder spotting potential partners when you're gay. If a guy asks a girl for a date, about the worst that can happen is that she laughs at him. If he asks another guy, he might get his face pounded in."

That thought had crossed my mind more than once as I was trying to figure myself out over the last year—and not only in regard to dating. I would have been happy just to have someone I felt safe *talking* to about this.

"Is this gaydar something you can learn?" I asked.

He furrowed his brow for a moment, then said, "I don't think so."

"It must be lonely," I muttered, more to myself than to him.

"It doesn't have to be," he replied sharply. "If gay people hadn't been forced to hide for so long, if we could just openly identify ourselves, there would be plenty of people you knew that you could ask for advice. Everybody knows gay people; they just think they don't."

"What do you mean?"

"Listen, honey, the world is crawling with faggots. But most of them are in hiding because they're afraid they'll get treated the way you did about an hour ago."

I took in my breath sharply. Melvin must have seen the look of shock on my face, because he looked puzzled for a moment. Then he laughed. "That word bother you?"

"I was taught that it was impolite."

"It is. But if you live in a world that keeps trying to grind you down, you either start thumbing your nose at it or end up very, very short. Taking back the language is one way to jam the grinder. My friends and I called each other 'faggot' and 'queer' for the same reason so many black folks call each other 'nigger'—to take the words away from the people that want to use them to hurt us."

His eyes went dreamy for a moment, as if he was looking at something far away, or deep inside. "I walk and talk the way I do because I'm not going to let anyone else define me. I can turn it off whenever I want, you know."

He moved in his seat. I couldn't begin to tell you exactly what changed, but he suddenly looked more masculine, less...swishy.

"How did you do that?" I asked.

"Protective coloration," he said with a smile. "You learn to use it to get along in the world if you want. Only I got sick of living in the box the world prescribed; it was far too small to hold me. So I knocked down a few walls."

"Yeah, and look what happened. You ended up dead."

"They do like to keep us down," he said, stirring his coffee. Suddenly he smiled and looked more like himself again. "Do you know the three great gay fantasies?" he asked.

"I don't think so," I said nervously.

He looked at me. "How old are you?"

"Sixteen."

"Skip the first two. You're too young. It was number three that I wanted to tell you about anyway. We used to imagine what it would be like if every gay person in the country turned blue for a day."

My eyes went wide. "Why?"

"So all the straights would have to stop imagining that they didn't know any gay people. They would find out that they had been surrounded by gays all the time, and survived the experience just fine, thank you. They'd have to face the fact that there are gay cops and gay farmers, gay teachers and gay politicians, gay parents and gay kids. The hiding would finally have to stop."

He looked at me for a moment. "How would you like to have the sight?" he asked.

"What?"

"How would you like to have gaydar for a while? You might find it interesting."

"Does this count as a wish?" I asked suspiciously.

"No, it's education. Comes under a different category."

"All right," I said, feeling a little nervous.

"Close your eyes," said Melvin.

After I did as he requested, I felt him touch each

of my eyelids lightly. My cheeks began to burn as I wondered if anyone else had seen.

"Okay," he said. "Open up, big boy, and see what the world is really like."

I opened my eyes, and gasped.

About a third of the people in the café—including the guy that Melvin had winked at—were blue. Some were bright blue, some were deep blue, some just had a bluish tint to them.

"Are you telling me all those people are gay?" I whispered.

"To some degree or other."

"But so many of them?"

"Well, this isn't a typical place," said Melvin. "You told me the theater crowd hangs around in here." He waved his hand grandly. "Groups like that tend to have a higher percentage of gay people, because we're so naturally artistic." He frowned. "Of course, some bozos take a fact like that and decide that *everyone* doing theater is gay. Remember, two-thirds of the people you're seeing *aren't* blue."

"What about all the different shades?" I asked.

"It's an indicator of degree. I set it up so that you'll see at least a hint of blue on anyone who has a touch of twinkiness. And a lot of blue on...well, you get the idea. Come on, let's go for a walk."

It was like seeing the world through new eyes. Most of the people looked just the same as always, of course. But Mr. Alwain, the fat guy who ran the grocery store, looked like a giant blueberry—which surprised me, because he was married and had three kids. On the other hand, Ms. Thorndyke, the librarian, who everyone *knew* was a lesbian, didn't have a trace of blue on her.

"Can't tell without the spell," said Melvin. "Straights are helpless at it. They're always assuming someone is or isn't for all the wrong reasons."

We were in the library because Melvin wanted to show me some books. "Here, flip through this," he said, handing me a one-volume history of the world.

My bluevision worked on pictures, too!

"Julius Caesar?" I asked in astonishment.

"Every woman's husband, every man's wife," said Melvin. "I met him at a party on the other side once. Nice guy." Flipping some more pages, he said, "Here, check this one out."

"Alexander the Great was a fairy?" I cried.

"*Shhhhh!*" hissed Melvin. "We're in a library!"

All right, I suppose you're wondering about me—as in, was I blue?

The answer is, slightly.

When I asked Melvin to explain, he said, "The Magic 8 Ball says, 'Signs are mixed.' In other words, you are one confused puppy. That's the way it is sometimes. You'll figure it out after a while."

———

Watching the news that night was a riot. My favorite network anchor was about the shade of a spring sky—pale blue, but very definite. So was the congressman he interviewed, who happened to be a notorious Republican homophobe.

"Hypocrite," I spat.

"What brought that on?" asked Dad.

"Oh, nothing," I said, trying to figure out whether I was relieved or appalled by the slight tint of blue that covered his features.

Don't get the idea that everyone I saw was blue. It broke down pretty much the way the studies indicate—about one person in ten solid blue, and one out of every three or four with some degree of shading.

I did get a kick out of the three blue guys I spotted in the sports feature on the team favored to win the Super Bowl.

But it was that congressman who stayed on my mind. I couldn't forget his hypocritical words about "the great crime of homosexuality" and "the gay threat to American youth."

I was brushing my teeth when I figured out what I wanted to do.

"No," I whispered, staring at my bluish face in the mirror. "I couldn't."

For one thing, it would probably mean another beating from Butch Carrigan.

Yet if I did it, nothing would ever be the same.

Rinsing away the toothpaste foam, I whispered Melvin's name.

"At your service!" he said, shimmering into existence behind me. "Ooooh, what a tacky bathroom. Where was your mother brought up, in a Kmart?"

"Leave my mother out of this," I snapped. "I want to make my second wish."

"And it is?"

"Gay fantasy number three, coast to coast."

He looked at me for a second, then began to smile. "How's midnight for a starting point?"

"Twenty-four hours should do the trick, don't you think?" I replied.

He rubbed his hands, chuckled, and disappeared.

I went to bed, but not to sleep. I kept thinking about what it would mean when the rest of the world could see what I had seen today.

I turned on my radio, planning to listen to the news every hour. I had figured the first reports would come in on the one o'clock news, but I was wrong. It was about 12:30 when special bulletins started announcing a strange phenomenon. By one o'clock, every station I could pick up was on full alert. Thanks to the wonders of modern communication, it had become obvious in a matter of minutes that people were turning blue from coast to coast.

It didn't take much longer for people to start figuring out what the blue stood for. The reaction ranged from panic to hysterical denial to dancing in the streets. National Public Radio had quickly summoned a panel of experts to discuss what was going to happen when people had to go to work the next day.

"Or school," I muttered to myself. Which was when I got my next idea.

"Melvin!" I shouted.

"You rang?" he asked, shimmering into sight at the foot of my bed.

"I just figured out my third wish." I took a breath. "I want you to turn Butch Carrigan blue."

He looked at me for a moment. Then his eyes went wide. "Vincent," he said, "I like the way you think. I'll be back in a flash."

When he returned he was grinning like a cat.

"You've still got one wish left, kiddo," he said with a chuckle. "Butch Carrigan was already blue as a summer sky when I got there."

If I caused you any trouble with Blueday, I'm sorry. But not much. Because things are never going to be the same now that it happened. Never.

And my third wish?

I've decided to save it for when I really need it—maybe when I meet the girl of my dreams.

Or Prince Charming.

Whichever.

THE METAMORPHOSIS OF JUSTIN JONES

Justin Jones shot out the front door of the house where he lived—not *his* house, just the place where he was forced to live—and ran until he could no longer hear his uncle's shouts. Even then he didn't feel safe. Sometimes Uncle Rafe's anger was so powerful it propelled the man onto the street after Justin. So the boy ran on, stopping only when the stitch in his side became so painful he could go no farther.

He leaned against a tree, panting and gasping for breath. The air burned in his lungs.

It was late twilight, and stars had just begun to appear, peeking out of the darkness like the eyes of cats hiding in a closet. Justin didn't see them. He was pressing his face against the tree, wishing he could melt into its rough bark and be safe.

When he finally opened his eyes again, Justin noticed an odd mist creeping around the base of the tree—a mist that somehow seemed to have more light, more color, than it should.

Curious, he stepped forward to investigate.

As he circled the tree he heard an odd whispering sound and felt a tingle in his skin. The mist covered the street ahead of him—a street he had never seen before, despite the fact that Barker's Elbow was a very small town.

He walked on.

At the end of the street he saw a strange, old-fashioned-looking building. In the window were the words ELIVES MAGIC SUPPLIES—S. H. ELIVES, PROP.

I could sure use a little magic about now, thought Justin. He glanced at his watch. Most of the stores in town were closed by this time of the evening. But this one had a light in the window.

He tried the door. It opened smoothly.

A small bell tinkled overhead as he stepped in.

Justin smiled. He would never have dreamed that Barker's Elbow could hold such a wonderful store. Magicians' paraphernalia was scattered everywhere. Top hats, capes, scarves, big decks of cards, and ornate boxes covered the floor, the walls, the counters, even hung from the ceiling. At the back of the shop stretched a long counter with a dragon carved in the front. On top of the counter stood an old-fashioned brass cash register. On top of the cash register sat a stuffed owl. Behind the counter was a door covered by a beaded curtain.

Justin wandered to one of the counters. On it stood an artillery shell, thick as his wrist. To his disappointment, the shell had already been fired. Attached was a tag that said LISTEN.

Remembering the big seashell his mother used to put to his ear so he could "hear the ocean," Justin lifted the empty metal shell and held the hollow end to his ear.

He could hear the sound of cannons, explosions, the terrified neighs of horses, the screams of wounded men.

He put the shell down. Quickly.

Next to it stood a French doll. When Justin reached for her, the doll blinked and cried, "Ooh-la-la! Touch me not, you nasty boy!" Then she began a wild dance. When Justin pulled his hand back, the doll froze in a new position.

Deciding he should just *look* at the merchandise, Justin crossed to another counter. A broom resting against the edge of it blocked his view. Justin picked it up so he could see better.

The broom began to squirm in his hands.

Justin dropped it. He was about to bolt for the door when the owl he had thought was stuffed uttered a low hoot.

"Peace, Uwila," growled a voice from beyond the beaded curtain. "I'm coming!"

A moment later an old man appeared. He was shorter than Justin, with long white hair and dark eyes that seemed to hold strange secrets. His face was seamed with deep wrinkles. The old man looked at Justin for a moment, and something in his eyes grew softer. "What do you need?"

"I don't think I need anything," said Justin uncomfortably. "I just came in to look around."

The old man shook his head. "No one comes into this store just to look around, Justin. Now what do—"

"Hey, how do you know my name?"

"It's my job. Now, what do you need?"

Justin snorted. What did he need? A real home. His mother and father back. He needed—

"Never mind," said the old man, interrupting Justin's bitter thoughts. "Let's try this. Have you ever seen a magician?"

Justin nodded.

"All right, then what's your favorite trick?"

Justin thought back to a time three years ago, back before his parents had had the accident. His dad had taken him to see a magician who did a trick where he locked his assistant in handcuffs, put her in a canvas bag, tied up the bag, put it in a trunk, wrapped chains around the trunk, and handed the keys to a member of the audience. Then he had climbed onto the trunk, lifted a curtain in front of himself, counted to five, and dropped the curtain. Only, when the curtain fell, the assistant was standing there, and the magician was inside the bag in the trunk, wearing the handcuffs. Justin had loved the trick, half suspected it was real magic.

It had had a special name, something scientific.

"The metamorphosis!" he said suddenly, as his

mind pulled the word from whatever mysterious place such things are kept.

The old man smiled and nodded. "Good choice. Wait there."

Justin felt as if his feet had melted to the floor. The old man disappeared through the beaded curtain—and came back a moment later carrying a small cardboard box. Clearly it didn't have a big trunk in it. What, then? Probably just some instructions and... what? Justin was dying to know.

But he also knew the state of his pockets.

"I don't think I can afford that," he said sadly.

The old man started to say something, then paused. He looked into the distance, nodded as if he was listening to something, then blinked. His eyes widened in surprise. After a moment he shrugged and turned to Justin.

"How much money do you have?"

Though he was tempted to turn and run, Justin dug in his pocket. "Forty-seven cents," he said at last.

The old man sighed. "We'll consider that a down payment. Assuming the trick is satisfactory, you will owe me..." He paused, did a calculation on his fingers, then said, "Three days and fifty-seven minutes."

"What?"

"You heard me! Now do you want it or not?"

Something in the old man's voice made it clear that "not" was not an acceptable answer. Swallowing hard, Justin said, "I'll take it."

The old man nodded. "The instructions are inside. We'll work out your payment schedule later. Right now, it's late, and I am tired. Take the side door. It will get you home more quickly."

Justin nodded and hurried out the side door.

To his astonishment, he found himself standing beside the tree once more. He would have thought the whole thing had been a dream...if not for the small cardboard box in his hands.

Justin walked home slowly. The later it was when he got there, the greater the chance his uncle would be asleep.

Luck was with him; Uncle Rafe lay snoring on the couch, a scattering of empty beer cans on the floor beside him.

Justin tiptoed up the stairs to his room. He set the box on his desk, then used his pocketknife to cut the tape that held it shut. He wasn't sure what he would find inside; clearly it was too small to hold the entire trick. Probably he'd have to go out and buy the trunk and stuff, which would mean that he'd never get to try it.

The box contained two items: a small instruction book and a bag that—to Justin's astonishment—shook out to be as large as the canvas sack the magician had used.

The fabric was smooth and silky, and the colors shifted and changed as he looked at it. It was very beautiful, and at first he was afraid that it would be easy to tear. But it felt oddly strong beneath his fingers.

He opened the instruction booklet.

The directions were written by hand, in a strange spidery script. On the first page of the booklet were the following words: WARNING: DO NOT ATTEMPT THIS TRICK UNLESS YOU REALLY MEAN IT. DO NOT EVEN TURN THE PAGE UNLESS YOU ARE SERIOUS.

Justin rolled his eyes…and turned the page.

The directions here were even weirder:

To begin the metamorphosis, open the bag and place it on your bed. Being careful not to damage the fabric, climb inside before you go to sleep. Keep your head out!

After you have slept in the bag for three nights, you will receive further instructions.

Justin stared at the bag and the booklet for a long time. He was tempted to just stuff them back in the box and take the whole crazy thing back to the old man. Only, he wasn't sure he could find the store again, even if he tried.

He rubbed the whisper-soft fabric between his fingers. It reminded him of his mother's cheek.

He climbed inside the bag, feet down, head out, and slept. That night his dreams were sweeter than they had been in a long, long time. But when he woke he felt oddly restless.

Justin slept in the bag for the next two nights, just as the directions said. In his dreams—which grew more vivid and beautiful each night—he flew, soaring far away from his brutal uncle and the house where he had felt such pain and loss. He came to long for the night, and the escape that he found in his dreams.

On the morning of the fourth day, Justin felt as if something must explode inside him, so deep was the restlessness that seized him. Eagerly, fearfully, he turned to the instruction booklet that had come with the silken sack. As he had half expected, he found new writing on the page after the last one he had read— a page that had been blank before.

Sometimes a leap of faith is all that's needed.

Wondering what that was supposed to mean, he went to the bathroom to get ready for school.

His shoulders itched.

The next morning they were sore and swollen.

The morning after that, Justin Jones woke to find that he had wings. They were small. They were feeble. But they were definitely there.

Justin had two reactions. Part of him wanted to shout with joy. Another part of him, calmer, more cautious, was nearly sick with fear. He knew Uncle Rafe would not approve.

He put on a heavy shirt and was relieved to find that the weight of it pressed the wings to his back.

The next morning the wings were bigger, and the morning after that, bigger still. Justin wouldn't be able to hide them from his uncle much longer.

The wings were not feathered, nor butterfly delicate, nor leathery like a bat's. They were silky smooth, like the sack he slept in. To his frustration, they hung limp and useless. Late at night, when his uncle was asleep, Justin would flex them, in the desperate hope that they would stretch and fill, somehow find the strength to lift him, to carry him away from this place.

Exactly one week after the first night he had slept in the sack, his wings became too obvious to hide. When he sat down to breakfast that morning, his uncle snapped, "Don't slouch like that. Look how you're hunching your shoulders."

Justin tried sitting up straighter, but he couldn't hide the lumps on his back.

"Take off your shirt," said his uncle, narrowing his eyes.

Slowly, nervously, Justin did as he was told.

"Turn around."

Again, Justin obeyed. He heard a sharp intake of breath, then a long silence. Finally his uncle said, "Come here, boy."

Turning to face him, Justin shook his head.

His uncle scowled. "I said, come here."

Justin backed away instead. His uncle lurched from the table, snatching at a knife as he did.

Justin turned and ran, pounding up the stairway to his room. He paused at the door, then went past it, to the attic stairs. At the top he closed the door behind him and locked it.

A moment later he heard his uncle roaring on the other side of it. For one foolish moment Justin hoped he would be safe here. Then the door shuddered as his uncle threw himself against it. Justin knew it would take only seconds for the man to break through.

He backed away.

Another slam, another, and the door splintered into the room. Stepping through, Uncle Rafe roared, "Come here, you little heathen!"

Shaking his head, mute with fear, Justin backed away, moving step-by-step down the length of the attic, until he reached the wall and the small window at the far end. His uncle matched his pace, confident in his control.

Justin knew that once Uncle Rafe had him, the wings would be gone, ripped from his shoulders. Pressing himself against the wall, letting all his fear show on his face, he groped behind him until he found the window latch. With his thumb, he pulled it open, then began to slide the window up. It hadn't gone more than half an inch before his uncle realized what he was doing and rushed forward to grab him.

"Don't!" cried Justin, holding out his hands.

The wings trembled at his shoulders, and he could feel some strange power move out from them. His uncle continued toward him, but slowly now, as if in a dream. Moving slowly himself, Justin turned and opened the window.

He glanced behind him. His uncle's slow charge continued.

Taking a deep breath, Justin stepped out.

He fell, but only for a moment. Suddenly the wings that had hung so limp and useless for the past few days snapped out from his shoulders, caught the air, slowed his fall.

They stretched to either side of him, strong and glorious, shining in the sun, patterned with strange colors. As if by instinct he knew how to move them, make them work. And as his uncle cried out in rage and longing behind him, Justin Jones worked his wings and flew, rising swiftly above the house, above the trees, his heart lifting as if it had wings of its own.

Justin flew for a long time, as far from Barker's Elbow and the home of his brutal uncle as he could manage to go. He changed course often, preferring to stay above isolated areas, though twice he flew above towns, swooping down just so that he could listen to the people cry out in wonder as they saw him. Once he flew low over a farm, where an old woman stood in her yard and reached her arms toward him, not as if to catch him, but in a gesture that he knew meant that she wanted him to catch her up. He circled lower, and saw with a start that tears were streaming down her face. Yet when he flew away, she made no cries of anger as his uncle had, only put her hand to her mouth, and blew him a kiss.

And still he flew on.

Though Justin had no idea where he was heading, he could feel something pulling him north, north and west. After a time, he saw a cloud ahead of him. It was glowing and beautiful, and without thought, he flew into it.

The air within seemed to be alive with light and electricity, and as Justin passed through the cloud he felt a tingle in his skin—a tingle much the same as the feeling he had had just before he found the magic shop.

When he left the cloud, he had come to a different place. He had been flying above land when he entered it, a vastness of hills and forest dotted by small towns that stretched in all directions for as far as he could see. But though it had taken no more than a minute or two to fly through the cloud, when he left it he was above water—a vast sea that, like the hills and forest, stretched as far as the eye could reach. Panic-stricken, Justin turned to fly back. But the cloud was gone, and the water stretched behind him as well.

Justin's shoulders were aching. He wasn't sure how much longer he could stay aloft.

And then he saw it ahead of him: a small island, maybe two or three miles across, with an inviting-looking beach. The wide swath of sand gave way to a deep forest. The forest rose up the flanks of a great mountain that loomed on the island's far side.

With a sigh of relief, Justin settled to the beach. He threw himself face forward on the sand to rest.

Soon he was fast asleep.

When Justin opened his eyes, he saw three children squatting in front of him.

"He's awake!" said the smallest, a little girl with huge eyes and short brown hair.

"I told you he wasn't dead," said the largest, a dark-haired boy of about Justin's age. "They never are, no matter how bad they look."

"Come on, then," said the girl, reaching out to Justin. "Lie here in the sun all day and you'll get burned."

Justin blinked, then glanced back at his shoulders. The wings were still there. Why didn't these strange children say anything about them?

"Maybe I should just fly away," he muttered, pushing himself to his knees. He did it a little bit to brag, a little bit to see if he could get the children to say something about the wings.

"Oh, you can't do that," said the little girl, sounding very sensible. "Well, you could. But it wouldn't be smart. Not until you've talked to the old woman."

"She's right," said the biggest boy. "Come on, we'll show you the way. But first you ought to eat something."

"So you've seen people with wings before?" asked Justin.

"Silly!" giggled the girl. "We all had wings when we came here. Were you scared when you went through the cloud? I was."

Justin nodded, uncertain of what to say. He realized someone else seemed to be in the same condition. "Doesn't he ever talk?" he asked, gesturing to the middle child, a dark-eyed boy who looked to be about nine.

"Not yet," said the girl. "I think he will someday. But he was in pretty bad shape when he got here."

"Come on," said the biggest boy. "The old woman will tell you all about it."

Justin followed the three strange children up the beach and into the forest, a forest so perfect that it almost made him weep. It was not that it was beautiful—though it was. Nor that the trees were old and thick and strange—though they were. What made it so wonderful, from Justin's point of view, was that it was filled with tree houses...and the tree houses were filled with children. Happy children. Laughing children. Children who scrambled along rope bridges, dangled from thick branches, and swung from tree to tree on vines.

"Hey, new boy!" they cried when they spotted him. "Welcome! Welcome!"

No one seemed to think it odd that Justin had wings, though a few of them gazed at the wings with a hungry look.

Justin's own hunger, which he had nearly forgotten in the strangeness and the wonder of this new place, stirred when the children led him to a platform built low in a tree, where there were bowls of fruit and bread and cheese. He ate in silence at first, too hungry to talk. But when the edge was off his appetite, he began to ask questions.

"Ask the old woman" was all they would tell him. "The old woman will explain everything."

"All right," he said, when his hunger was sated. "Take me to this old woman, will you please?"

"We can't take you," said the boy. "You'll have to go on your own. We can only show you the way."

Justin walked through the forest, following the path the children had shown him. The trees were too thick here for him to spread his wings, which annoyed him, because the path was steep, and his legs were beginning to grow tired. He wanted to fly again. Where did this old woman live, anyway? A tree house, like the children? That didn't seem likely. Maybe a cottage in some woody grove or beside a stream? Maybe even a cave. After all, he did seem to be climbing fairly high up the mountainside.

It turned out that all his guesses were wrong. The path turned a corner, and when he came out from between two trees he found himself at the edge of a large clearing, where there stood a huge, beautiful house.

The door was open. Even so, Justin knocked and called out.

No one answered.

Folding his wings against his back, he stepped through the door.

"Old woman?" he called.

He felt strange using the words instead of a name, but that was the only thing the children had called her.

"Old woman?"

"Up here!" called a voice. "I've been waiting for you."

Justin climbed the stairs, flight after flight of them, going far higher than the house had looked from the outside. At each level he called, "Old woman?" And at each level the voice replied, "Up here! I'm waiting for you!"

At last the stairs ended. Before him was a silver door. He put his hand against it, and it swung open.

"Come in," said the old woman.

She was sitting before a blue fire, which cast not heat, but a pleasant coolness into the room. Her hair was white as cloud, her eyes blue as sky. A slight breeze seemed to play about the hem of her long dress.

"Come closer," she said, beckoning to him.

He did as she said.

She smiled. "I'm glad you're here. Do you like your wings?"

Justin reached back to touch one. "They're the most wonderful thing that ever happened to me," he said softly.

The old woman nodded. "I'm glad. It's not easy getting them out there, you know. I can't do nearly as many as I would like."

"Who are you?" asked Justin.

She shrugged. "Just an old woman with time on her hands, trying to do a little good. Now listen carefully, for I have to tell you what happens next. The wings will only last for one more day. However, that will be long enough for you to fly home, if you should wish."

Justin snorted. "Why would I want to—"

"*Shhh!* Before you answer, you must look into my mirror. Then I will explain your choice."

Standing, she took his hand and led him across the room. On the far side was a golden door. Behind it, Justin could hear running water. When she opened the door, Justin saw not a room, but a cave. Four torches were set in its walls.

In the center of the cave was a pool. A small waterfall fed into it from the right. A stream flowed out to the left.

"Kneel," said the old woman. "Look."

Justin knelt, and peered into the water. He saw his own face, thin and worn, with large eyes where the fear was never far beneath the surface. From his shoulders sprouted wings, huge and beautiful.

The old woman dipped her finger in the water and stirred.

The image shifted. Now Justin saw not a boy, but a man. Yet it was clearly his face.

"The man you will become," whispered the old woman.

Justin stared at the face. It was not handsome, as he had always hoped he would become. But it was a good face. The eyes were peaceful and calm. The beginning of a smile waited at the corners of the mouth. Laugh lines fanned out from the eyes. It was a strong face. A kind face.

Outside, far down the mountain, Justin could hear the laughter of the children.

The old woman stirred the water again. The man's face disappeared. The water was still, showed no image at all.

"Come," she said quietly.

Justin followed her back to the room.

"Now you must choose," she said. "You can stay here. This place is safe and calm and no one will hurt you, ever again."

Justin felt his heart lift.

"But…you will stay just as you are. Never change, never grow any older." She sighed. "That's the trade. There's always a trade. It's the best I can do, Justin."

He looked at her, startled, then realized that given everything else that had gone on, the fact that she knew his name should be no surprise at all.

Justin went to the window. It looked out not onto forest or mountains, but clouds. He stood there a long time, looking, listening. Finally he turned to the old woman.

"Can I ask a question?"

"Certainly—though I can't guarantee I will know the answer."

He nodded. "I understand. Okay, here's the question. The man I saw in the pool. Me. What does he do?"

The old woman smiled. "He works with children."

Justin smiled, too. "And what about my uncle? Will things be better with him if I go back?"

The old woman shook her head sadly.

Justin blinked. "Then how is it possible I can turn out the way you showed me? How can *that* be me?"

The old woman smiled again. "Ah, that one is easy. It is because no matter what happens, you will always remember that once upon a time…you flew."

Justin nodded and turned back to the window. Far below he could hear the children at play.

He ached to join them.

But then he thought of the others he knew.

The ones who never laughed.

The ones who still needed wings.

"How would I find the way back?"

"Take the side door," said the old woman softly. "It will get you home a little more quickly."

Tucking his wings against his back, Justin stepped through the door—and found himself on top of the mountain. He could see the entire island spread out below him, could hear, even from this height, the laughter of the children.

Justin took a deep breath. Then he spread his wings and leaped forward. Catching the air in great sweeps, he soared up and up, then leveled off and flew.

Not toward home; Justin Jones had no real home.

Flexing his wings, he pointed himself toward tomorrow.

Then he flew as hard as he could.

PERMISSION ACKNOWLEDGMENTS

"The Box" copyright © 1986 by Bruce Coville; originally published in *Dragons and Dreams* (HarperCollins), edited by Jane Yolen, Martin H. Greenberg, and Charles Waugh. "Duffy's Jacket" copyright © 1989 by Bruce Coville; originally published in *Things That Go Bump in the Night* (HarperCollins), edited by Jane Yolen and Martin H. Greenberg. "Homeward Bound" copyright © 1987 by Bruce Coville; originally published in *The Unicorn Treasury* (Doubleday), edited by Bruce Coville. "With His Head Tucked Underneath His Arm" copyright © 1993 by Bruce Coville; originally published in *A Wizard's Dozen* (Jane Yolen Books/Harcourt, Inc.), edited by Michael Stearns. "Clean as a Whistle" copyright © 1994 by Bruce Coville. "The Language of Blood" copyright © 1994 by Bruce Coville. "Old Glory" copyright © 1991 by Bruce Coville; originally published in *2041* (Delacorte Press), edited by Jane Yolen. "The Passing of the Pack" copyright © 1988 by Bruce Coville; originally published in *Werewolves* (HarperCollins), edited by Jane Yolen and Martin H. Greenberg. "A Blaze of Glory" copyright © 1994 by Bruce Coville. "The Golden Sail" copyright © 1999 by